The Savage Heart

L. E. SMOOT MEMORIAL LIBRARY
KING GEORGE. VA. 22485

Diana Palmer

The Savage Heart

L. E. SMOOT MEMORIAL LIBRARY
KING GEORGE, VA. 22485

Copyright © 1997 by Susan Kyle.
All rights reserved.

Published in Large Print by arrangement with Ballantine Books, a division of Random House Inc. in the United States and Canada

Wheeler Large Print Book Series.

Set in 16 pt Plantin.

Library of Congress Cataloging-in-Publication Data

Palmer, Diana.
The Savage Heart / Diana Palmer.
p. (large print) cm.(Wheeler large print book series)
ISBN 1-56895-573-1 (softcover)
1. Large type books. I. Title. II. Series
[PS3566A513S28 1998]
813'.54—dc21

98-024000
CIP

To Dr. Nestor R. Carabajal,
Dr. Winston H. Gandy, Dr. F. Stuart
Sanders, Dr. David A. Bray, and
Dr. Michael J. Maloney.
Thank you all, most sincerely.

—Mrs. James E. Kyle
(aka Diana Palmer)

PROLOGUE

MONTANA
SPRING 1891

There was lightning in the distance where dark clouds settled low over the buttes. Spring storms, all lightning display at first, were common here, and Tess Meredith loved to watch them—especially now that she had a companion who seemed to have a legend about every one of these natural occurrences... and every unnatural one, too.

But even more than watching summer storms with her new and treasured friend, Tess liked to ride fast, hunt and fish, live in the outdoors enjoying nature and what she called "adventure." Her father despaired of her ever marrying. Who would appreciate a young woman who had such accomplishments, not one of which had anything to do with traditional domestic occupations?

Today Tess looked quite different from the way she usually did and quite grown-up for a fourteen-year-old. Her blond hair was piled neatly on top of her head, rather than flying free; she was wearing a long cotton dress with a high neck, rather than rolled-up dungarees and one of her father's shirts. Polished lace-up shoes replaced the scuffed boots she always wore. Her father had beamed when he'd seen her earlier. Of course, he wouldn't say a chastising word to her on the subject of her dress or her unladylike pursuits. He was far too kind to do such a thing. It was the kindness in him, so deep and so sincere, that made him such a wonderful doctor, Tess believed, for many who practiced medicine had skill, but few had his way with patients.

She sighed and glanced over at Raven Following, the only man she'd ever known who treated her as an equal, not a silly child—or worse, a silly girl. He was a Sioux who had lived at Pine Ridge until about eight months ago. His shoulders, wide and powerful, did not move under the buckskins he wore. His long, thick black hair was braided and wrapped with narrow bands of ermine skins, and his strongly boned, handsome face was free of expression.

Looking at him, Tess was filled with melancholy and curiosity. What did Raven see—for he seemed to see all manner of things around and in the far distance that she couldn't? Sometimes it was difficult for her to believe he was only six or seven years older than she.

"Are you scared?" she suddenly asked.

"A warrior never admits fear."

She smiled. "Oh, pardon me. Are you nervous, then?"

"Uneasy." His lean, graceful fingers held a stick that he alternately toyed with and used to draw symbols on the ground. Now he was idly moving it from hand to hand. "Chicago is far away from here. I've never been to a white man's city."

"Papa says you'll be educated there and afterward you can get a job. He knows a man who will give you work."

"So he has told me."

She touched his shoulder lightly. He didn't like to be touched, not since he'd been so badly wounded in the massacre at Wounded Knee Creek, South Dakota, where the fury of the Hotchkiss guns of the soldiers had taken the lives of more than two hundred of his people, including his mother and two sisters. But Tess's touch was different, and, she thought, tolerable to him, since she'd help nurse him through the agonizing recovery from having his body riddled with U.S. Army issue bullets.

"It will be all right," Tess said, her voice gentle and, she hoped, reassuring. "You'll like Chicago when you get there."

"You are so very sure of that?" His black eyes were glittering with humor.

"Of course! After Mama died and Papa told me he was going to take a job doctoring on the reservations, I was scared to death. I didn't know anybody out here, and I had to leave all my friends and relatives behind. But once I got to the West, it wasn't bad at all." She rearranged her skirt. "Well, it wasn't too bad," she amended. "I didn't like the way the soldiers treated your people."

"Neither did we," he said dryly. He paused, studying her, finally looking intently into her clear green eyes. "You father will be relieved when I am gone. He permits me to teach you things, but he grimaces when he sees you doing them."

"He's old-fashioned." Tess laughed. "And the world is changing." She looked at the distant buttes. "I want to help it change. I want to do things that women have never done."

"You already do things that few white women do—skin a deer, track a doe, ride without a saddle, shoot a bow—"

"And sign and speak Lakota. All thanks to you, Raven. You're a good friend and a good teacher. How I wish I could go to Chicago with you. Wouldn't we have fun?"

He shrugged and began to draw symbols in the dust at his feet.

How graceful his hands were, Tess mused. His fingers were strong, yet lean, and his wrists were so finely boned, they appeared delicate beneath the long corded muscle of his forearm. He leaned forward, and her gaze traveled over his back. Tess winced. Beneath the buckskin shirt his flesh was puckered and pocked with scars, scars that would be there always to remind him of Wounded Knee.

It was a miracle, Tess's father Harold had said, that Raven had survived. Half a dozen bullets had torn into his upper back; one had punctured his lung, causing it to collapse. And that was not the worst of his injuries. Harold Meredith had done everything his medical training had taught him and then some to save Raven's life, but at last he'd sought the help of a practitioner from a tradition far different from his own: he smuggled a Lakota shaman into Raven's bedchamber.

Whether it was Harold's or the shaman's skill—or the skills of both—they would never know. But soon the Great Spirit smiled, and

Raven began to recover. It was a long and painful journey back to health, and through it all Tess was at Raven's side.

"Will you miss me?" she asked.

"Of course," he said, smiling easily. "You saved my life."

"No. Papa and your shaman did that."

Raven Following was not a demonstrative man, but now he took her small white hand in his large, dark one and held it. "You did it," he said firmly. "You saved my life. I lived only because you cried so hard for me. I felt sorry for you and knew I could not be so rude and thoughtless as to disappoint your hopes by dying."

She chuckled. "That's the longest sentence I've ever heard from you, Raven—and the only one the least bit deceitful." Her eyes sparkled.

He stood up, stretched lazily, then pulled her up beside him. His gaze slid over her flushed face. She was almost a woman, and she was going to be very pretty, perhaps beautiful. But she worried him. She felt things so deeply... with such strong emotion.

"Why?" she asked suddenly. "Why, why?"

He did not need to ask where her thoughts had carried her. Without hesitation, he said, "Because of what the Lakota did to Custer, I think. I have reflected on Wounded Knee for several months now, Tess. Some of the soldiers who opened fire on us, on the children"—his body stiffened for a moment as if he might be hearing once again the wails of terror and screams of pain from those children—"some of those soldiers," he went on, "were from Custer's surviving companies." He looked at her intently. "I was six when we fought Custer, and I remember how the soldiers looked there, on the battlefield. Many of the women had lost sons and fathers and husbands to those men. My own father died there. The women took out their grief on the bodies of the dead soldiers on the Greasy Grass. It was bad."

"I see."

"No. And it is good that you don't," he replied, his face curiously taut. "I teased you before, Tess, but truly I would not have lived if you and your father had not been so brave... and so swift."

"We left for the battlefield the instant we heard there had been fighting and that many were dying on that frozen ground." Tess shivered and tears filled her eyes. "Oh, Raven, it was so cold, so bitterly cold. I shall never forget it, and I thank God we found you."

"As I thank the Great Spirit that you and your father rescued me and tended my wounds and hid me in your wagon until we were out of South Dakota."

"Lucky that Dad was being transferred to the Northern Cheyenne Reservation. It was easy to pretend we'd found you on the roadside in Montana near Lame Deer. No one ever questioned our story—well, not to our faces anyway."

He smiled. "I was not so lucky in my decision to visit my cousins in Big Foot's band, though, was I?"

She shook her head. "You could have been safe in your lodge in Pine Ridge..."

"And my mother and sisters, too." His voice had trailed off. Now, suddenly, he shook off his enveloping grief. "Come," he said, "let us go back. Your father will be wondering where you are."

She started to protest, but his gaze was even and quiet, and she knew that it would be like talking to a rock. She gave in with good grace and smiled at him.

"Will we ever see you again after you go?" she asked.

"Of course. I'll come back and visit from time to time," he promised. "Don't forget the things I've taught you."

"As if I could," she replied. She searched his black eyes. "Why do things have to change?"

"Because they do." In the distance, the sky became misty as the threatening clouds released a curtain of rain.

"Come. The rain will overtake us if we don't hurry."

"One more minute, Raven. Please, tell me something."

"Anything," he murmured.

"What did Old Man Deer do when we sat up here with him last week?"

Raven's body stiffened slightly and he glanced away. "He performed a ritual. A very sacred one." He looked fully at Tess. "It was a way of protecting you," he said enigmatically. Then he smiled. "And we will say no more about it... now."

Chapter One

Chicago, Illinois
November 1903

The telegram read: "Arriving Chicago depot 2:00 P.M. Saturday. Tess."

Matt Davis had read the telegram several times and cursed it several times more. Tess Meredith had no business moving to Chicago. Her father had died only two months ago. Matt hadn't got the news until long after the funeral was over when he returned from working in another state. He'd written Tess right away, of course, and she'd written back. But she'd never so much as hinted that she had this in mind.

He'd visited Tess and her father many times and kept up a regular correspondence with them all through the years after he'd gone east to be educated, then changed his name to begin work as a Pinkerton detective. Raven Following had become Matt Davis and changed in a hundred other ways, too, but never in his regard for Tess and Harold Meredith. They were all the family he could claim. And he'd looked forward to each visit with them more than anyone would ever know.

Tess at sixteen hadn't been quite so outgoing as she had been two years before. She'd become somewhat shy, remote. Tess at eighteen had been a very different proposition. Mature, pretty—and more reckless than he remembered. Last year, he'd made another pilgrimage to Montana, which he combined with work on a case for his own new private detective agency, and the sight of a grown-up Tess of twenty-four had shocked him speechless. No longer the grinning fourteen-year-old sprite, no longer the shy sixteen-year-old or the reckless eighteen-year-old, Tess was mischievous, forceful, outspoken—and so beautiful that she made him ache. And she was driving her father wild. He'd confessed to Matt that she wouldn't even allow talk of marriage... that she'd ridden her horse through town wearing pants and a shirt and carrying a sidearm... that she'd organized a women's suffrage group in town... and that she'd actually attacked a local man with a pistol when he tried to get fresh with her. The aging doctor had asked Matt for advice. But, confronted by this new and challenging Tess, Matt, too, had been at a loss.

Now her father was dead and he was inheriting Tess, a legacy of feminine trouble he knew was going to change his life. It was a worrying and exciting proposition.

The train pulled into the station, huffing and puffing clouds of smoke. Wary of the cast-off cinders from the engine, elegantly dressed men and women began to disembark, porters came and went unloading baggage, but there was no sign of Tess.

Matt sighed irritably as he stared around the platform. Suddenly, a shapely woman clad in natty green velvet, wearing a Paris creation of a hat with a veil, and impatiently tapping a prettily shod foot, ceased to be a stranger to him. The years fell away and the elegant woman was again the girl with long blond pigtails he'd known so long.

At that very moment Tess spied him. All her elegant poise vanished, and she raced across the platform shouting his name, then hurled herself at him.

His arms swallowed her and he lifted her high, laughing as his dark eyes met her green, green ones through the misty veil.

"Oh, Matt, I've missed you so," she crooned. "You haven't changed a bit."

"You have," he said, slowly lowering her back to her feet.

"Only because I have breasts now," she said.

His cheeks went ruddy, he knew, for he could feel the heat in them. "Tess!"

She propped her hands on her hips and stared up at him. "It's a new world. We women are done with hypocrisy and servitude. We want what men have."

He couldn't help it. He grinned. "Hairy chests?"

"Yours isn't hairy," she said belligerently. "It's very smooth." She looked at him soberly. "Does anybody here know who you really are, where you came from?"

Matt's brow lifted just enough to make him look arrogant. "It depends on which version of my past you prefer. My banker is convinced I'm exiled Russian royalty. My old Pinkerton buddies believe I came here from

Spain. The elderly Chinaman who does my laundry thinks I'm an Arab."

"I see."

"No," he said, his eyes narrowed. "You don't. You have the right to speak your native language and dress in clothing familiar to your forebears. A Sioux isn't even allowed to participate in a native religious ceremony, not even the Sun Dance."

He straightened the tie that so beautifully complemented his elegant vested suit. He wore a derby, his long hair contained in a ponytail that rested under the neck of his shirt. Few people in Chicago knew that he was Sioux. "Let people think what they like about me," he said, refusing to admit that it disturbed him to reveal his ancestry. "I'm a mystery man, Tess," he said gleefully. Then he sobered again and added, "Nothing will ever be the same because of Wounded Knee. Now it's illegal for an Indian at a government school or holding a government job to wear his long hair or dress in native clothing or speak his own language."

"And," Tess added morosely, "you can't even vote in your own country." She brightened. "Just like me. Well, Mr. Davis-Following, we're going to have to change all that."

His onyx eyes regarded her somberly. She was delightfully pretty. But underneath the beauty, there was character and an independent spirit. "I'm sorry about your father," he said. "I know you must still miss him."

"Don't get me started," she said through stiff lips, glancing around her to stay the tears. “I’ve tried very hard to be brave, all the way here. Even after two months, it’s still very new, being an orphan.” Her small gloved hand went to his waistcoat pocket and rested over it. “Matt, you don’t mind that I came?” she asked abruptly. “I had no one in Montana, and one of the soldiers was pestering me to marry him. I had to get away before I gave in out of sheer exhaustion.”

“The same soldier your father mentioned in his last letter to me, a Lieutenant Smalley?”

“The very one.” She withdrew her hand and twisted the handle of her frilly parasol. “You remember the name very well, don’t you?”

“It’s hard to forget the name of a man who helped kill most of my family at Wounded Knee,” he said harshly.

She looked around them, finding people going their own way. Nobody paid undue attention to them. It would have been a different story back in Montana, where the sight of a young blond woman with a full-blooded Sioux would have raised more than just eyebrows. Lord, she thought, everyone would have been glaring furiously at them—as they had in the past.

“I remember the way you were,” she said gently. “Dressed as a warrior, on horseback, with your hair flying in the wind and your arrows winging toward the center of a bull’s-eye.” Watching her watch Raven, her father had teased her that she was losing her heart.

Matt didn’t like remembering his past. “I remember you trying to skin a deer and throw up at the same time.”

She held up a hand. "Please, I'm a gentlewoman now."

"And I'm a detective now. Shall we agree to let the past lie without further mention?"

"If you like."

"Where are your bags?"

"The porter has them on the cart, there," she pointed toward a steamer trunk and several smaller bags. She glanced up at him. "I suppose I can't live with you. Or can I?"

He was shocked. Did she know more about the past than she had ever let on? He held his breath.

"I don't mean *with* you," she said, embarrassed at her own phrasing of the question. "I mean, you live in a boardinghouse, and I wonder if there's a vacancy?"

He let out his breath and smiled with relief. "I imagine that Mrs. Mulhaney could find a room for you, yes. But the idea of a young single woman living in a boardinghouse is going to make you look like a loose woman in the eyes of the community. If anyone asks, you're my cousin."

"I am?"

"You are," he said firmly. "It's the only way I can protect you."

"I don't need protecting, thank you. I'm quite capable of looking after myself."

Considering that she'd handled her father's funeral alone and gotten here, halfway across the country, without mishap, that was apparent.

"I believe you," he said. "But you're a stranger here and totally unfamiliar with life in a big city. I'm not."

"Aren't we both strangers here, really?" she asked, and there was a deep sadness in her tone. "Neither of us has anybody now."

"I have cousins, in South Dakota and in Montana," he replied.

"Whom you never visit," she shot back. "Are you ashamed of them, Matt?"

His eyes glittered like black diamonds. "Don't presume to invade my privacy," he said through his teeth. "I'll gladly do what I can to see you settled here. But my feelings are my own business."

She grinned at him. "You still strike like a rattler when you're poked."

"Be careful that you don't get bitten."

She dropped him a curtsey. "I'll do my best not to provoke you too much."

"What are you planning to do here?" Matt asked. He'd arranged with the station agent to have her bags stored until he could settle Tess and send for them.

"I'm going to get a job."

He stopped dead in his tracks and stared at her. "A job?"

"Certainly, a job. You know I'm not rich, Matt, and besides, it's 1903. Women are getting into all sorts of professions. I've read about it. Women are working as shop girls and stenographers and in sewing plants. I can turn my hand to most anything if I'm shown how. And I'm quite an experienced nurse. Until Papa died"—her voice broke and she took a few seconds to compose herself—"I was his nurse. I can get work nursing in a hospital here. I know I can." She abruptly looked up at him. "There is a hospital here, isn't there?"

"Yes." He remembered making a keen shot of her with both bow and rifle. She was a quick study, and utterly fearless. Had he started her down the road to nonconformity? If he had, he knew in his bones that he was about to regret it. Nursing was not considered by many as suitable for a genteel woman. Some would raise eyebrows. Of course, it would raise eyebrows, too, if she worked in a shop, or—

"The very notion of a woman working is—well, unconventional."

Her brows rose. "What would you call a Sioux Indian in a bowler hat pretending to be exiled Russian royalty—*traditional*?"

He made an irritated sound.

"You shouldn't debate me," she muttered. "I was first in my class in my last year in school."

He glared at her as they started to walk again down the broad sidewalk. Exquisite carriages drawn by horses in decorated livery rolled along the wide street, whose storefronts were decorated for the holiday season.

Tess caught sight of a store window where little electric trains ran against a backdrop of mountain scenery that had actual tunnels running through. "Oh, Matt, look. Isn't it darling?"

"Do you really want me to tell you how I feel about iron horses?"

"Never mind, spoilsport." She fell into step beside him once more. "Christmas isn't so very far away. Does your landlady decorate and put up a tree in the parlor?"

"Yes."

"How lovely! I can crochet snowflakes to go on it."

"You're assuming that she can find room for you."

She gnawed at her lower lip. She'd come here on impulse, and now for the first time, she was uncertain. She stopped walking and looked up. "What if she can't?" she asked.

Even through the veil, Matt could see plainly the expression of fear on Tess's face. He was touched in a dozen ways, none wanted. "She will," he said firmly. "I won't have you very far from me. There are wicked elements in this city. Until you find your feet, you need a safe harbor."

She smiled. "I'm a lot of trouble, I guess. I've always been impulsive. Am I trading too much on our shared past, Matt? If I'm in your way, just tell me, and I'll go back home."

"Home to the persistent lieutenant? Over my dead body. Come on."

He took her arm and guided her around a hole in the boardwalk that looked as if a rifle had made it. Matt recalled reading about a fight between a city policeman and a bank robber recently. The bank was close by.

"Mrs. Blake told me that Chicago is very civilized," Tess said. "Is it?"

"Occasionally."

She looked over at him. "Now that you have your own detective business, what sort of cases do you take?"

"Mostly I track down criminals," he replied. "Once or twice I've done other sorts of work; I've taken on a couple of divorce cases, getting evidence to prove cruelty on the part of the men." He glanced at her. "I suppose you have no qualms about divorce, being modern."

"I have a few," she confessed. "I think people should try to make a marriage work. But if a man is abusive or cheats or gambles, I think a woman is more than entitled to be rid of him."

"I think she's entitled to shoot him," he murmured, remembering vividly a recent case, where a drunken husband had left vicious bruises on a small child and her mother. Matt had knocked the man down and taken him to the police himself.

"Good for you!" Tess peered up at him through her veil. "You're still wickedly handsome."

He gave her a mocking smile. "You're my cousin," he reminded her. "We're relatives in Chicago. You can't leer at me, regardless of how modern you feel."

She made a face at him. "You've become absolutely staid!"

"I work in a staid profession."

"I'll bet you're good at it, too." She eyed his waistcoat. "Do you still carry that enormous bowie knife around with you?"

"Who told you about that?"

"It was in a dime novel I read about you."

"What?"

She bumped into him because he stopped so abruptly. "Don't do that!" She straightened her hat. "There was a dime novel about you, didn't you know? It came out close to a year ago, just after that case where you caught the ringleader of some bank robbery gang and shot him. They called you Magnificent Matt Davis!"

"I'm going to be sick," he said, and looked as if he meant it.

"Now, now, it can't be so bad to be a hero. Just think, one day you can show a copy of that novel to your children and be a hero to them, too."

"I won't have children," he said shortly, staring straight ahead.

"Why not?" she asked. "Don't you like them?"

He looked down at her evenly. "Probably as much as you do. Isn't twenty-six about the right age to be called a spinster?"

She flushed. "I don't have to get married to have a child," she informed him haughtily. "Or a lover!"

He gave her a speaking look.

Odd, she thought, how that look made her feel. She swallowed hard. It sounded good at suffragist meetings to say such things, but when she looked at Matt, she thought of how it would be to have him as a lover, and her knees went wobbly. She actually knew very little about such things, except that one of her suffragist friends had said that it hurt a lot and it wasn't fun at all.

"Your father would beat you with a buggy whip if he heard you talk like that!"

"Well, who else can I say such things to?" she demanded, glaring at him. "I don't know any other men!"

"Not even the persistent soldier?" he asked venomously.

She shifted. "He never bathes. And there were crumbs in his mustache."

He burst out laughing.

"Never mind," she grumbled, and started walking again. "I'll just keep my scandalous thoughts to myself until I can find a group of suffragists to join." She looked at him from the corner of her eyes. "Do you know where they meet?"

"I never attend suffragist meetings myself; I'm much too busy with my knitting."

She punched his arm playfully.

"I'm sure you'll find them," he said quickly.

"I expect they have a low tolerance for liquor, as well," she mused aloud. "Do you have a hatchet?"

"Only Indians carry hatchets," he informed her. "I'm a detective. I carry a .32 caliber Smith and Wesson double action revolver."

"You never taught me to shoot a pistol."

"And I never will," he said. He gave her a wry glance. "One day, the temptation might be too much for you. It wouldn't look good on my record if you shot me. We're here."

Matt took her elbow and guided her up the steps of a brownstone house with long windows and a huge door with a lion's head knocker. He escorted her inside, then paused outside a closed door and knocked.

"Just a minute," a musical voice called. "I'm coming."

The door opened and a tiny woman with gray-streaked blond hair in a bun looked way up at Matt and then at his companion.

"Why, Mr. Davis, have you found a wife at last?"

Tess flushed scarlet and Matt cleared his throat.

"This is my cousin, Tess Meredith, Mrs. Mulhaney. Her father has died, and she has no relatives except me. Is that room on the third floor still vacant?"

"Yes, it is, and I'd be delighted to rent it to Miss Meredith." She smiled at Tess, a thousand unspoken questions in her blue eyes.

Tess smiled back. "I'd be very grateful to have a place to stay near Matt." She looked up at him with sickening adoration. "Isn't he just the sweetest man?"

"Sweet" wasn't an appellation that had ever connected itself with the enigmatic Mr. Davis in Mrs. Mulhaney's mind, but she supposed to a kinswoman he might be.

"He is a kindhearted soul," she agreed. "Now, Miss Meredith, you can have meals with us. Mr. Davis will tell you the times, and there's a laundry just three doors down run by Mr. Lo."

Matt stifled a chuckle. "I'll show her where it is," he promised.

"Let me get the key and I'll take you to your room, Miss Meredith. It has a very nice view of the city."

She went off, mumbling to herself, and Tess lifted both brows as she looked up at Matt. "And what was so amusing about the laundry?"

"Don't you remember? Whites used to call

us Mr. Lo."

She frowned.

He made an exasperated sound. "Lo, the poor Indian... ?"

She laughed. "Oh, good heavens. I'd forgotten our jokes about that."

"I haven't," he murmured. "You and I joked. Everywhere else being called Mr. Lo or 'John' most of my life was not funny."

"Well, you're anything but a *poor* Indian now," she said pointedly, her gaze going over his rich paisley vest in shades of magenta and the dark gray suit and white shirt he was wearing with it. Even his shoes were expensive, handmade. For feet that size, she thought wickedly, they'd have to be handmade! She searched his dark eyes with a smile in her own. "You look filthy rich to me!" she whispered.

"Tess!"

"I'll reform," she promised, but hadn't time to say more because Mrs. Mulhaney was back with the key.

Chapter Two

Chicago was big and brash, and Tess loved to explore it, finding old churches and forts and every manner of modern building. Lake Michigan, lapping at the very edge of the city and looking as big as an ocean, fascinated Tess, who had spent so many of her formative years landlocked in the West.

She rather easily got a nursing position at the hospital in Cook County. Her experience and skill were evident to a number of the physicians, who maneuvered to get her on their services. Since she wasn't formally trained, however, she was classified a practical nurse.

The matrons who lived at the boardinghouse were less approving. They considered nursing a dreadful profession for a well-brought-up single woman and said so.

Tess took their comments with smiling fortitude, mentally consigning them to the nether reaches. They couldn't really be blamed, though, considering their upbringing. Change came hard to the elderly.

Fortunately, she discovered a group of women's rights advocates and joined immediately. She eagerly worked on every plan for a march or a rally aimed at getting the vote for women.

Matt kept a close eye on her. He often saw her as an unbroken filly that no hand was going to tame. He wouldn't have presumed to try. There was much to admire in Tess, and much to respect.

Tess made a good friend right away in Nan Collier, the young wife of a telegraph clerk, who attended suffragist meetings with her. Matt had insisted that she not go out at night unaccompanied. It was the only restriction he'd placed on her, and since she didn't consider it demeaning, she abided by it. And Nan was good company, too. She wasn't an educated woman, as Tess was, but she was intelligent and had a kind heart.

As they grew closer, it became obvious to Tess that Nan had problems at home. She never spoke of them, but she made little comments about having to be back at a certain time so that her husband wouldn't be angry, or about having to be sure that her housework was done properly to keep him happy. It sounded as if any lapse in what her husband considered her most important duties would result in punishment.

It wasn't until the end of her first month in Chicago that Tess discovered what Nan's punishment was. She came to a suffragist meeting at a local matron's house with a split lip and a black eye.

"Nan, what happened?" Tess exclaimed, her concern echoed by half a dozen fierce campaigners for women's rights. "Did your husband strike you?"

"Oh no!" Nan said quickly. "Why, this is nothing. I fell down the steps, is all." She laughed nervously, putting a self-conscious hand to her eye. "I'm so clumsy sometimes."

"Are you sure that's all it is?" Tess persisted.

"Yes, I'm sure. But you're sweet to worry about me, Tess," Nan said with genuine affection.

"Don't ever let him start hitting you," Tess cautioned. "It will only get worse. No man has the right to beat his wife, regardless of what she's done."

"I fell down the steps," Nan repeated, but she didn't quite meet Tess's eyes. "Dennis gets impatient with me when I'm slow, especially when those rich friends of his come over, and he thinks I'm stupid sometimes, but he... he wouldn't hit me."

Tess had seen too many victims of brutality to be convinced by Nan's story. Working as a nurse was very informative—too informative sometimes.

She patted the other woman's shoulder gently. "Well, if you ever need help, I'll do what I can for you. I promise."

Nan smiled, wincing as the motion pulled the cut on her lower lip open. She dabbed at it with her handkerchief. "Thanks, Tess, but I'm okay."

Tess sighed. "Very well, then."

The meeting was boisterous, as often happened, and some of the opinions voiced seemed radical even to Tess. But the majority of the members wanted only the right to be treated, at least in the polling booth, as equal to men.

"The Quakers have always accepted women as equals," one woman said angrily. "But our men are still living in the Dark Ages. Most of them look upon us as property. Even the best men think a woman is too ignorant to render an opinion on any matter of public interest."

"Yes!" came cries of assent.

"Furthermore, we have no control over our own bodies and must bear children again and again, whether we're able or not. Many of our sisters have died in childbirth. Many others are so overburdened by children that they have no energy for any other pursuit. But if we mention any sort of birth control, especially abstinence, men brand us heretics!"

There were more cries of support.

"We cannot even vote," the woman continued. "Men treat us either as children or idiots. A woman is looked down upon if she even shops for her own groceries!"

"Or if she works away from the home!" another added.

"It is time, past time, that we demanded the rights to which any man is legally entitled at birth. We must not accept being second-class citizens any longer. We must act!"

"Yes, we must!"

"Yes!"

They were all in agreement that they should march on city hall as soon as possible. A date was set and leaders designated.

"I can't go," Nan said with a long sigh. "Dennis will be home all day." She barely repressed a shudder. "I wouldn't dare leave the house."

"You could sneak away," a woman standing nearby suggested.

"Oh, I couldn't do that," Nan said quickly. "He doesn't even like me coming to one of these meetings each week. I have to be so careful to make sure he doesn't know how involved I am. So it's best if he isn't home when I creep off for a rally or an added meeting." Her thin shoulders rose and fell as if they bore a heavy burden. "He works an extra job away from the telegraph office on Mondays and Thursdays, and he's real late getting home, so I can get out and he doesn't know."

What a horrible way to have to live, Tess thought. She wondered, not for the first time, what sort of home life poor Nan had. Men could be such brutes!

She was still fuming about Dennis's treatment of Nan when she got home. Matt was on his way out, and she met him on the front steps. He looked gloriously handsome in his expensive vested suit. She remembered how his hair used to look hanging straight and clean almost to his waist, and wondered if it was still that long. Since he hid his braid these days, she couldn't judge the length.

"You work all the time," she accused gently, smiling.

"I'm addicted to fancy gear," he teased. "I have to make enough to support my expensive tastes." His large black eyes went over her, in her neat skirt and blouse under a long overcoat. "Another meeting?"

"Yes."

"Where's the friend who goes with you?" he asked, frowning when he noted that she was on the street alone.

"On her way home in the carriage I hired," she explained. "It lets me off first."

He nodded. "You be careful," he cautioned. "You're a daisy back east."

"I can still shoot a bow and arrow." She winked. "Skin a deer. Track a cougar." She leaned closer. "Use a bowie knife."

"Stop that."

"Sorry. It slipped out."

He glowered. "I don't use it. I threaten to use it."

"There's a difference?"

"There certainly is. A very *big* difference, miss."

"I'll reform," she promised, smiling. There were deep lines around his mouth and nose, and dark circles under his eyes. "Poor Matt. You're tired to death."

"I spend long nights watching people I'm hired to watch." He studied her face under the wide-brimmed felt hat she was wearing. "You don't look much better."

"Nursing is a tiring profession, too, Matt. I spent my day sitting with a patient who had a leg amputated. He was knocked down and run over by a carriage. He's barely my age."

"Young for such a drastic injury."

"Yes. And he was a baseball player."

He grimaced.

"He wants to commit suicide," she said. "I talk and talk, hoping I'll dissuade him."

He touched her cheek. It was cold from the winter wind. "I felt that way myself, once," he murmured. "Then this pretty little blond girl came and held my hand while her father dug bullets out of my hide. And soon life grew sweet once more."

"Did I make you want to live?" she asked. "Really?"

He nodded. "My whole family was dead. I had nothing to look forward to beyond hating the white soldiers or trying to avenge my people. I was in such terrible pain. But the pain grew manageable, and I saw the futility of trying to fight a veritable ocean of whites. What is it you say, better to join than fight them?"

"If the odds are against you." She liked the feel of his strong, warm fingers on her cheek. She stood very still so that he wouldn't move them. "Is it so bad, the way you live now?"

He studied her face. "If I were a poor man, it might be. I have too many advantages here to feel sorry for myself." His eyes narrowed. "Tess, try not to get too embroiled in the women's movement, will you? Some of these women are very radical."

"I promise not to go wild with a hatchet in any local bars," she said demurely. "Does that reassure you?"

"Not a lot," he said. "Your father worried about you."

Her pale eyes became sad. "Yes, he did. I miss him terribly. But I couldn't very well stay on at the reservation. The job was his, not mine."

"They'd probably have hired you to teach, if you'd asked," he commented.

"Possibly. Still, there was the persistent lieutenant. What a temptation he presented."

His brow rose. "Temptation?"

"I was tempted to put a bullet through him," she clarified. "I was at Wounded Knee, too, Matt. I know he shot women and children and old men."

His hand slowly lowered. "You should go inside. It's too cold out here for idle conversation."

"You can't imagine how you look when I

mention the massacre," she said softly. "I'm sorry. However painful the memories are for me, I know they're a hundred times worse for you."

He gazed down at her with his heart twisting inside him. She was pretty, but her attraction went so far beyond the physical. She had a soft heart and a stubborn independence that made his breath catch. She had, he mused, a savage heart.

"Why are you smiling?" she asked.

"I was thinking how you go headfirst into a fight," he replied. "And how soft your heart is." He became solemn. "Don't wear it on your sleeve, little one," he said softly. "The world can be a cruel place."

She saw the lines in his hard face and reached up hesitantly to touch the ones between his dark eyes. He flinched and she jerked her fingers back.

"Sorry!" she cried, flustered.

His expression grew even more grim. "I'm not used to being touched. Especially by women."

She laughed nervously. "So I noticed!"

He relaxed, but only fractionally. "I've grown a shell since I've been here," he confessed. "And now I'm trapped in it. I'm rich and successful. But under it all, I'm still a poor ragged Indian—to people more shortsighted than you are."

"I've only always thought of you as my friend."

"And I am," he said solemnly. "I'd do anything for you."

L. E. SMOOT MEMORIAL LIBRARY
KING GEORGE, VA. 22485

"I know that." She drew her old coat closer and smiled up at him, her gaze intent. "I'd do anything for you, too, Matt."

As she turned away, he suddenly caught her arm and swung her back to him. The unexpected movement made her lose her balance. She fell heavily against him. His hand at her back steadied her, and she rested against him, breathing in soap and cologne and a faint scent of tobacco from the occasional cigar he smoked.

His eyes were turbulent, and the hold he had on her was new and exciting.

A little startled, she asked huskily, "What is it?"

His gaze roamed over her face, then stopped on her mouth. Her lips were full and soft and he wondered not for the first time in their long relationship how they would feel under his. The hunger he felt made his heart race.

"Matt, you're scaring me," she said all in one breath.

"Nothing scares you," he returned. "You walked right into the thick of the wounded, even before the soldiers had stopped hunting the people who escaped the Hotchkiss guns. A young girl with her whole life ahead of her, completely blameless. You and your father were kind... and so courageous."

The contact with his hard chest was making her knees weak. She bit her lower lip, trying to regain some sort of control over her wandering senses. Her hands pressed gently into the silky stuff of his vest.

"This is... unconventional."

"Working as a nurse isn't?"

She punched him in the ribs. "Don't you start. I get enough guff from those old ladies in there." She scanned the dark windows of the boardinghouse. Did a curtain move?

"They're probably clutching the windowsills, dying to see what happens next."

"What happens next is that you let go of me so that I can get in out of the cold," Tess said with far more confidence than she felt. Her reaction to Matt's closeness was surprising and a little frightening. She hadn't thought herself vulnerable to any man's touch.

His lean, strong hands moved down to her tiny waist and rested there while he continued to look intently at her.

"You aren't like any other woman I've ever known," he said after a long, breathless silence.

"Do you know a lot of women in Chicago who shoot bows and speak Sioux?"

He shook her gently. "Be serious."

"I don't dare." She laughed. "I have... I have my life planned. I intend to devote it to the women's movement."

"Totally?"

She fidgeted in his grasp. "Yes."

"Have they convinced you that men are superfluous? Or, perhaps, suitable only for the purpose of breeding?"

"Matt!"

"Don't look so outraged. I've heard members of the women's rights groups say such things. Like the mythical Amazons, they feel that men are good for only one purpose, and that marriage is the first step to feminine slavery."

"It is," she said vehemently. "Look around you. Most married women have a child a year. They're considered loose if they work outside the home. They must bend to the husband's will without thought of their own comfort or safety. There is nothing to stop a man from beating his wife and children, from gambling away all they own, from drinking from dawn till dusk... Oh, Matt, can't you see the terror of this from a woman's point of view, even a little?"

"Of course I can," he replied honestly. "But you speak of exceptions, not the rule. Remember, Tess, change is a slow thing in a large society."

"It won't happen by itself."

"I agree. But I also feel that it can't be forced in any drastic fashion. Such as," he continued coldly, "taking children away from their parents on the reservations and sending them away to government schools, making it illegal for them to speak their own language"—he paused, smiling now—"even making it illegal to wear their hair long."

Her hands itched to touch his hair, as she had only once, in the early days of their relationship, when he was teaching her the bow. She searched his dark eyes, a question in her own. "Do you miss the old days?"

He laughed shortly and let her go. "How can I miss something so primitive? Can you really see me in buckskins speaking pidgin English?"

She shook her head. "No, not you," she said. "You'd be in a warbonnet, painted, on horseback, a bow in hand."

He averted his head. "I'll be late. I have to go."

"Matt, for heaven's sake, you aren't ashamed of your heritage?"

"Good night, Tess. Don't go out alone. It's dangerous."

He strode away without a single look over his shoulder. Tess stood and watched him for a moment, shivering in the cold wind. He was ashamed of being Sioux. She hadn't realized the depth of it until tonight. Perhaps that explained why he rarely went home to South Dakota, why he didn't speak of his cousins there, why he dressed so deliberately as a rich white man. He hadn't cut his hair, though, so he might retain a vestige of pride in his background, even if he kept it hidden. She shook her head. So many of his people had been unable to do what he had, to resign themselves to living like whites, and the policies forbidding them their most sacred ceremonies and the comfort of their shamans were slowly killing their souls. It must have been easier for Matt to live in Chicago and fan the fires of gossip about his true background, than to go to the reservation and deal with it.

She recalled the way soldiers and other white men had spoken to him when he lived with her and her father, and she bristled now as she had then at the blows to his enormous pride. Prejudice ran rampant these days.

Nativism, they called it. Nobody wanted "foreigners" in this country, to hear white people talk. Tess's lip curled. The very thought of calling a *native* American a *foreigner* made her furious. Out west, one still could hear discussion about eradicating the small remnant of the Indian people by taking away all their remaining lands and forcefully absorbing them into white society, absorbing them and wiping out their own culture in the process.

Did no one realize that it was one hairbreadth from genocide? It turned Tess's stomach. She'd always felt that the government's approach to assimilating the Indians was responsible for the high rates of alcoholism, suicide, and infant mortality on the reservations.

She turned away from the cold wind and went inside the boardinghouse, her mind ablaze with indignation for Indians and women. Both were downtrodden by white men, both forbidden the vote.

The two old ladies who lived upstairs, Miss Barkley and Miss Dean, gave her a cold stare as she tried to pass quickly by the open door to the parlor where they sat.

"Decent young ladies should not stand in the street with men," Miss Dean said icily. "Nor should they attend radical meetings or work in hospitals."

"Someone must tend the sick," Tess said. "I daresay it might do you both good to come to one of our meetings and hear what your sisters in life are bearing because society refuses to accept women as equals!"

Miss Barkley went pale. "Miss... Meredith," she gasped, a hand at her throat, "I do not consider myself the equal of a man, nor should I want to!"

"Filthy, sweating brutes," Miss Dean agreed. "They should all be shot."

Tess grinned. "There, you see, Miss Dean, you and I have much in common! You simply must come to a meeting with me."

"Among those radicals?" asked Miss Dean, scandalized.

"They aren't," Tess returned. "They're honest, hardworking girls who want to live life as full citizens of this country. We are a new type of woman. We will never settle back and accept second-class citizenship."

Miss Barkley was red in the face. "Well, I never!"

Miss Dean held up a hand. "A moment, Clara," she told her companion. "Miss Meredith presents some interesting arguments. These meetings are open to anyone?"

"Certainly," Tess said. "You may go with me next Tuesday, if you like, and see what they are about."

"Ida, don't you dare!" Miss Barkley fumed.

"I should have gone, were I twenty years younger," came the reply, and a smile. "But I am too old and set in my ways, Miss Meredith."

"Tess," she corrected.

The older woman's eyes twinkled. "Tess, then. I hope you achieve your goals. My generation will not live to see it, but perhaps yours will eventually gain the vote."

Tess went to her own room, happily having diverted them from any discussion of her surprising interaction with Matt. It wouldn't do to have people in the boardinghouse speculate about the two of them. She refused to do any speculating on her own, either. She buried Matt's odd behavior in the back of her mind and got ready for bed.

Outside the wind was blowing fiercely; snow-flakes struck the windowpane. She closed her eyes, hoping for a heavy snowfall. She always felt curiously happy, often content, too, on snowy days.

Chapter Three

Saturday's march was lively. It was held after dark with torches to light the path of the marchers. More than four hundred women showed up, carrying placards. Tess marched between two women she knew vaguely, but she missed the company of her friend Nan.

"Isn't this exciting?" the girl beside her asked. "We're bound to win with such large numbers of us demanding the vote now."

Tess agreed, but less wholeheartedly. She'd learned one terrible truth in her young life, and that was the bullheadedness of government in the face of demands for change. Regardless of how just the cause, the people in power in Washington were avid in supporting the status quo. Roosevelt was keen on creating a safe place for wildlife and showing pride in the American spirit. But he was also a believer in Manifest Destiny, and a manly man. Tess wondered if he shared the same attitude toward women that most men of his generation harbored—that women were created only to keep house and bear children and look after men.

Demonstrations inevitably attracted spectators; Tess glanced around at them. A man waving a flag that read UP WITH LABOR stepped from the street into the ranks of the women, bringing a small body of cohorts with him.

"This is not your group!" one woman yelled at him.

"This struggle is also the workers' struggle!" the man yelled back, and kept marching. "We support your cause! Down with oppression of all kinds!"

"You see?" one of Tess's companions grumbled. "We cannot even hold a rally without having a man step in and try to lead it. Well, I'll just show him a thing or two!"

The small, matronly woman turned in the throng with her placard held like a club and beaned the advocate for laborers with it right on his bald spot.

He yelped and dropped the banner, and the few men and women who were in his group started attacking the women's rights marchers.

Tess stood very still and gave a long sigh as she heard the first of many police whistles start to sound. The authorities had looked for a way to break up this march, and the communist had given it to them. The small scuffle became a melee.

As she tried to move back from the combatants, Tess was aware of a newcomer who didn't seem to be part of either group. He was tall and young, expensively dressed, and he carried a cane. He seemed to be looking straight at her. While she was wondering about the odd incident, she was suddenly knocked down and all but trampled as the fighting accelerated.

She never lost consciousness, but she heard a metallic sound through the commotion of loud voices. She rolled to avoid being stepped on, and as she did, her arm was hit a mighty blow. It throbbed, and even though the light was dim, she could see that the sleeve of her jacket and blouse seemed to be ripped through.

Two policemen were on either side of her when she looked up again. One of them, kindly and older, assisted her to the sidewalk. Muttering about people who couldn't live and let live, he left her on the stoop of an apartment house. Two small boys played with a hoop and gave her curious stares.

She wished that she could open her blouse and look at her arm because it felt wet as well as bruised under her torn jacket, but to do something so indecent in public would start another riot. She wondered how she was going to find the carriage and driver Matt had insisted on hiring to take her to and from the hospital and her suffragist meetings as soon as she'd received the nursing position and found the group of women she wanted to join. Her driver, Mick Kennedy, was a prince of a fellow, and she'd asked him to wait a number of blocks away from the demonstration for her. Now the streets were in such an uproar and she was feeling so very disoriented that she wasn't sure precisely where he was or how to find him.

As luck would have it, Mick Kennedy found her. Worried by what he'd seen on the fringes of the demonstration, he'd hitched his team to a street lamp, plunged into the crowd, and spent the last fifteen minutes or so searching for her. He was visibly relieved to find her.

"Hurt in all this, were you?" At her nod, he added, "Some mess, I'll say. Shall I get you back to your boardinghouse?"

"Oh yes, thank you, Mick."

"Well, now, just take me arm and I'll have you back there in no time, or me name's not Mick Kennedy!"

In short order they were out of the crowd, and Mick was helping Tess into the carriage. His fine team was swiftly under way, drawing the impressive black carriage through the thinning crowd.

By the time they reached the boardinghouse, Tess's arm was much worse.

"Shall I help you up to your door, ma'am?" Mick offered.

"No, thank you. I can manage." She smiled, then made her way slowly up the steps.

Mrs. Mulhaney met her at the door. At the sight of Tess, dirty and disheveled, her hat askew and her hair coming down, she exclaimed, "Why, Miss Meredith, whatever has happened?"

"A man from the workers' party infiltrated

our ranks and provoked one of our number to violence." Tess groaned. She leaned against the wall, wincing and nauseated, as she regarded the staircase with uneasy eyes and wondered how she was going to get to her room.

"Is my cousin Matt in this evening?" she asked suddenly.

"Why, I'm sure he is. I haven't seen him go out. You wait here, my dear; I'll fetch him!"

Mrs. Mulhaney rushed upstairs and quickly came back down with Matt, who was shrugging into a jacket as he walked. He eyed Tess with an expression she was too wounded to contemplate.

"Are you hurt? Where?" he asked immediately.

"My arm," she said, breathing unsteadily. "I was trodden on, and I think it may be cut, as my sleeve is."

"Can you send for Dr. Barrows?" he asked Mrs. Mulhaney.

"I can—and shall. At once. Can you take Miss Meredith to her room?"

"Yes."

Without another word, Matt swung Tess up in his arms and climbed the staircase as easily as if he were carrying feathers.

She clung to his neck, savoring his great strength as he covered the distance to her door.

"Who did this?" he asked under his breath.

"There was a riot," she explained. "I don't know who did it. Several people were fighting, and I seem to have got in the way. My arm throbs so!"

"Which one?"

"The left one, just above the elbow. I didn't even see how it happened. I rolled away from a very heavy man who was about to step on me. I remember a man with a cane looking at me before I fell, just before something stabbed at my arm. I think it might have been his cane. I wish I'd bitten his ankle."

The mental picture of Tess with her teeth in a man's ankle amused Matt and he chuckled softly.

"Here, open the door for me, can you?" he asked, lowering her.

She turned the crystal knob with her good hand and pushed the door open, trying not to notice the faint scent of his cologne and the warm sigh of his breath close to her lips. Matt shouldered into the room and carried her to her bed. He put her down very gently on the quilt that covered the white-enameled iron bedstead.

Wary of Mrs. Mulhaney's return, he closed the door and then matter-of-factly began taking off Tess's jacket.

She was panting, but not from the pain. "Matt, you... mustn't!" She feverishly tried to stay the lean, strong hands that were unfastening her blouse.

His black eyes met hers with a faint twinkle. "Feeling prudish, Tess? You saw as much if not more of me after I was shot at Wounded Knee."

"I was fourteen then," she said, aware even as she spoke that it was a nonsensical answer. "And you mustn't handle me... like this."

"Where are all those slogans you were spouting about a woman's rights?" He glanced down again at the buttons. "Don't your more radical sisters even advocate free love?"

"I am not... that radical! Will you please stop undressing me?"

He didn't even slow down. "With the best of luck, it will take the doctor a little time to get here," he said as he worked buttons through the dainty holes. "I smell the blood."

She started, having forgotten about Matt's remarkable sensory powers, honed from childhood. If he'd ever been a child. Sioux males trained to be warriors from a very early age, learning the knife and bow and horsemanship as young boys, and getting a taste of battle by accompanying war parties as water carriers.

"Matt..." she protested, both hands going to the buttons to stop him.

He brushed her fumbling fingers aside. "I never imagined you to be such a prim woman," he chided. "You and I know more about each other than many husbands and wives do."

That was true. Intimacy had been forced into their relationship because she nursed him so long after his devastating wounds. Not that her father hadn't had many qualms. It violated his sense of morality and decorum, but he had been unable to withstand her tearful pleas to be allowed to help.

"But this is... different," she tried to explain.

His hands stilled for an instant while he looked into her eyes and saw the shyness there.

"I would do the same for anyone," he said evenly.

She bit her lower lip.

He moved her hands aside very gently. "No one will ever know," he said softly. "Does that reassure you?"

It was odd that she trusted him so much. The thought of any other man's hands on her was sickening. But not Matt's. They were immaculate hands, always clean and neat and so very strong, yet gentle.

The problem was that her heart reacted violently to the touch of those hands on her bare skin over her collarbone. She ached for him to do more than unbutton her clothing, though she couldn't imagine what that "more" might be.

He pretended not to notice, and unbuttoned the last of the buttons on her blouse. Visible beneath it was a whalebone corset and, above that, a lace-decorated muslin chemise. At the sight of the dark points of her nipples through the muslin Matt's hands stilled. A faint glitter claimed his dark eyes for an instant.

"You mustn't stare at me like that," she whispered.

His eyes lifted to hers. "Why not?"

She wondered that herself. While she was struggling for a rational reason, his eyes went back to her bodice and seemed bent on memorizing how she looked.

"Oh, this is very unconventional," she protested weakly.

"And wickedly pleasurable," he murmured. His hand slid from the buttons of her blouse to the edge of the muslin and she jumped as if his lean fingers burned her soft skin.

"You rake!" she gasped, catching his hand.

"All right." He chuckled, letting her move his curious fingers back to the task at hand. "If I had any lingering doubts about your modern ideas, they're gone now."

"What do you mean?" she asked indignantly.

"All that talk about free love and liberated morals," he chided. "You're a fraud."

She glowered, but she didn't deny it. He lifted her and moved her arm gently to free it from the long sleeve of her blouse. It hurt dreadfully.

He whispered to her in Sioux, a tender command to be still. Once the arm was free, leaving her only in the sleeveless muslin chemise, he turned her arm gently so that he could see the wound. It was a long, deep cut on her upper arm, made not by a cane, but almost certainly by a sword. A sword concealed in a cane? Whoever had wielded it had meant to do damage, perhaps even more damage than he'd accomplished with this wound.

"This is deep," he said angrily. The rent in her otherwise perfect white skin was sluggishly discharging blood. He took a cloth from the washstand, applied pressure, making her wince, and held it until the bleeding began to stop.

"I wish I knew who did it," she muttered.

"No more than I do." He held her hand above the cloth he'd placed over the wound and left her long enough to fetch a basin of water and soap and a fresh cloth. He bathed the wound gently, watching her posture go rigid as he performed the necessary chore. He put the basin aside to fetch a bottle of rubbing alcohol and some cotton flannel. "This is going to hurt like hell," he told her.

She held her arm steady and looked at him with her teeth locked, then nodded.

The sting was almost unbearable. She made a sharp little cry and bit her lip as he flooded the wound with the alcohol.

"Sorry," she said at once, pale but game. "That was shameful, to cry out like that."

"Considering the pain, it was hardly shameful," he said honestly. He covered the wound with another piece of clean flannel and went to fetch her lacy robe from the clothes closet. Gently, he enfolded her in it.

"No, Matt, it's the only one I have! The blood will stain it!"

"Robes are easily replaced," he said indifferently. "Put it on."

And without argument she did so, docile, he supposed, because of the pain. He drew the front edges together, his knuckles just barely brushing the curve of her breasts above the chemise, and she gasped at the contact.

He hesitated, searching her eyes. Under his hands, he could feel the frantic whip of her heart; he could see the erratic beat of the pulse in her neck. Her lips parted and everything she felt was suddenly visible. A scarlet flush ran from her cheeks down her white throat to the silky white skin of her throat and shoulders and breasts.

Something was happening to her. She felt her breasts draw, as if they'd gone cold. Inside her, there was a burst of warmth, a throbbing that made her feel tight all over. Matt's hands contracted on the lace of the robe, and if she wasn't badly mistaken, they moved closer to her skin, the warm knuckles blatantly pressing into the soft flesh.

His eyes were on a level with hers, and her heart raced even faster as she saw the heat in them. They were a liquid black, steady and turbulent, unblinking on her rapt face. For seconds that dragged into minutes, they simply looked at each other in hot silence.

Just as his hands moved again, just as she felt the chemise give under their insistent but almost imperceptible downward pressure, footsteps on the staircase sounded like thunder, breaking the spell.

Matt stood up at once and turned away from her, leaving her to close the robe and fasten it frantically. Her hand went protectively to the flannel she was holding over the wound.

There was a perfunctory knock and the door opened.

The doctor glanced from one to the other. "Matt Davis? And this would be your cousin?" he added with a smile, closing the door behind him. "What happened?"

She told him in a jerky voice.

"I brought her some water and soap to bathe the wound and some flannel and alcohol to clean it thoroughly," Matt said. "But it will need more tending."

"Of course it will. Wait outside again if

you don't mind, young man," he added, assuming, as Matt had meant him to, that Tess had done the treatment herself.

"Certainly," Matt said formally, and went out of the room.

The doctor pulled the robe aside and probed the wound carefully. "What did this?"

She winced at the unpleasant examination. "A cane, I believe."

"No, ma'am. More probably the point of a sword cane," he corrected. "A nasty deep cutting wound, too. I'll do what I can, but you're going to be very sick for a few days, young woman. This wound will have to be carefully watched for sepsis. I'm to be called at once if you see red streaks on your arm... or a greenish discoloration around the wound."

"I'm a nurse, sir," she said in a strained tone. "My father was a physician."

"Indeed!"

"I work in the Cook County Hospital," she added.

"I thought you looked familiar. What a small world. And how fortunate that you knew what to do for this. I shan't need to lecture you on how to tend it, shall I?" he added with a small chuckle.

He swabbed the wound with more alcohol, then began to take stitches while she recited the alphabet through gritted teeth.

"I have only a small amount of suturing material with me," he explained. "That wound could do with a few more stitches, but I think the three I've made will hold just fine." He applied a neat bandage.

"You'll send for me if there are any problems," he said, rising. "And you won't work until the wound heals," he added firmly.

"Yes, sir," she said with a resigned sigh, wondering how she was going to earn her crust of bread. She still had a little of the nest egg her father had left her. Hopefully, she wouldn't have to use too much of it. "You'll send your bill?"

"My wife will," he said kindly. "And now I'll give you something to make you sleep."

He left a bottle of laudanum with instructions on its use, gave her a polite nod and a smile as he snapped his bag shut, and left.

Somber and quiet, Matt entered only minutes later. "The doctor said that he gave you something to make you rest."

"Yes. This." She indicated the cork-stoppered brown bottle.

"I'll fetch a spoon."

"Can't I have it in water?"

"All right."

There was a glass carafe near the bed. He poured water from it into its matching cup, mixed the drug for her, and watched her gulp the bitter-tasting draft.

"If you have fever, and you probably will, you'll have to be sponged down," he said. "I'd prefer to stay with you myself, but it just wouldn't be acceptable, Tess. You know that. Mrs. Mulhaney already has complained about your nursing and your work in the women's movement. We don't dare make matters worse."

She felt very sick, and her arm was hurting

badly. She looked up at Matt, only half hearing him. "I feel terrible."

"No doubt." He brushed wisps of hair back from her face. "I'm going to find someone to sit with you. I'll be back as quickly as I can."

Her hand caught his, and she held it to her cheek. "Thank you," she whispered wearily.

His face was unreadable, but his fingers lightly caressed her cheek before he drew them away. "Try to sleep," he said. "The laudanum should help."

"Yes."

He eased out the door and closed it behind him, his dark face taut with anger. It made no sense at all that someone should deliberately stab her, but that was the only logical explanation for what had happened. And he had a sick feeling that wounding her had not been the goal of her attacker. Far from it. She'd mentioned rolling away from trampling feet just before she felt the pain. Had he been aiming at another target on her body? If she hadn't rolled over, would she be dead now?

He was being fanciful, he told himself. Tess had been in Chicago a very brief time. Why would anyone want to kill her? No, it had to have been some renegade, perhaps a disgruntled husband or son who hated all women and found an outlet for his anger in attacking a member of the women's movement. But why Tess?

By the time Matt located an elderly woman who made her living caring for the sick and infirm to sit with Tess, the patient was long since fast asleep on her pillows, still in her clothing. Matt looked in on her briefly and then left her with the sitter, Mrs. Hayes, confident from his knowledge of the woman that she'd take good care of Tess. It was much too late for him to be sitting in the room, and Tess still had to be put into her night clothing, asleep or not. He didn't like leaving her, but there was very little he could do for her right now. He daren't risk her reputation.

On his way back to his own room, he was intercepted by a flustered Mrs. Mulhaney.

"Mr. Davis, two of my tenants are very, very upset by all this," she said worriedly. "Please don't think that I haven't every sympathy for your cousin's wound, but these suffragists do bring such things on themselves... marches and torchlight parades, and working around hospitals and living alone. It's so scandalous!"

Matt had to bite his tongue to keep from making a harsh reply. Mrs. Mulhaney was a victim of her own advanced age and her upbringing. She wouldn't move easily into the twentieth century.

"She's my cousin," he said. "I won't turn my back on her."

He didn't smile. At times he could look quite formidable. This was one of them.

"Well, and I wouldn't expect you to!" she said, reddening. She made an odd gesture. "I'm sure that she'll be discreet in the future—I mean, I do hope that she'll be all right. If there's anything I can do..."

"I've employed a woman to sit with her," he said. "She'll be taken care of."

Matt Davis made her feel uncharitable, Mrs. Mulhaney thought. Those black eyes of his could chill her bones. She often wondered about his background. There were so many rumors about his origins. He didn't have an accent, so she discounted those who credited him with European ancestry. However, the thought occurred to her that he might have studied English so thoroughly that he had no accent. She'd seen an African at the World's Columbian Exposition in 1893, and he spoke perfect English with a British accent!

"If there's anything I can do..." she reiterated.

Matt only nodded and went into his room, closing the door firmly behind him. Mrs. Mulhaney hovered, but only for a moment, then rushed downstairs, trying to put the troubling Matt Davis and his beautiful maverick cousin out of her mind.

Sunday, Matt sat with Tess and Mrs. Hayes for most of the day, not caring what the other tenants or Mrs. Mulhaney might think. Tess was much worse, and quite feverish, as the doctor had predicted. She was pale as death except for her flushed cheeks.

Mrs. Hayes spent a good deal of her time wetting cold cloths to put over Tess's feverish forehead.

"My husband was shot once," she confided, "in a riot. Acted just like this, he did, delirious and tossing and turning and saying all sorts of crazy things. Poor child. She keeps muttering about birds. Ravens."

He was not going to tell her that he'd once been known as Raven Following, or about the superstitions of his people concerning that large black bird.

"Delirious, I suppose," he said, his eyes on Tess's drawn face.

"She's been like this for most of the night and a good deal of the morning," Mrs. Hayes said. She put another cloth in place. "I'll keep this fever at bay, don't you worry, Mr. Davis. This child will be fine."

He didn't answer. One lean hand reached down to touch Tess's flushed cheek.

Her pale green eyes opened, and she looked up at him through a mist of fever and laudanum. "My arm... hurts. Where is my father?"

Matt hesitated. "He isn't here," he said finally. "You're going to be fine. Try to sleep."

"I can't... sleep. The birds come. They tear at my flesh." She shivered as she looked at him. "The bullets," she whispered frantically. "They tore the flesh like giant talons, and the people lay there, in the snow... in the snow!"

Wounded Knee. The fever would accentuate the horrible memories.

"Crazed in the head." Mrs. Hayes nodded. "Birds and bullets and snow. Poor thing. Where is her father?" she asked Matt when Tess had slipped back into oblivion.

"He died," he replied bluntly, "just a couple of months ago. She came here because I'm the only family she has left." It made him warm inside to say it that way. It felt so true. She was the only family he had, too. They weren't related—well, not by blood, at least—a fact that he didn't dare share with anyone.

"Well, it's good that you have each other," Mrs. Hayes said. She frowned as she studied Tess. "Odd that she hasn't married, and her such a pretty girl."

"Yes," he said.

She glanced at him. "No beau at all?"

"No," he replied, hating the thought of Tess with another man. He'd often worried about what he'd do if she ever decided to marry anyone else. The situation hadn't arisen, though, thank God. "She's never mentioned a special man."

"Would she, to her own cousin?" Mrs. Hayes asked. "But, then, perhaps not. It is a shame, though."

Matt changed the subject adroitly by asking what Mrs. Hayes thought of President Roosevelt. She was good for an hour on that topic, as it happened, and Matt was able to avoid any more discussion of Tess's love life.

The next morning, after only a few hours of sleep, Matt shaved and dressed for work.

He went in to see Tess, who was sleeping and still looked feverish. "I have to go to my office," Matt said reluctantly. "Take good care of her. She's a fighter, but it won't hurt to remind her that she is."

"I'll do that." Mrs. Hayes frowned. "That arm's bleeding," she pointed out.

Matt felt his stomach do an uneasy flip. "I'll call at Dr. Barrows's office on my way," Matt said with a grim sigh. "She's probably tossed and turned enough to tear the stitches."

"T'ain't but three stitches," Mrs. Hayes said curtly. "I had to retie the bandage early this morning. That's why it's opened again."

"What?" Matt's lips pressed into a thin line. "Good Lord, the cut's almost four inches long! It needed more than three stitches! I'll speak to him about that as well," he said. He nodded, took one last look at Tess, and went out the door. His stride was enough to make two gentlemen on the street step right back to give him room.

Dr. Barrows was on his way out when Matt caught up with him at the office he maintained at the side of his elegant residence.

"Tess is restless, and has torn the wound open," he told the physician curtly. "And Mrs. Hayes says that there were only three stitches to keep it from reopening."

Dr. Barrows fidgeted, his black bag right in his hand. "Yes, yes, I know, I had barely enough sutures for that many stitches. I was sleepy, and it was very late... I have plenty of sutures this morning, though, and I'll attend to it. Is she feverish?"

"Very." Matt's eyes narrowed. "I'll take it personally if she doesn't improve," he added, and with an almost imperceptible movement of his arm, his jacket drew back from the bright paisley vest to disclose a leather belt that held a long, broad knife with a carved bone handle.

The doctor was used to threats, and he didn't take them seriously. But this man wasn't like those he routinely dealt with. And he hadn't seen a knife like that since a boyhood trip out to the Great Plains. One of the cavalry scouts, a half-breed, had carried something similar. It was a great wide gleaming blade of metal with which, a sergeant told him, that very scout had lifted a scalp right in front of his eyes.

His hand tightened on his bag. "Of course you will, Mr. Davis," he said curtly. "But your cousin is going to improve. I'll take excellent care of her!"

"I know you will," Matt replied, and the very words carried a soft, dangerous threat that was only emphasized by the faint smile on his thin lips.

Dr. Barrows watched the tall man walk away, his eyes narrowed on that odd gait. Davis didn't walk like a city man. Like many other Chicagoans, he wondered where the mysterious Mr. Davis came from. But it wasn't a question he was keen to ask the man. No, not at all keen.

He pulled his pocket watch out by its long gold chain and flipped the case open with a practiced movement. He was already late starting his calls, but he was going to see Miss Meredith first thing. He should have gone home for the sutures Saturday night. He certainly would properly stitch that wound today!

Chapter Four

Sitting behind his huge oak desk in a swivel chair, Matt whirled toward the fair, younger man who had just entered at his call.

"Stanley, I want to find somebody," he said curtly. "A well-dressed man with a cane who was at the women's movement torchlight parade Saturday night. He'd probably be with the workers' party people who muscled in on the women."

"Yes, sir," Stanley Lang said eagerly. Stanley was only twenty-two, a tall and gangly man who reacted with enthusiasm to any sort of job he was given. He was also the youngest of Matt's six agents. "Do we have any identification for this man?"

"None," was the deep reply. "He stabbed my cousin. I want his name."

Stanley's eyes opened wide. He'd worked for Matt Davis for two years, and he'd heard from the other agents that their boss never spoke of family. This was news indeed.

"Was he badly hurt?" Stanley asked.

"She," Matt corrected. "She was stabbed in the arm. But I think the man meant to do her worse harm. I must know who he is."

"Well, I'll certainly do my best, sir," Stanley returned. "And I hope your cousin will be all right."

"So do I," Matt murmured. He glanced up. "Get going, man."

"Yes, sir, and thank you for the opportunity—"

"Out, Stanley."

"Yes, sir, but I really do appreciate—"

"Out!"

Stanley withdrew at once with a wide grin and closed the door to discourage any flying objects that might come from that quarter. Matt Davis was known to throw things when he was in one of his black moods. Usually it was something soft. But one never knew.

Matt brooded for half the day while he pursued his own pending cases, sending his agents out on various routine tasks. Most of his cases involved criminal activities of some sort. But one man had required an agent to follow a young woman—his wife, presumably—whom he suspected of infidelity. The Pinkerton Detective Agency, of which Matt had been an agent until two years before, had refused to accept cases that involved public or private morals. However, Matt had taken what business he could get when he started his own agency. He'd been amazed at how rapidly his clientele grew, and how wealthy he'd become in a relatively short time. Although he was able to be selective now, he also accepted cases on an individual basis, and his acceptance depended on his assessment of the client.

A rich widower wanted his daughter's shady new boyfriend checked out because he suspected that the man was a gigolo. The girl was very young and innocent, and the man had a shady reputation. Matt had accepted the case because he felt sorry for the girl.

There were other assorted jobs on the books, none of the current ones very interesting. He leaned back in his swivel chair and remembered the exciting times he and the other Pinkertons had had chasing down yeggs, safecracking burglars who robbed banks across the country. They moved around like tramps, hiding by day and working at night. They used nitroglycerin to get into the safes and generally led the agency on a merry chase. One gang of yeggs was still operating and had achieved legendary status. Almost every Pinkerton man had some anecdote about the yeggs. One of the more ironic was that of a poor law enforcement officer whom a gang of safecrackers had taken with them at gunpoint when they went to blow up a safe at a post office somewhere out west. They'd tied him up in a canvas mail bag and stamped him for travel, leaving him otherwise unharmed.

Matt didn't do much work on robberies anymore. He seemed to spend more and more of his time trapped in his second-floor office, dictating letters and talking to contacts and prospective clients. His men did most of the legwork now, and Matt missed the excitement of tracking down suspects, of extracting information. He must be getting old, he thought, to have allowed himself to get into such a rut.

He put the paperwork aside, still fuming about the attack on Tess. He didn't like remembering how sick she looked when he left for work this morning, or how careless that doctor had been about her wound. Wounds brought on fever and infection and sometimes led to gangrene. He'd seen men die of it. He was worried and he was angry at himself for not checking the doctor's work at the time. He could have punched that doctor for doing such a haphazard job. If Tess wasn't better by morning, he was going to find another physician for her.

Why had Tess been attacked? He couldn't answer that question. But he could make some reasonable assumptions. The assailant had to know her on sight. That narrowed down the possibilities. It could be someone from the hospital, which was highly unlikely, or someone connected with a woman who participated in the women's rights rallies.

As he considered that last possibility, it began to make good sense. Tess had told him that she had a young friend who attended the meetings with her, whose husband disapproved of his wife's involvement.

He shoved his chair back and stood up. Yes. That would be the most likely source.

He jerked open his office door in time to catch Stanley putting on his derby. "Stanley!"

"Yes, sir?"

"Hold on a minute. Before you go any further with your hunt for the man who attacked my cousin, I want to stop by my boardinghouse and check with her. I think I may have an easier way to find the culprit."

"Yes, sir!"

Minutes later, Matt tapped briefly on Tess's door and waited for Mrs. Hayes to admit him.

The older woman was chuckling as she shut him in the room with Tess and herself.

"Must have lit a fire under that pill pusher, Mr. Davis," she mused, "because he treated herself here as if she were royalty. Looks better, don't she?"

Indeed, Tess did look better. She was still feverish, but she was conscious and seemed aware of her surroundings.

"Matt," she croaked, smiling through lips cracked with fever. "The doctor says my arm looks better. He put ten stitches in it this time."

"Did he?" Matt asked with a faint smile. "Feeling up to a question?"

She nodded. Her lovely long blond hair was loose and hung over her shoulders like a cloud of gold. Matt stared at her appreciatively for a moment before he moved closer to the bed and looked down into her wan face.

"That young woman who goes to meetings with you, who is she?"

"You mean Nan?"

"Yes."

"Her last name is Collier," she said in a strained tone, wincing as she moved her sore arm. "Her husband, Dennis, is a telegraph clerk somewhere. Why do you ask?"

She didn't know that she'd given him the information he wanted, without his having to pry it out of her.

"I wondered if you might like to have her visit you," he said, lying through his teeth. "She's the only real friend you've made since you came to Chicago."

"That's nice of you, Matt," she said. Her tongue felt almost too thick for speech. "But I don't think her husband would like it. He's very angry that she comes to our meetings, and forbids her to attend more than one a week. She has to sneak out if she comes to more than that. I'm sure he wouldn't approve of her coming here."

Another wealth of information. He scowled as he saw her face contort.

"It must hurt a lot," he said.

"My mouth is dry," she replied. "Could I have some water, Mrs. Hayes?"

"Certainly, dear. Here you go."

Matt took the cup from her with a smile. He lifted Tess's head, his hand buried in that thick, silky blond hair, and he held the glass to her lips, watching them move weakly as she drank. Her hair felt soft, he thought, and her eyelashes were long and thick, too. Under them, her pale green eyes were the color of the leaves on the cottonwoods early in spring.

"Had enough?" he asked.

"Yes, thanks." She smiled up at him, but the look in his eyes froze the smile. She couldn't look away. Even in her weakened condition, Matt at close range was overwhelmingly attractive to her.

His face filling her eyes, his breath on her mouth, he eased her very slowly down onto the pillow. His eyes were black and unblinking. He hesitated there, the glass forgotten in his hand, as he searched Tess's soft, shocked eyes.

"Mind that glass, Mr. Davis," Mrs. Hayes murmured as she searched for her knitting needles. "I've already spilled one glass of water over her this morning and had to air the bedclothes."

He stood up abruptly, putting the glass down on the bedside table with too much deliberation. "She does look better," he said after a minute. His voice sounded hoarse. Tess's heartbeat was visible at her throat.

"I told you so." Mrs. Hayes chuckled. She took out her yarn and sat down in the rocking chair beside the bed. "Mrs. Mulhaney is fixing some nice chicken dumplings for supper this evening. Tess said she thinks she can eat something today."

"Not too much," Matt cautioned. "She's still pretty frail."

Tess smiled at him, all the fight gone out of her as the fever fluctuated. "Thanks for coming home to see about me," she said. "When I get better, can I borrow your knife?"

The unexpected question threw him off balance. "Why?"

"I want to have a conversation with the man who cut me," she murmured weakly. "You can hold him while I talk to him with your... your knife in my hand."

"Tess, I'm shocked!" he lied.

She chuckled weakly and closed her eyes. "Isn't he lucky... that I was on the ground and helpless?" she asked wearily. "I still remember how to throw people. You taught me, remember?" She murmured softly in Sioux and Matt smiled.

"There she goes, babbling again," Mrs. Hayes said with a sigh, having failed to recognize that Tess was speaking another language.

Tess had reminded Matt that he'd once taught her how to throw him, unbeknownst to her father, who would have thought the close physical contact between them indecent.

"I never babble," Tess denied with a sleepy chuckle. "Do I, Cousin Matt?"

"Only when you're recovering from sword wounds," he said dryly. He pulled out his watch, checked the time, and slid it back into the watch pocket of his silk vest. "I'd better get back to work. I've used up my lunch break," he added, leading the women away from the real reason for his presence. "I'll check on you later, Tess. Take care."

He smiled at Mrs. Hayes, put his hat back on, and closed the door behind him.

"He's a fine figure of a man," Mrs. Hayes remarked as she began to cast on stitches for the woolly cap she was knitting. "Good to have around in an emergency, and that's for sure."

"Yes, he is, isn't he?" Tess was still feeling the heat of that look he'd given her, and even in retrospect it was exciting. Matt was like a volcano. Only a very little fire escaped until an eruption was imminent. She wondered what violent passions he hid behind that calm face, and colored as she realized the track of her errant thoughts.

Mrs. Hayes glanced at her patient, put her wool aside, and stood up. "You're flushed again. I'll wet some more cloths. Poor child, you've had a terrible time of it."

"I feel more fit, though," Tess assured her

companion. "Tomorrow, if the fever goes down, I'd like to get up a little, so that I won't be so weak." She smiled ruefully. "After all, I have to earn my living."

Mrs. Hayes put another cool cloth on Tess's forehead. "May I ask you something?"

"Of course," Tess murmured.

"Why have you never married? Surely you've had many chances."

"I've had one, but from a man for whom I had no respect, none at all," she added, recalling the cavalryman in Montana with his studied arrogance and persistence. "I should have stayed single forever rather than marry such a bounder."

"Wise girl. I married for love, but I was one of the lucky ones. My husband and I have three children living, out of the ten that I birthed." She sat back down and concentrated on her knitting. "We've had hard times, but we always had each other when things got bad." She smiled at Tess. "I don't suppose you and Mr. Davis... ?"

"Matt is my cousin," Tess said evasively, and closed her eyes. She didn't like remembering Matt's views on marriage, as well as the mixing of races.

All the same, it was hard to put out of her mind the look in Matt's black eyes when he came close to her. He was attracted to her; she knew that. But a man could be attracted and still not love. Physical attraction alone was never enough. She loved him. Nothing short of a love as powerful as her own being reciprocated would be enough. Tess closed her eyes. She might as well try to sleep. Lamenting the future was fruitless.

She concentrated on breathing slowly and evenly. Minutes later she drifted off into a restless sleep.

Matt visited five telegraph offices before he found one with a clerk named Collier. He wrote a telegraph to one of his operatives whom he'd dispatched to an outlying town, mentioning that his cousin Tess Meredith had been wounded by an unknown assailant and that he wouldn't be in the office for two days, and instructing the man to contact Senior Agent Riley Blair if he needed assistance before Thursday. Then he signed his name.

He handed the message to the clerk and watched closely as Collier read it and noted Tess's name. There wasn't much response. Only a mere twitching of the muscles in the man's hands and an almost imperceptible flutter of his eyelids. But it was enough. The man had recognized Tess's name—and now he knew her "cousin" was a detective.

Matt covertly scanned the office. First he spotted a fancy cane in the umbrella stand, along with an expensive topcoat on the rack. Matt was willing to bet that there was a sword in that cane. He had to fight down an impulse to go right over the counter after the man who'd wounded Tess. But he controlled himself. Not yet. Not until he had enough evidence to have the man arrested. He had to be able to prove that Collier had deliberately attacked her, and why.

Collier finished tallying the cost of the telegraph and told Matt. He handed the man a bank note and waited for him to make change. Collier botched it—a sure sign of nerves—and had to count out the change again.

He smiled wanly at Matt. "It will go off immediately, Mr. Davis."

"Thank you," Matt said. As he started to put the change in his pocket, he made sure that his jacket opened enough to give the man a look at the knife.

Collier's eyes widened like saucers.

Matt's chin lifted. His eyes narrowed. "Haven't you ever seen a bowie knife?" he asked coldly. "I find it much handier than a pistol in my line of work."

The younger man couldn't seem to stop staring. "Ever use it on anybody?"

Matt's thin lips tugged up a cool smile. "Yes."

Collier averted his eyes. "Thank you for your business, sir."

"Not at all. I like to patronize friends of my cousin."

The man froze in place. "Friends?"

"Well, not you, of course, Collier," he added pleasantly. "But I believe your wife, Nan, is a friend of my cousin Tess."

The man hesitated and then turned around. He was noticeably paler. "Yes. Nan knows her. They go to those accursed women's meetings together. You might as well know, I've discovered that Nan was sneaking out of the apartment on the two nights when I was at work, and I've forbidden her to attend any more meetings." Brazenly, to Matt's ear, he added, "There was a riot Saturday night, and those women were right in the middle of it. Everybody was talking about it. I'm very thankful that Nan was home with me when it happened, and that I didn't let her out of my sight."

It was a long speech, calculated, Matt thought, to make him believe that Collier had an alibi for the time when Tess was stabbed. Matt didn't buy it for a minute, but he wasn't in a position to challenge the other man yet.

"You're very lucky," Matt agreed. His face went hard. "The same can't be said for the man who wounded Tess. I'll find him. And when I do, I'll skin him alive."

Collier swallowed. "That wouldn't be legal."

"What he did to Tess wasn't legal, either. Only a coward attacks a woman."

Collier, visibly shaken now, said quickly, "I hope you'll convey my best wishes to your cousin. And Nan's best wishes, too, of course. I don't know your cousin, but I certainly wish her no harm."

Matt said nothing. He merely stared. "I'll tell Tess that she won't be seeing Nan at any more meetings. She'll be sorry, I'm sure."

Collier shifted restlessly and his face was sullen. "Some women just use those meetings as an excuse to play around," he muttered. "Damned women. Always scheming."

Matt wasn't about to get into any argument on that score. But he was grateful for the insight into why Collier might have attacked

Tess. He tipped his hat mockingly. "Good day, Mr. Collier."

"Good day."

Once out of the telegraph office and across the street, Matt looked at Collier. He wasn't sending the telegram. He was sitting at his desk with his head in his hands. He looked as if the world were sitting on him.

Good enough for him, Matt thought angrily. The damned coward, pretending that he knew nothing about Tess's attack. Odd, that last statement he'd made, about women using the meetings as an excuse to run around on their husbands. Could the young Mrs. Collier be duping Tess? Suppose she really was running around on her husband, and Collier thought that Tess was helping her? In fact, Tess had said that Nan was allowed to come to only one meeting a week, but Collier had said that she was sneaking out two additional nights.

It put a whole new complexion on the business. He'd have to look into the matter. Tess would be safe enough; Collier wouldn't dare risk arousing Matt's ire now that he knew he was up against a detective. But what about Collier's wife? If he wouldn't hesitate to brutally attack a stranger, what might he do to a wife he suspected of philandering? He wondered if Collier beat his wife, and if Tess knew anything personal about her. He made up his mind to ask her about it that night.

Tess was sitting propped up in bed in her lacy robe, which Mrs. Hayes had washed for her, with her hair tied back by a yellow ribbon. She looked very young, still pale and in some pain, but improving.

Her face lit up when he came into the room. "You're early tonight," she commented.

"I gave myself the evening off," he said, chuckling as he removed his hat and overcoat. "Let me put these in my room, and I'll be back."

He returned a minute later, frowning when he noted the absence of Mrs. Hayes.

"She went home to make supper for her husband. He's a tugboat skipper," she elaborated. "They move those big ships around when they come into port. He and two of his sons have their own business. They aren't rich, but they make a nice living."

"Who's the detective around here?" he asked.

"I could learn to be one."

"I don't doubt it for a minute. How do you feel?"

"Sore and mad," she told him. "Have you found out who did it?"

"I have a lead," he said evasively, and pulled up a chair. He'd left the door wide open for the sake of propriety. He crossed his long legs. "Tess, has Mrs. Collier ever said anything to you about a man other than her husband?"

Tess eyed him warily. "Now, why on earth would you ask me such a question?"

"Indulge me. This is important."

She sighed and sank back into the pillows. "I don't know if she's seeing anyone," she confessed after a minute. "Once or twice she's darted into a meeting just as it ended. A couple of nights she didn't share the carriage home with me. I assumed that she'd come with someone else and was leaving with her, too." She looked squarely into Matt's eyes. "If she's running around on her husband, I wouldn't blame her. He's a bully and a brute and I think he beats her. But I don't know for a fact that she's doing anything immoral."

Steps sounded outside the room, and Mrs. Mulhaney stopped, looked in, and smiled nervously.

"Oh, so you're visiting with your cousin, are you?" she asked Matt, pointedly noting the open door with approval. "Can I bring you anything, Miss Meredith?"

"Thank you, Mrs. Mulhaney, but Mrs. Hayes is coming back any second with some of her oyster stew. I've never had it before. It sounded quite interesting."

"I forget that you used to live far inland," Mrs. Mulhaney said. "What did your father do, dear?"

"He was a physician."

Mrs. Mulhaney smiled. "Why, how nice!"

Matt stared at her, unblinking. She shifted, smiled again, and excused herself, walking quickly on down the hall.

Tess muffled a giggle. "Wicked man," she taunted in a whisper. "What a chilling expression!"

He grinned at her. "I practice in the mirror twice daily." He stood up. "I think she's trying to make the point that I shouldn't be in here alone with you."

Her eyes sparkled mischievously. "You're my cousin, aren't you? Do tell why you shouldn't be alone with me."

He actually moved close to the head of the bed, and, propping a long arm against the white iron rail, he leaned down to within inches of her face. "Because God only knows what a man might do with a helpless woman should she be left alone with him and at his mercy!" he whispered.

She chuckled. "How exciting!"

He touched the tip of her nose with his finger. "Excitement is the last thing you need, my girl. Close your eyes and rest until your companion returns. I have book work to do."

"Thank you," she said, momentarily solemn. "You must have been very firm with the doctor. He was quite thorough."

"Why didn't you tell me that he hadn't stitched that arm properly?"

"I kept going in and out," she replied. "I can't remember ever feeling quite so sick and helpless."

His jaw tautened. "You won't be hurt again, I promise you," he said curtly.

She looked up at him with soft, affectionate eyes. "You take very good care of me. It's strange for you, isn't it, having someone depend on you even in a small way?"

"Yes, it is, since I've been alone so long."

"And you like it. I know. I'll try not to let anything like this happen again. Normally I'm quite self-sufficient."

Her face was wan and drawn. He knew the pain of wounds from his own experience.

"Try to get some rest. If you need me, sing out."

"I won't, but thanks." Her eyes searched his face. "You're tired, aren't you? I'm sorry I've cost you so much sleep... "

His fingers pressed back the words, lingering against her soft, warm mouth. "I don't want gratitude."

Her eyes lowered. His fingers made her lips tingle. She had to fight the urge to kiss them.

The already familiar sound of Mrs. Hayes's step on the staircase sent him away from the bed, so that he was standing by the door when the elderly woman appeared with a jar, bowl, spoon, and napkin on a wooden tray. "Borrowed from the kitchen here," she said with a grin. "Hello, Mr. Davis. Care for some of my oyster stew? I made it fresh this evening."

"Thank you, but no. I've eaten. Sleep well, Tess."

"You, too, Matt."

He went out, and this time he closed the door. Tess enjoyed the stew and Mrs. Hayes's conversation, but she was beginning to worry about the attitude of Mrs. Mulhaney. The woman obviously didn't approve of Tess—or anything about her. The landlady seemed to be looking for an excuse to toss her out. It was enough to keep her awake most of the night. She didn't know how she'd cope if she had to live away from Matt. Their relationship was so different that she tingled all over just thinking of the pleasure it gave her to be near Matt. She'd have to find some way to make friends with her disapproving landlady while there was still time.

Chapter Five

By the end of the week, Tess was up and about and feeling almost as good as new. Except for a twinge now and again from the stitches, which were due to be taken out the following Wednesday, she felt very well indeed.

Matt took her to a nearby soda parlor on Saturday and bought her an ice cream sundae, which was served in a tulip glass with mounds of whipped cream and a cherry on top. It was the most magical concoction she'd ever seen, much less tasted, and Matt found himself enjoying her reaction to it. When she was excited about something, Tess looked young as a child.

He approved of her well-fitted black suit with its green trim, although he wasn't enamored of the huge wide-brimmed feather-covered hat that she wore with it. Women and their queer ideas of fashion, he thought. Every time the wind blew, the hat shed feathers worse than a shot quail.

He stirred his own chocolate malt soda and smiled at Tess's uninhibited pleasure in the sundae.

She was glancing around her with evident curiosity, and something in the intentness of her action puzzled him.

"Why the gawking, Tess?"

She met his eyes with a start. "Oh, it was just something one of the girls at the meetings said," she replied, laughing with faint embarrassment despite herself. "I don't know if I should tell you, especially in public."

His dark eyebrows lifted and he smiled sweetly. "Go ahead. Be a devil."

She leaned toward him, so that her lips were scant inches from his ear and she could smell the spicy shaving lotion he used. "They say that ice cream parlors, especially those run by foreigners, are dens of iniquity. The white slave trade operates out of their back rooms, and also in amusement parks and at skating rinks!"

He burst out laughing, and other people in the ice cream parlor looked over.

"Do stop," she muttered, tapping him lightly on the sleeve. "People are staring at us."

He leaned forward. "You forgot to mention railroad depots," he whispered.

She sighed. "Well, what do I know? I spent most of my life in the wilderness"—she lowered her voice—"with uncivilized people!"

His black eyes twinkled. "Like me?"

She studied his handsome face. It was hard to forget the Raven Following of her very young womanhood, wearing a trailing warbonnet—a visual statement of his bravery because each feather stood for an act of courage—and his face painted with his own mystical symbolism, like his war pony.

"What are you thinking?" he asked.

She shook her head. "I was remembering,"

she corrected softly. "And you probably wouldn't like knowing what I was remembering, so you shouldn't ask."

He took a sip of his soda and then stirred it absentmindedly with a long spoon. "It was a long time ago, wasn't it?" he murmured, and he looked up, catching her eyes. "We were different people then."

"You were," she agreed, and wondered just how brave she felt like daring to be.

"In what way?"

"You weren't ashamed of your people."

It was a mistake; she knew it instantly. His hand clenched around the thick tulip glass. He didn't speak, but his black eyes did. Her gaze fell before his hot intensity.

"I told you that you shouldn't ask." She felt very uncomfortable. "I'm sorry."

He didn't say a word. He sat very still and finished his soda. "Are you through?" he asked in a curt, deep tone a few minutes later.

She nodded.

He got up, left a tip, and escorted her out the door.

"I said that I was sorry," she said after they'd gone half a block.

"You can't imagine what I feel," he said under his breath, "to be part of such a nation. They sit and starve on the reservations, freeze to death, drink illegal whiskey, and complain about the lack of rations and the poor quality of the blankets." He stopped, his eyes on the city skyline. "I came here with nothing. I scrimped and saved and studied. I learned.

I did whatever mean little job I was offered, anything that would help me to advance in my work. Two years ago—almost three years, now—I quit Pinkerton and opened my own detective agency, and I've become well-to-do because I was willing to work for what I wanted."

"You've had advantages that the others haven't," she said, lifting her face. She had to look up, a long way up. "Some of them have tuberculosis and some are crippled. Others have lost so much family that they're afraid to take a chance. Still others don't want to have to depend on the whites for survival, but they have no other options. They're too weak in numbers to fight, too proud to beg, too poorly educated or informed to know even where to begin to try for a new way of life. You were lucky."

"Too lucky," he ground out. "For God's sake, don't you understand?" He looked down at her with anguished eyes. "I don't belong anywhere now! I can't go back to warpaint and hunting buffalo, but I'll never be white either."

She put a gloved hand on his arm and let it rest there. "You carry an air of mystery around with you. No one knows exactly where you come from, or what your background is. That won't change unless you want it to. Chicago is big."

"Not big enough to escape prejudice," he said harshly. "Or haven't you noticed?"

She sighed. "Of course I've noticed. I can't change the world. I can only do my best to help keep it going around. Women aren't having an easy time either. You know what I've gone through trying to work as a nurse. I still can't imagine why people think it so indecent a profession."

His grim look began to dissolve. His lips tugged up into a reluctant smile. He bent. "You get to look at naked men," he said teasingly.

Flustered, she colored. "I most certainly do... do not!" she said. She couldn't look at him. She was carrying around a secret about their shared past that he didn't know.

"How does one avoid it?"

"One calls an orderly or a physician!" She pressed her fingers agitatedly against her wide-brimmed hat. "Of all the outrageous things to say!"

He chuckled. "We seem to have become addicted to saying outrageous things to each other." He shifted and took her arm. "Perhaps we're both too sensitive."

"One of us is," she agreed.

He pinched her arm—the uninjured one—gently and made her jump. "I am not sensitive."

"And cows fly," she muttered.

He walked her to the corner and then across the wide street, avoiding carriages and the occasional motorcar, because there was a sprinkling of the newfangled inventions loose in the city. Matt had hated the inventions since he'd been forced inside one in Atlanta, working on a case for a friend.

"Have you ever met Nan's husband?" he asked when they were safely across.

"Nan Collier's husband, Dennis? No. I

wanted to visit her, but she said that it wouldn't be a good idea at all. Since her husband doesn't approve of the women's movement, I think he might be rude to any of her friends who called."

He hesitated, uncertain about how much he should tell her. She was just getting over the attack, which had made her unsettled enough. She didn't really need to know. But it was hard not to tell her. Suppose the man tried again? Or she went home unexpectedly with her friend Nan? Matt couldn't protect her, under those circumstances, and Collier would have unrestricted access to her.

"You're holding back something," she said, eyes narrowed.

He stuck his hands in his pockets and looked down at her. "Yes, I am. I know who stabbed you."

Her heart seemed to skip a beat. "You do? Who?"

"It was your friend Nan's husband, Tess," he replied grimly.

She put a hand to the lace at her throat and mentally cursed the corset that made her even shorter of breath than the surprise did. "Heavens! Are you sure?"

"Yes. I tracked him down and satisfied myself that he was the one. I made some veiled threats, Tess, and I don't believe he'll bother you again."

She shook her head. "I can't believe it. I just can't believe it. Why?"

"Because he thought you were an accomplice."

"I beg your pardon?"

He looked around them. They weren't being watched by the passersby, but he didn't like to discuss private matters in public places. "Come with me."

He drew her along to a wrought-iron bench among some trees and sat her down, taking his place beside her.

"How much do you really know about Nan Collier?" he began.

"A lot less than I know about you," she volunteered.

He ignored the faint teasing note in her voice. "I suspect she might be having an affair, Tess."

Her face felt stiff. "An affair? You mean she's seeing someone besides her husband?"

"Yes, and using the women's meetings to cover up. Collier may have suspected or actually caught her at it and blamed you as an accomplice. He could believe you were helping her meet her lover."

"As if I would ever be party to such a sordid thing!" she exclaimed, furious.

"I know that, but you're a complete stranger to Collier. The man was beside himself when he alluded to it."

"Do you know who it is, the man she's involved with?"

"Not yet. But I will. One of my detectives is watching your Mrs. Collier. And you're not to warn her, Tess," he added firmly. "You're involved in something dangerous: A man who won't hesitate to attack a woman with a sword cane in a crowd means business.

And I don't think wounding you was his objective at all. I think that he meant to kill you." Matt's expression was grim.

Tess's breath escaped in a soft, ragged sigh. "But I knew nothing of any affair," she said huskily.

"I realize that. But my word alone, and even a threat, might not be enough to dissuade him. Even worse, he seems to have some connections—" He broke off, pausing for a second, then added, "I assigned one of my brightest young detectives to this case, Tess. Late this afternoon he reported some information that's... well, alarming, if true. I'm not going to say more until we've had a chance to sift through all this, evaluate it, and follow up leads."

Tess's mind was whirling with these revelations.

"Now that you know," he continued, "you'll be more careful, and more alert. I saw no reason to protect you; knowledge *is* freedom, Tess."

"I should have been furious if you had withheld all this. I'm not afraid of hard facts."

"I know."

She looked up at him from under the brim of her hat, her green eyes searching. And in that moment she knew that Matt was as eager as she to be free for a few minutes at least from this worrying new situation. Lightly, then, she said, "Maybe you'd better lend me that terrible knife of yours."

"You'd cut your hand off," he said, chuckling.

"I can shoot a bow and skin a deer."

"When you were fourteen."

"Do you think I stopped doing those things because you left for Chicago?" she asked haughtily. "You had cousins at Lame Deer who also left South Dakota after the massacre. I became well acquainted with some of them."

"Did your father know?"

"Of course."

"Did he approve?"

"My father was never able to stop me from doing anything that I really wanted to do, as you well know. He never thought it was ladylike for me to do the things you taught me, but then, I never pretended to be a lady."

"Yet you are one, Tess." He stared at her with appreciation. "Despite that terrible temper and outrageous independence."

"I do not have a temper, sir. It's just that I sometimes have strong opinions." Suddenly she couldn't sustain the banter any longer. Her expression serious, she asked, "Matt, what about Nan?"

"What do you mean?"

"Will he hurt her? I mean, if he was willing to stab me... even kill me, shouldn't we fear for Nan? I mean, won't he be even worse to her, if he thinks she's cheating on him and—"

"I was able to find out that he's been beating her fairly regularly," he said. "The neighbors even appealed to her elder sister to intervene on one occasion, but when she and her husband arrived, Nan swore that she'd fallen down the stairs. She refused to leave or allow her sister to call in the police." His face became set. “Amazing, isn’t it, the lengths a woman will go to in her efforts to protect a brute of a husband?”

“She might be afraid that he’ll kill her if she has him put in jail, then he gets out. Many women tolerate brutality as the lesser evil to being murdered. In other cases it’s a woman’s own security she’s protecting,” Tess added sadly. “Many of these mistreated wives have children and no hope of supporting themselves, no family to turn to. If they have the husband locked up, what are they to do—go on the… well, on the streets to earn a living?”

“A hellish living,” he said coldly, since he’d seen the way such women ended their young, miserable lives.

“Which is why our group is working so hard to change the way society treats women,” she said. “Men, most of them, will turn a blind eye to a woman’s bruises and humiliation because they convince themselves the women brought such punishment on themselves. Men stick together like glue when one of them is threatened with the law.”

“Not all of us.”

She lifted her eyes to his. “Not you,” she said softly. “Regardless of the provocation, you aren’t the sort to hurt anything or anyone who is defenseless.”

He laughed without humor. “You think you know me so well.”

“Part of you is a closed book,” she replied thoughtfully. “But I know that you would never attack an enemy, even a hateful enemy, who couldn’t fight back.”

He didn't answer her. Unseeing, his eyes seemed to be focused on distant buildings.

She handled her purse restlessly. "In years past, you weren't so reticent and hard to talk to."

"In years past, you were a child."

"I don't understand."

He turned toward her. "Why did you refuse the advances of the soldier back in Montana?"

"He was a butcher!" she exclaimed.

"You are in your mid-twenties," he persisted. "Your father told me several times that you had no interest in men whatsoever, that you refused invitations to social occasions and even to dances. Why?"

Her gloved fingers clutched her purse, distorting its contours. "I find most men irritating."

"No answer at all," he returned.

She managed to drag her gaze from his obsidian eyes to his firm mouth and then to his tie. Her heart was beating madly. She wanted to get up and run, an impulse so unlike her normally fearless state that it shocked her.

His long arm slid along the bench behind her and he bent his head closer so that he could see under the brim of her hat. His eyes were relentless on her flushed face.

"Am I the reason you never married?"

For a few seconds, the sound of his breath at her temple was all she could hear.

Her docility betrayed her to Matt. Tess wasn't docile. She was fiery and outspoken.

To see her like this was electrifying. He touched her softly rounded chin, turned it, tilting her face up.

His thumb ran gently across her full lower lip, a whisper of sensation that made her tremble visibly and almost cost him his control. In that instant, without a word being spoken, everything became clear to him. Her lack of enthusiasm for suitors, her arrival in Chicago, her refusal to become involved with local society. She averted her eyes.

He dropped his hand with a rough breath and withdrew. He might have been in another city suddenly, his remoteness was so complete. He was stunned. Speechless. He could hardly dare to let himself believe what he'd seen in her lovely face.

Gamely Tess ignored the implications of that stare and the sigh that had followed it. She got to her feet, pretending that nothing out of the ordinary had happened.

"I must go back to the boardinghouse," she said stiffly. "I am still a little weak from the wound."

"As you wish."

He didn't take her arm. He walked silently beside her, buried in his own tormented thoughts.

He opened the gate for her and remained on the other side when it closed. "I won't be at home very much for the next several days because of a case I'm working on. Don't linger at the hospital after your shifts end," he said as if nothing of any import had happened. "Get straight into the hired carriage, making sure the driver is Mick Kennedy—and only Mick Kennedy. Do you understand?"

She nodded.

"It's dangerous for you to be out alone," he said firmly.

"As if you'd care if I landed in a ditch with a knife in my ribs!" she exclaimed unfairly, surprising him with a burst of fury. His pointed lack of interest in her deepest feelings hurt terribly. "As for staying out late, I'll do what I please, and you can... you can... Oh!" she ended in a burst of pure fury as her struggle for the right words fell flat.

She didn't look back as she mounted the steps and went into the house. Perhaps if she acted normal, she might begin to feel normal. It was more than she could bear to look at him again after his pointed, humiliating question about her love life. Well, he certainly didn't love her. He'd made his opinion of white women blatantly clear over the years, and even strangers knew how he felt about mixed-blood children. She'd been building sand castles in the surf, and it had to stop.

She smiled politely at Mrs. Mulhaney and went quickly up the staircase before the woman could speak to her. She was feeling more and more uncomfortable under this roof. Soon, she decided, she was going to have to move farther away from Matt and his overly conventional landlady.

That would require some care, she thought, since there were more boardinghouses with bad reputations than good. She didn't want to end up in the white slave trade herself! Perhaps one of the nurses or even one of the women in her group might know of a respectable place where she could lodge.

Everything she felt was suddenly out in the open. It was visible. Matt knew how she felt, and he'd said nothing at all about it. He was ignoring it because she was white. She couldn't bear to have him look at her with pity. Better to break her own heart than give in to settling for crumbs.

Tess was welcomed back to the hospital Monday after a weekend of not even catching a glimpse of Matt. Despite the twinges in her arm, she enjoyed her work. It was good to stay busy when nursing a broken heart.

The young amputee, Marsh Bailey, was happy to see her. "I've been desperate for a sight of you," he said, his sad eyes lighting up when she paused by his bed. "The older nurses are very unsympathetic."

They'd had years to become hardened, Tess thought, as any good nurse had to be or lose her sanity. She was already unsettled by this young man's clinging nature. He had been becoming obsessed with her before she was hurt; apparently his feelings about her had become even more charged in her absence. She felt extremely uncomfortable with him now. He was only a patient to her, but he wanted more than her nursing skill.

"I've been thinking," he said in a quick, agitated tone, "that we might live in a smaller town north of here when we marry."

"Marsh," she burst out, "I won't marry you."

He was perspiring rather profusely, and his eyes had a glassy, glazed quality. "You must," he said earnestly, clutching at her hand. "You've kept me alive. Only you. You must marry me, or I have no reason to want to live! They have taken my leg, Tess. I shall be a cripple. I need you!"

She pulled away from him and made rather a thing of checking the thermometer before she placed it in his mouth. "Be a good boy," she said in a gentle but neutral voice. "Let me take your pulse."

His eyes were turbulent, and his pulse mirrored it. She grimaced as she felt it at his wrist under her firm, cool fingers. His agitation was puzzling.

"Have they given you anything, Marsh, any medication?" she asked as she let go of his wrist to make a note of the pulse rate on his chart. There was no indication of any recent drug having been given him.

"No," he mumbled around the thermometer.

She took it out of his mouth and checked it. He had no fever. Those glazed eyes puzzled her.

He caught her hand. "You must marry me! I'll... I'll do something desperate if you don't!"

She gently disengaged her fingers. "Now, Marsh, you don't mean that."

"I do! I swear I do!"

She was dismayed by her own stupidity in

allowing this situation to develop. An impulse to be kind to a frightened young man, to listen to his fears, to make him comfortable, to soothe him—and it had led to this! She hadn't meant to encourage him in any amorous way, but the consequences of her actions were frightening.

"Marsh, you've been very ill," she said. "You'll get better. It's natural for a man to become fond of his nurse, just as it's natural for a desperately ill woman to feel an attachment to a physician who saves her life. It will pass."

He looked wild-eyed, overexcited. "It isn't an attachment. I love you!"

"You think you do," she said evenly. "I promise you, it will pass. I have other patients to attend, Marsh, but I'll check on you later." She gave him a cool, remote smile, and left the bedside with his chart. This was the only way to control the situation now, to ignore it. She couldn't allow his obsession to continue.

She went about her duties woodenly for the rest of the day, vaguely aware of Marsh's accusing eyes on her from the other end of the ward. He'd get over it, she told herself. He had to. He was being released in a few days. He'd go home to the uncle and aunt with whom he lived upstate and forget her. He must, because she had nothing in her to give him. Every thought and feeling she possessed, all she was, had belonged to Matt since she was fourteen years old. Even if he didn't want them.

But she did, at least, have an outlet for

her anguish. She would devote her life to nursing and advancing the women's movement, and try never to grieve for Matt. There would be no children, no home, no husband to cherish. Her life would be one of service and sacrifice. And if she wept for her losses of an evening, then no one would know except herself.

There was a certain nobility about sacrifice, she thought sadly. Perhaps it would compensate for the things she could never have.

She finished her tasks, and at the end of her duty hours, she went to change back into her street clothes in the room provided by the hospital. When she came out again, neatly dressed in a black suit with a white lacy blouse and simple hat, she noticed a commotion at the end of the ward where she worked.

Curious, she moved swiftly down the hall and stopped where a doctor was just lifting his head.

"Gone," he pronounced. "There's nothing more we can do." He started to pull up the sheet, paused, and scowled. "Here, what's this?"

He produced a small dark bottle with a cork stopper. He took the stopper out and sniffed. "Opium," he said angrily. "He's taken the whole bottle!"

Tess's white face told its own story. The elder nurse saw her and came forward, her rigid features softening just a little when she saw the effect of Marsh's demise on Tess's face.

"Tess, he was an addict," she said. "Didn't you know?"

Tess shook her head, speechless, her face as white as flour.

"He had this smuggled in, of course," the doctor added angrily. "There should be a law against this foul substance! It was the opium which caused the accident in the first place, you know. He was so drugged that he didn't even see the carriage coming; he walked right out in front of it. And now, knowing he might be unable to hold down a job and pay for this filthy stuff, he ended his life."

"You mean, it wasn't... because of me?" Tess asked weakly.

The doctor saw her pallid features and came closer. "No, my dear. Of course not," he assured her. "It was his own weakness that killed him." He left abruptly then.

Tess watched as the nurse covered Marsh. The open-eyed contorted face with its gaping mouth mirrored the convulsive final moments of death. She gave a small cry and turned, almost running in her haste to get out of the hospital, away from her own guilt.

Chapter Six

It was dark and very late. Cold, yet oblivious to the wind, Tess stood on the hospital steps, staring past the gas lamps into the street. It was unlike Mick to be late. In fact, this was the first time she'd emerged from the hospital and not found the jaunty Irishman perched on the driver's box of his carriage and eager to see her home safely.

At last Mick Kennedy came into view, skillfully managing his team and halting them only inches from the curb. Mick had taken it upon himself to be her protector. As he liked to say, he took the same care of her that he would have of his own daughter, if she'd lived, God rest her tiny soul. He worked hard for his living and had mentioned to Tess that he sent money home to his mother and father in County Cork, Ireland. Judging by the way he dressed, Tess thought, there was precious little left over after he paid his stable fees and rent. She'd grown rather fond of him, and she trusted him—no mean thing in a city the size of Chicago.

Mick leapt down, and she let him put her into the carriage. "Don't take me right home," she told him in a subdued tone. "Drive me around the city for a few minutes first, if you don't mind."

"Right-o, me lass. Bad night, eh? Sure, and I wouldn't want to work in no such place meself, all them sick folk. We'll drive a bit, then. Yes, we will. Wrap up in that robe, so ye'll not catch a chill."

Mick shut the carriage door, and Tess pulled the bearskin robe around her. The gift of a grateful patron, the bearskin was "the pride of my hired carriage," Mick had told her. The thick black fur brought back memories for Tess of Montana winters, of accompanying her father in the buggy on his visits to the sick on the reservation. Just such a robe kept the winter chill from them.

The sound of the steady clip-clop of the horses' shoes on the hard road comforting her, Tess closed her eyes and in that dark privacy let the tears come. Poor Marsh Bailey. He'd thought he needed only her... and everything in his life would be set right. The doctor swore that it was the opiate that killed him, but Tess knew better. Her rejection had brought on his anger and despair and caused him to take that fatal dose. Perhaps he wanted to punish her for being only a kind nurse and not a lover; perhaps he wanted only to escape his tragic and desperate situation. She would never know. Would she ever know why Matt could not love her the way she wanted—just as Marsh Bailey did not know her heart and mind?

She wiped at the hot tears on her cheeks with her gloved hand and felt as if her heart would crack. Nursing was no profession for the weak-willed or soft-natured, her father had told her many times. While doctors and nurses had to be compassionate, they also had to be in control of emotion at all times while maintaining a sense of separation from the patient. Otherwise, he'd said, one couldn't perform one's tasks. Imagine these poor, sick people depending on a weeping nurse, her father had chided her during an outbreak of diphtheria. She was weeping copiously over a dead infant when he said, "You have to toughen up, Tess, or you're no good to me." He hadn't hugged her or patted her or tried to comfort her in any other way. He'd been stern. "You don't stop caring—not ever. But you have to wall up your feelings so they don't interfere with your work. The practice of medicine requires a strong constitution and cool nerve. Now dry those tears and come here. I'm going to need you to hold this young man while I swab out his throat!"

These memories of the lessons she'd learned from her father's words and actions helped restore her perspective. Little by little, Tess regained control of herself, so that by the time she finally told Mick to drive her home, she was almost back to her old self. Her red eyes and nose gave her away, of course.

"Now you just go in there and get yourself a good night's sleep, me dear," Mick told her, tipping his hat. "In the morning, sure, everythin' will look bright and new again!"

"Thanks, Mick," she said in a subdued tone.

"A good evenin' to you!"

He climbed back into the driver's seat and with a smile and a nod went his way.

Tess slowly climbed the steps to the front door, and cried out softly when a shadow detached itself from the depths of the porch and confronted her.

"It's about time," Matt said angrily. "Where the hell have you been? Didn't I tell you to come straight home? For God's sake, woman, must you put your life in danger just to spite me?"

She caught the pungent scent of the cigar he'd been smoking, mingling with his cologne. He wasn't wearing a hat, and his jacket was unbuttoned. He looked furious in the dim light pouring out the long windows of the boardinghouse.

"I had Mick drive me around a bit before I came home," she said quietly. "I had a long and difficult shift, Matt. Now I'm very tired, and I want to go to bed."

He caught her arm in a steely grip as she started past him and held her so close that she could feel the heat of his body.

"You were off duty at least an hour and a half ago," he continued relentlessly. "I want to know where you were."

She tugged at his grip, but she couldn't move him. "I don't have to tell you anything!"

"The hell you don't."

He pulled her back into the shadows. His arms contracted, riveting her body to his in a contact that shocked her speechless. While she grappled with the implications of the embrace, his head bent and his hard mouth found hers unerringly in the darkness.

It wasn't at all how she'd thought her first kiss would feel. He wasn't gentle or particularly considerate. His lips hurt. His arm encircled her nape, so that the force of his hard mouth pushed her head back against the solid muscle of his upper arm. Her fingers plucked weakly at his sleeve while she stood, frozen against him. Even the pain was sweet after so many long years of dreaming about passionately kissing Matt.

All at once, the pressure of his mouth eased. Then his lips lifted away from hers. She stared up into the darkness at the blurry outline of his face.

His breath sounded strained and rough. She felt his free hand move and come to rest on her face, his fingers touching as if their tips might see her expression. His thumb caressed the contours of her lower lip. She was hypnotized. His thumb slipped to the crease between her lips, continuing its rhythmic stroking. She was breathless.

She gasped as he gently pried her lips apart, his head dipped lower, and his mouth replaced his thumb with a gentle suction that set her heart pounding. His hand smoothed her cheek, her neck, lightly caressing the soft skin. When she sagged against him, soft and compliant, his mouth became more insistent, tenderly exploring, coaxing, provoking.

Something very strange was happening, Tess realized. She was entranced. Her knees felt too weak to support her. Her small hand clung high on his sleeve. She felt him shift her so that she was lifted even closer to him, her arm going naturally around his neck.

He moved just enough to find the support of the porch rail. He leaned against it, adjusting Tess's body until she was suddenly between his legs in an intimacy that shocked her with its newness.

She moaned, afraid of these hot, drugging sensations that were being born in her. Matt's mouth was making her senseless. She couldn't bear the thought of letting it part from hers, so when he began to lift his head, she followed his mouth, her body trembling as she stretched it against his.

She needed... something. Something more. Her arms tightened around his neck, and she moaned again, a little sob of noise that seemed to cause an explosion of feeling in Matt. His arms contracted bruisingly and his mouth opened. She felt his tongue probing inside her lips, and she let him invade that warm darkness, more demanding now. She was shaking all over as if with a fever. She shuddered with the force of these new feelings, and involuntarily she moved her body against Matt's in an instinct that brought a similar movement from him.

One of his arms still held her securely while his hard mouth devoured hers, but the free hand was against her side, under her jacket. It moved up and up and she stiffened, though not with fear. She gasped and twisted her body so that his searching fingers could find what they were seeking: the soft, exquisite smoothness of her breast under the jacket, under the blouse, right above her corset in its brief muslin cover...

Footsteps inside the house forced them to spring apart. Matt pulled her farther into the shadows. Two residents walked past the glass-paned front door into the parlor.

Matt was holding Tess against him, struggling to slow his breathing. She was all but collapsed in his arms, her body softly trembling with the newness of passion.

His hand pressed her cheek against his

shirt beneath his open jacket. She could feel the beating of his heart.

His fingers smoothed against her cheek, her throat. It took all his remaining control to keep from letting them slide back to the softness of her breast.

She was overexcited. And she was confused. She felt wonderful. She felt strange, as though a different woman inhabited her body. Tears coursed down her cheeks. Suddenly all her profound new feelings of wonder and surprise and embarrassment coalesced into a violent sensation of shame. She'd encouraged Matt, provoked Matt, led him to these intimacies that he detested... at least with her. She tried to stifle a sob, but failed.

His hand pressed her face closer to his chest. "Shhh," he whispered. "Don't cry."

"I'm so ashamed," she muttered.

His lips touched her eyelids. "Stop listening to your Victorian upbringing. You're a modern woman. Haven't you told me so a dozen times?"

"Not modern enough." She sniffed.

He chuckled deep in his throat. "Coward," he taunted softly. "Are you really naive enough to believe that good girls and boys don't do this?"

She stiffened a little. "They don't. And I'm not. Good, that is."

"They do, and you are," he countered. "We both lost control. It's nothing to cry about."

"I led you... I encouraged you—" She

stopped, too embarrassed to finish the sentence.

"Yes, I know," he mused wickedly. "I'll strut for a week."

She shivered. "It was wrong!"

"It doesn't feel wrong," he replied. His hand smoothed her disheveled hair, and he noticed that somewhere in the tempestuous heat of the past few minutes, her hat had been dislodged, pins and all. "We'll find your hat in a minute," he said, "when my legs stop trembling."

"Oh, are they?" she asked impulsively. "So are mine."

He laughed again, his misgivings gone in the delight of the moment. "Tess, have you never felt a man's mouth before?"

"Well, no," she confessed. "And certainly not... not like that!"

Her embarrassment made him feel protective. "Like what?"

She hid her face against his chest. "You know."

His hand soothed her nape. His lips brushed her temple. "Oh, for the wild, free days," he whispered huskily, "when we could have lain together in the tall grass by the river and learned each other by touch and taste with no household of strangers to barge in on us!"

She found a glimmer of humor in the frustration in his voice and laughed. "Snakes would have slithered over us, and we'd have been eaten alive by mosquitoes."

He chuckled, too. "I suppose so." He touched her earlobe. "Feel less shaky now?"

"A little."

He released her, bending to pick up her hat. "I can't see the pins in the dark. How many had you?"

"Only one, with a pearl on the end. Oh, dear, Father gave it to me for my birthday last year. I hope it isn't lost."

He was still feeling around the floor. "Aha."

He produced it and placed it in her hand, along with the hat. "You'd better try and get that back on, or we'll become the focus of some lively gossip when we go inside."

She felt for her bun, and then placed the hat, spearing through it with the hatpin. "I'll bet I look flushed."

"I should hope so," he said haughtily.

She hit at his sleeve. "Masher."

"Good God, you're delicious to make love to," he said in spite of himself.

"Never do that again," she said primly. "You aren't going to lead me into a life of sin."

"I wouldn't dream of it," he said with mock solemnity.

She moved into the light, nervous about how she must look. She turned. "How bad?" she asked worriedly.

He moved closer. He was as grim and severe as always, except for his eyes. "You've been crying," he said suddenly. "And before I ever touched you. Why?"

She sighed raggedly. "Because Marsh Bailey committed suicide today."

"Tess!"

"He had a bottle of opium. The doctor said it was an overdose, that he was an addict and his amputation would leave him unable to afford his habit." She wiped at another tear with the handkerchief crumpled and stuffed in her skirt pocket. "Oh, bother, I can't help feeling that I helped bring it about, Matt. I let him depend on me... and he came to think he loved me... and asked me to marry him. This very afternoon, he asked. And I turned him down, of course. I don't really feel it was my fault exactly, Matt, but oh—"

He hugged her tight. "I'm sorry, so sorry," he said as he pushed her to arm's length. "I wouldn't have been angry if I'd known. I thought you were staying out deliberately to spite me. I was half out of my mind, thinking about all the dire things that could have happened to you, alone in the city, especially after the close call you already had."

"I don't hold grudges," she replied. "I wouldn't have been so low as to stay out late just to worry you." She hesitated and looked up at him. "You were worried about me? Truly?"

"Why else would I have been angry enough to manhandle you?" He grimaced. "I forgot your poor arm, too. I'm sorry, Tess."

"It's not very sore now. The doctor took my stitches out Friday. I've healed quite well, he said."

"You didn't tell me Saturday."

"I didn't think of it."

He recalled the things he'd said to her with faint regret. "I was rude to you."

"I was obnoxious," she replied. "You had every right to be rude. I didn't even thank you for my ice cream."

"Still, I had no right to treat you as I did then—or tonight," he said through his teeth. "Especially in your overwrought condition."

"Is that why it felt the way it did?" she asked, openly curious. "I mean, because you were angry and I was so upset?"

He hesitated. "How did it feel?"

"It's hard to describe," she said. "Throbbing, hot, shaky, weak. I haven't experienced those feelings before."

She heard him draw a long breath. "Those feelings," he began, "are desire. A woman's desire to... lie with a man."

"To be intimate with him," she ventured.

"Yes."

She could have gone through the floor. "Oh."

"Civilization covers desire with a veneer of romantic love," he continued cynically, "to make it respectable. It's only after marriage, as a rule, that a man permits himself to show desire. I'm sorry that I lost my temper and treated you in such a familiar manner."

"It's all right," she said. She wrapped her arms around her rib cage. "Most women of my age are already married and know about such things. In the normal course of events, I should never have known how it felt to be... to want..."

His lean hands took her arms gently from behind. "Don't be ashamed," he said quietly. "I regret having shocked you, but nothing of any real import happened. Certainly nothing happened that should shame you."

She sighed. "It's rather wicked, isn't it, to feel such pleasure?"

He let his hands drop. "I think we should stop talking about it," he said. His body was ignoring the cold reason of his mind.

"As you wish. But I can't help being curious about such things. Despite having worked as a nurse for some years, there are still many aspects of life I know very little about."

"You were made for marriage," he said bluntly, holding a guilty secret in his heart.

"Better to live alone than with a man whom I couldn't love," she said simply, which made her think again of Marsh and brought the stinging tears back. "I must go inside."

She moved ahead of him and opened the front door just as Mrs. Mulhaney came into the hall.

She gasped as she saw Tess's face. "My dear, whatever has happened to you?" she exclaimed, glancing suspiciously over Tess's shoulder at Matt.

"One of my patients committed suicide this evening," Tess said at once. "I'm very sorry to be seen in such a state, but he was very young and..." A sob stopped the words.

"Oh, my dear." Mrs. Mulhaney was at once all sympathy and concern, any trace of suspicion gone from her manner. She put her arm around Tess. "You come right along to the kitchen with me and I'll fix you a nice cup of tea. You poor dear, you must tell me all about it!"

Tess dared not glance back at Matt. Her embarrassment had grown to unmanageable proportions, and she was glad of Mrs. Mulhaney's intervention. She didn't know how she would ever be able to talk normally to Matt after the glimpse of heaven he'd just shown her.

Mrs. Mulhaney's sympathy was shot full of morbid curiosity. A genteel woman with no real knowledge of the world outside her home, she listened raptly while Tess told her about the young amputee who hadn't been able to cope with life before his accident and had convinced himself he'd be even less able to do so as a cripple.

"Such a pity," the older woman said, shaking her head. "And him so young, as you say." She eyed Tess covertly. "Working in a hospital must be... revealing. I mean, you must learn a great deal about men. About their bodies. Oh dear, I didn't mean to sound like that."

Tess smiled at her. "Mrs. Mulhaney, we do what we're told by the physicians, but there are male orderlies to deal with the men when they need bathing or, er, other assistance. We're actually quite sheltered in most ways."

Mrs. Mulhaney put a hand to her heart. "Heavens, what a relief," she said. "We didn't know, and there's been so much speculation—well, my father always said that women had no business outside the home anyway. When my husband was alive, I had a washerwoman and a cook. He insisted." She straightened her skirts. "I know nothing of these modern ways in the city." She looked embarrassed. "I think it unwise to work in a shop or even a hospital." She wrinkled her brow. "Tess, aren't you afraid to be out unescorted of an evening?" she asked bluntly.

"Not with Mick driving me," Tess assured

the other woman. She chuckled. "He's the same age my father would have been. He lost his wife and child to pneumonia, and he drives me to and from work and my meetings. He carries a huge crooked stick which he calls a shillelagh, and he tells me that he knows how to use it on any man who might get fresh with me."

Mrs. Mulhaney's eyes were twinkling. "My goodness. You do miss your father, don't you?"

"Very much. I was his nurse, too, for some years," she added sadly. "My mother died when I was very young. Dad and I were close. It's very lonely without him."

"At least you have your cousin here, to comfort you," she said. The comment was almost a question.

"We're not close relations." Tess was surprised at how easily the lie rolled off her tongue. "Matt and I are friends, too. He's been very kind to let me come here and stay near him. I have to make my own living, you know," she said solemnly. "My father had nothing to leave me, and I have no other family."

"My dear, I had no idea," Mrs. Mulhaney said, shocked. "I thought your job was nothing more than a social statement, a way of emphasizing your views about the emancipation of women."

"It's much more than that, I'm afraid," Tess confided. "I can hardly expect Matt to support me, however kind he is. I must manage to make my own way in the world. Nursing is the only thing I know how to do."

The conversation was very enlightening

for the elderly woman, who had a new picture of Tess and her independence. The poor thing, too proud to accept charity even from her cousin Matt, having to slave away in that horrible place to earn her crust of bread. It saddened Mrs. Mulhaney, who had gone from the protection of her father directly into the protection of marriage at the age of fifteen. While she did need the income from taking in boarders, she also needed the company, liveliness, and sense of purpose they lent to her life. She had never considered herself an emancipated working woman.

She patted Tess's hand where it lay on the table. "Well, I'm sorry that things are so brutal for a nice young woman like you. It does explain why you've never married as well. You have no dowry at all, have you?"

Tess had to bite back a tart reply. The dowry was at least a bribe, more usually a price for selling a girl to a man in marriage, she thought. She had the utmost contempt for the whole process. She'd heard that girls from rich families back east were literally sold to impoverished European noblemen for the sake of having a title in the family.

She wondered what Mrs. Mulhaney would say if she told her that, by Sioux custom, the dowry was paid to the parents by the prospective bridegroom. And under different circumstances, she'd have loved letting Matt pay her father ten horses for her hand in marriage. She stifled a burst of hysterical laughter. As if Matt would have offered to marry her, horses or no horses.

"No," Tess answered the question with forced solemnity. "I have no dowry."

"I wouldn't worry," Mrs. Mulhaney said. "You'll find a husband one of these days, regardless. I'm sorry about your young friend at the hospital. But really, my dear, what sort of life would he have had, an amputee? A man's physical strength is his livelihood. And there is, too, the matter of his pride. Charity is a hard pill for any man to have to swallow."

That was true. A legless man had few options but the poorhouse or the beneficence of a church or some social organization. And that would be a huge blow to his ego, to his very manhood. He could hardly expect to make a living at manual labor. He would never have played his beloved game of baseball again either.

"You go on up to bed. I hope I've helped you to feel better."

Tess smiled at the older woman, who couldn't begin to understand the new world that was opening at her toes.

"Yes, you certainly have," Tess lied. "Thank you for the tea and the sympathy, Mrs. Mulhaney. I do feel better."

"I'm so glad. You were pitiful when you came in tonight, your eyes all red and tears running down your cheeks, and your hair in such a state." She laughed a little hollowly. "You won't believe this, but for a few seconds, I thought you might have been outside spooning with a man. So silly. There was only Mr. Davis out there with you, your own cousin!"

She'd turned away to put the dishes on the washboard of the sink and fortunately missed seeing the expression on Tess's face.

"Silly indeed," Tess murmured. "Good night, Mrs. Mulhaney. Thank you."

"You're very welcome, my dear. Sleep well."

"You, too."

Tess moved quickly out into the hall without looking around her. She went straight upstairs to her room.

But she didn't sleep. Her mouth still tasted of Matt. Her body was one long ache for something she couldn't even name. She was restless and hungry, and every time she closed her eyes, she could hear Matt's rough breath at her ear, feel his hands touching her...

She put the pillow over her head. She wasn't going to think about this. She was going to pretend that it never happened, which was surely what Matt would do. He'd lost his temper and something had happened that neither of them had expected; that was all.

As for those hot kisses, they could both forget that they'd tasted each other in the darkness of the porch. Matt had probably forgotten already. Having lived in the city for so long, such encounters must be a regular thing for him.

Her face flamed and she moaned. The thought of Matt with other women made her ill. She closed her eyes and started reciting the alphabet. Eventually she slept.

Chapter Seven

Morning came far too soon for Tess, and she looked it when she went down to breakfast. She flushed when Matt's dark, searching eyes met hers. Almost painfully ill at ease with him across the table from her, she couldn't still the tremor in her hands as she lifted her coffee cup. And merely looking at him made her lose her breath. Her lack of control over her senses embarrassed her almost to the point of tears. How humiliating, to love a man who didn't return the feeling, and have no way to hide it from him.

Matt was much the same as always, except that he put sugar in his coffee for the first time in memory and ate ham—which he detested. But his emotions were almost always under impeccable control. Last night had been the exception. This morning, he was himself again, on the outside at least.

Tess felt her body tingle at the near contact of their hands when they reached for the salt cellar at the same time. The look they exchanged was so potent, so unexpected and disquieting that Tess left half her breakfast sitting on the table.

Apparently Matt's answer to the small dilemma was to pretend that it never happened. He was polite and wished her a good day on his way out the door, looking as remote as the moon.

Tess returned his greeting in kind, and

then went on to her job, trying not to hark back to the night before and the feel of Matt's hard arms around her in mingled anger and passion.

She'd known that he was passionate. Having lived near him for some time, she'd seen him go on hunts, and she'd seen him playing athletic ball games with other young men in the green, lush summer grass near the wide, shallow river. She'd seen him happy and sad, wounded and strong. She'd learned his moods, as he'd learned hers. They knew too much about each other to behave as strangers. And now that knowledge was much more than intuitive. It was physical.

Matt didn't have to tell her that it was much easier to forget a smile than a kiss. She learned it painfully in the days that followed as she tried desperately to live with the unknown hungers that Matt had created inside her untried body.

If she was suffering, he certainly didn't seem to be. He was outwardly as calm and courteous to her as he'd always been. Except for a few minutes that first morning after it had happened, he was completely normal. Tess wasn't. But she had to pretend.

In her grief after Marsh Bailey's suicide and Matt's unexpected ardor, she hadn't thought much about her friend Nan. But as Tess started out to her suffrage meeting the next Thursday evening, Nan was unexpectedly in Mick's carriage when it called at Mrs. Mulhaney's boardinghouse to pick up Tess.

"Why, Nan!" Tess exclaimed, breathless

after letting Mick help her inside the carriage and thanking him. "I didn't expect you to come to any more meetings."

"I'm not exactly going to the meeting," Nan said, shaken. "Dennis hit me again, and there was a terrible fight. I'm going to meet my sister and her husband there, where it's public and he can't do anything, and I'm going home with her."

"I don't understand. You said that he'd never touched you in anger."

Nan pushed back her hair. "I lied," she said bluntly, her whole demeanor unsettled and frightened. "I was afraid of him and I lied. I thought I should deny it. I thought I could appease him. But that's all changed now."

"What's happened?"

Nan looked worn but determined as well. "The end of the world." She laughed without humor. "But I have something to hope for now, something to live for, and it's given me the courage to walk out." she said. "He's not going to hurt me anymore."

"Good for you!" Tess exclaimed.

Nan sighed and leaned forward. "I've had a devil of a time," she said. "I didn't dare tell you before because I didn't know you well enough to be sure I could trust you. I've been hiding in the shadows like a thief, but no more." She stared at Tess. "Here's something I should have told you before. Maybe you'll hate me when you know. You mightn't want me for a friend anymore."

Tess put her gloved hand on Nan's. "Nothing you could say would stop us being friends."

"I've been seeing another man," Nan blurted out, flushing. "I didn't plan to; neither did he. It just happened. I said I was coming to the meetings with you these past few weeks and I didn't. I was with him. Dennis knows about it. He invited my friend to supper without telling me. I had to fix a meal and sit at the table with them... and then he started cursing us both and he hit me. He and... and the man fought. Dennis swore he'd kill me if I see the man again. I... I can't tell you his name, Tess. I promised I wouldn't. But the man got me out, telephoned my sister, and arranged all this. He got Mick to come for me." She slumped. "I won't go back; better to be disgraced or even dead than live in fear all my life, especially now! My... my friend has said that he'll help me. He isn't afraid of Dennis—he knows him very well, in fact." She folded her hands in her lap tightly. "Dennis is a bad man, Tess," she added worriedly. "People underestimate him because they don't see how he is when he's... when he uses that... stuff. He calls it his 'medicine,' but it's not medicine, and it makes him go crazy. That's why he raged so much tonight, although I guess maybe it was for the best, since he couldn't hide what he was doing to me anymore and accuse me of lying about it."

Opium was what he was using, Tess guessed, but she didn't say it aloud. "Can your sister protect you?"

"Yes," she said at once. "She's tried time and again to get me to leave, but I was never desperate enough to do it. Now I am." She smiled and her whole face was radiant. "Tess, there's to be a baby."

"Oh, Nan." Tess didn't know what to say. All this was far beyond her experience of life.

"It isn't Dennis's," she added a little uncomfortably. "I love the father more than my own life. I had to get away from Dennis before he hurts me, or the baby."

"Is there anything I can do to help?" she asked gently.

"Lord, I wouldn't put you at risk for anything!" Nan exclaimed. "You're the only friend I have!"

"There won't be a risk," Tess lied. She'd already come afoul of Dennis's crazy temper once, but Nan needn't know that. Matt would protect her and Nan, if she asked him to.

"Thank you," Nan said sincerely. "But it isn't my intention to involve you any more than you've been involved already. My sister's husband is a policeman." She added with a chuckle, "A big, mean cop. Let Dennis try anything with him, even when he's not sober, and he'll think he's been run over by a streetcar!"

"But what if he should find you before you can get away?" Tess asked.

Nan shifted. "That's why we arranged to meet at a public place. But if Dennis comes after me, I'll run."

Tess took Nan's gloved hands in hers. "Now, Nan... what's this?" She felt moisture under her fingers. As they passed a streetlight, she could see the color of it, staining Nan's gloves. It was red.

"Nan!" she exclaimed. "You're bleeding!"

Nan jerked her hands back and shivered. "Oh... oh, that," she said, hesitating. "It was when I prepared the chicken for supper. I had my gloves lying on the counter. I didn't realize..."

"Blood splatters, doesn't it?" Tess was relieved that it was something so simple. "You'll be all right, Nan. I'm sure of it."

"I hope so." The pure exhaustion in the woman's voice had a pathos all its own.

Sure enough, Edith Greene was at the meeting with her husband, officer Brian Greene, in full uniform. They looked vaguely uneasy in the crowd of fairly militant women, but they stayed through the business meeting and immediately took Nan away with them as soon as the meeting was over.

Edith, tall and thin and severe-looking and years older than her sister, paused to grasp Tess's hand and thank her for helping Nan.

"I did nothing," Tess said, smiling. "But Nan is my friend. I hope you know that I'd help her in any way I could."

Officer Greene was watching her with narrowed eyes. "You'd be the cousin of Matt Davis, would you not?" he asked.

She flushed at the sound of Matt's name. "Yes, I am," she said.

His blue eyes narrowed. "You were hurt at that last women's march."

Tess's face contorted, and her eyes pleaded with him to say nothing, although Edith and

Nan were frowning curiously at the statement.

"You never said," Nan began.

"I haven't seen you since then," Tess replied, which was the truth. She smiled. "I was hurt in the riot that followed, but only a little. I'm fine now."

Officer Greene's lips pursed, but he bit back the rest of what he was going to say. "You're a brave lass," he said. "If there's any further trouble, you just let me know. I can handle it."

She smiled warmly at him. He was big and burly and not at all handsome, but Edith clung to his arm and shot him admiring looks as if he were Adonis.

They left. Tess said her good-byes to the other ladies and climbed into Mick's waiting carriage. It had been a night of surprises. She hoped that Nan would be all right. Knowing what she did about Nan's husband and how dangerous he was, she felt that her concern wasn't misplaced.

Matt was waiting on the porch when Tess got home from the meeting. Just like last time, she thought. Her heart began to race wildly as she waved Mick off, opened the gate, and walked slowly up to the porch where Matt leaned against one of the posts.

"You're on time tonight," he remarked.

"I usually am when terrible things don't happen to me," she replied in a cool tone.

He had one hand in his pocket. The other

toyed with the long gold watch chain that dangled from his vest pocket. "Nothing happened tonight, then?"

She shook her head. "The meeting was rather ordinary, except that Nan came back."

He was instantly alert. "Alone?"

She frowned, puzzled by his reaction. "Well, yes. She's left her husband. She was going home from the meeting with her sister and brother-in-law, Brian Greene. He's a big Irish policeman," she added with a smile.

"I know him," Matt replied.

"Nan will be safe," she said. "I'm so glad she came to her senses. I thought I'd go by and see her tomorrow at her sister's house—"

"No, you won't," he told her flatly. "She isn't safe. And neither will you be if you go near her. You little fool, have you no idea what sort of man her husband is, even after what he did to you?"

She was taken aback by his vehemence. "But, surely, with her brother-in-law there—"

"Greene works days, Tess. Her sister will be no protection at all for Nan. Collier won't like having his wife run away like that. He'll kill her; maybe her sister with her. None of you seem to have any idea what she's up against."

She put a hand to her throat. "Is he really so dangerous?"

He didn't answer her directly. "She should have had him arrested first, before she left him," he said coldly. "It would have given her a chance. Greene would have checked with her neighbors, and when he learned how she'd been treated, Collier would have been put so far behind bars that he'd never get free."

She was about to tell him what Nan had said about the fight, but it didn't seem to have much importance now. "Poor Nan," she said in a subdued tone, worried as she hadn't been before. She looked up at him. "Matt, from what you've said about her and Collier, I gather you've done more checking on them. Do you know of anything we can do to help her?"

He paused. "Perhaps. She should be safe enough tonight, with Greene in the house. I'll go by the police station first thing in the morning and talk with the officer on duty in that precinct. He's a friend of mine, and Greene's superior."

She shifted her weight from foot to foot, reluctant to end the conversation despite the coolness of the evening and her light jacket, which was no barrier at all to the wind. "Thank you, Matt."

"It's no trouble to do you a kindness," he said. His eyes narrowed as he looked at her. "You're loyal to your friends. Absurdly so, sometimes."

She shrugged. "I don't have so many that I can afford to lose one."

"Even unpopular ones," he agreed, smiling faintly as he remembered the past.

She moved closer to the door, her bag clutched in her hands. "Are we still friends?" she asked suddenly. She didn't look at him. She was afraid to.

He was silent for so long that she thought he wasn't going to answer. She felt him at her back, amazed at how quietly he moved. He'd taught her to walk silently, too, but she'd forgotten. He hadn't.

"Don't torture yourself so over a minute's madness. We lost our bearings for a little while," he said finally, and his voice held a trace of resignation. "That's all. We didn't stop being friends because of it."

He couldn't have put it much plainer that he considered those hungry kisses they'd shared a mistake.

Her back straightened and she turned, forcing herself to smile. "Yes. Of course."

But when she started toward the door, he caught her waist and held her near him, his fingers warm and strong through the stuff of her jacket.

"Don't dwell on it," he said gruffly. "There wouldn't have been any future in it, anyway. Imagine a pretty little blonde parading around with a Sioux in Chicago."

"What an interesting remark from a man who deliberately hides his ancestry," she pointed out.

He dropped her arm roughly. "I don't."

"You do," she argued. "You enjoy watching people try to guess what your nationality is, where you came from. But you never bother to correct them."

His face gave no clue to his feelings, but his eyes glittered. "We've had this conversation before. How I deal with the past is my concern."

"How can I convince you that it isn't a past to make you ashamed?" she asked gently. "No, don't." She moaned when he turned away. She caught his arm and moved closer. "Matt, don't be like this!"

His arm was as rigid as a plank. He didn't even look at her. He'd distanced himself so completely that he might have been carved of wood, like one of those horrible facsimiles of Indians in front of cigar stores. She couldn't reach him.

"All right," she said, loosening her grip on his sleeve. "You win. We'll pretend that I never said a word. You don't want to talk about anything personal with me. I'll remember from now on."

She left him standing there and went into the house, aware of angry dark eyes following her. Perhaps she'd burned her bridges. Not that it mattered anymore. He'd made his position crystal clear. She hadn't realized how much it would hurt to have him shut her out. In the old days, he'd been enigmatic, yes. But warm and friendly with her. Of course, back then she'd been no threat to a grown warrior. Her adolescent self was someone to amuse and teach and indulge. But she was a woman now, and Matt couldn't manage a relationship that included the passionate kisses he'd given her in anger. He wouldn't risk his heart.

She went straight to her room, put her jacket and hat away, and sat down in the small rocking chair beside her window. Matt had noticed her physically for the first time since she'd come to Chicago, and it had made him wary of her. Now that he was seeing her as a threat to his peace of mind, there wouldn't be any more cozy chats, any more teasing exchanges. He'd keep her at arm's length, figuratively and physically. He'd never let her get close enough to threaten his peace of mind again.

It was a blow to her ego and to her vulnerable heart. Matt had been so much a part of her life, for so long, that it wasn't going to be easy to let him go. But he didn't want Tess, and he'd made it very plain that she wasn't going to be part of his future.

She began to doubt her instincts in coming to Chicago. It hadn't been fair to put the responsibility for her well-being on Matt, just because they'd been friends in Montana. She hadn't thought of how it was going to affect Matt's life, having her around all the time. Of course he'd feel some responsibility for her. Her father had saved his life, and she'd nursed him back to health. He would feel obliged to do anything he could for her. But it would be pity, not love; obligation, not pleasure in her company.

Matt might not want her in any permanent way, but that didn't wipe out years of friendship. And it didn't cure her of loving him. Her eyes closed as she rocked, and she felt the pain and need all the way to her toes. She'd been unfair. She'd been thoughtless and irresponsible. Now she had to make amends... somehow.

As usual of late, Tess didn't sleep well. She went to work the next morning worried and high-strung from a night of guilt and self-recrimination. She hadn't seen Matt when she left the boardinghouse that morning, but she hoped that he'd go ahead to the police station before anything could happen to Nan. She was so afraid for her. Not that she wasn't afraid for Matt, too.

She went about her duties conscientiously, all too aware that the matron on her ward didn't seem to like her and wasn't shy about letting her know it.

Miss Fish, or "the Barracuda" as she was known to her juniors, wore white gloves to test the dust on bedside tables and windowsills. She was meticulous about making sure that all instruments were faithfully boiled for the prescribed time after use, and that there were adequate supplies of bleached sheets and blankets for the patients on her ward. She starched her skirts so much that she rustled when she walked. Under them, barely visible, were spotlessly clean lace-up shoes. On her head was the cap that all nurses at the Cook County Hospital wore on duty. She was a credit to her profession and the very devil to work for.

Tess thought with bittersweet pleasure of the days when she'd been her father's nurse. There had been no Miss Fish to drive her mad. She'd had time to show concern and compassion for her patients. Here her day was one hectic rush to get things done. Often she felt that the patients got lost in the shuffle.

After a long morning counting instruments for the second time because Miss Fish didn't trust her first effort, Tess walked calmly back down the ward and found herself suddenly face-to-face with Matt.

He hadn't seen her in uniform before. He studied her trim, neat figure.

Despite the mad beating of her heart, she displayed a calm expression.

"You shouldn't be here," she said in a low voice. "Miss Fish will have a conniption fit if she sees you."

"Miss who?"

"Fish," she murmured, moving quickly into the hall. "She's my superior."

He scowled as he looked around. "What do you do here all day?"

"What I used to do back in Montana," she said. "Empty bedpans, make beds, take temperatures, boil instruments, and generally give assistance when asked."

His eyes narrowed. "Aren't you a little old for such a junior position?"

"I've never been formally trained, as most of these girls have been. I have only practical experience, and that's what sort of work I do here."

"You don't assist the doctors?"

"Heaven forbid. Miss Fish would faint."

He scowled. "Is she as prim as her name?"

She peered past him. "You're about to find out."

He had his bowler hat in hand. He turned as the older woman joined them. He thought of prunes when he saw that drawn face, which looked as if it never smiled.

"Miss Fish," he murmured politely, and made her a slight bow.

She was taken aback when he lifted her hand to his lips in a continental way, and she went red-cheeked.

"My cousin speaks of you with awe," he said pleasantly. "You must be very important to command such respect among your nurses."

Miss Fish almost babbled. She straightened her sleeve nervously. "You are a flirt, young man," she said, but in a distinctly pleased tone. She was visibly flustered. "I presume that you came to see Miss Meredith on some urgent matter?"

"A grave matter," he assured her. "Otherwise I should never have ventured to interrupt her work."

"In that case, you may have five minutes in which to speak to her. Don't dally when you finish, Meredith," the woman added in a strict tone. She always called them by their surnames, presumably to keep them in their place. She looked at Matt and actually smiled. "Don't detain her unnecessarily, young man. Even family has no privilege here, in the face of urgent work."

"Yes, ma'am," he said with a pleasant smile.

She flushed again, nodded curtly at Tess, and took herself off down the ward with a back like a fire poker.

Matt had to smother a grin at Tess's perplexed expression.

"What a nice touch," she said. "Did you practice in the mirror until you perfected that suave manner?"

"For weeks," he agreed. His face lost every trace of mirth, however, as he began to speak.

"I've been at the police station most of the morning. I didn't want to come until I had something optimistic to say. But that hasn't happened, so I've come anyway."

"Is it Nan?" she asked at once. "Is she all right?"

"That depends on your definition of well-being." He took a breath. "She's in jail."

It took Tess a moment to absorb what he'd said. She turned her head the least bit, confused. "In jail? Nan? On what charge?"

"Murder in the first degree," he said bluntly. "They found Dennis Collier in his living room this morning with a pair of scissors stuck through his neck. He was quite dead."

CHAPTER EIGHT

Tess felt Matt's hand on her arm, steadying her. "Don't take it like that," he said curtly. "She isn't guilty. I knew it the minute I spoke with her. Greene doesn't believe she did it either, but her sister went to sit with a sick friend, Greene was called out to work, and Nan was alone for several hours. She has no alibi for the time Collier was killed, and her neighbors heard her threaten to kill him before she left the house earlier last night."

"Oh, dear heaven," Tess said. She straightened her dainty white cap and pushed back a wisp of hair. "She couldn't kill a worm. She's not that sort of woman. I know she didn't do it." She looked up. "But can we prove it?"

"I don't know. Greene says it's doubtful, unless she was seen somewhere. Even that might not help." He glanced down the ward, where Miss Fish was looking at them pointedly.

"You must help her," Tess pleaded, wide-eyed. She touched his sleeve. "Please."

He stiffened and moved back from her until her hand fell. "You don't have to plead with me on her behalf," he said curtly. "Greene and his superior have already asked me to investigate the murder. I would have done it even if they hadn't."

She let out a relieved sigh. "I can help."

His eyebrows rose. "You can?"

She glared. "I'm not stupid or helpless. I can ask questions or follow people around for you."

His stiff posture relaxed as he looked down at her, and his sudden smile was indulgent. She looked belligerent and very pretty with her cheeks flushed and her big green eyes accusing as they met his. She was pretty. Too pretty. The smile faded as his eyes fell to her soft mouth and he remembered with an inconvenient ache how it felt to kiss her.

The cold glare, coming right behind the warm smile, made her uncomfortable. "I'd better get back to work. I'll do whatever I can to help. Nan is the only friend I have."

The wording hurt him. He knew that he'd alienated her, but he hadn't realized that he'd done it to this extent. There was another aspect that haunted him. Tess was the only "family" that he had. His cousins were so distant and foreign to him that he wouldn't have known them if he saw them on the street. But Tess was a part of his past... and very much a part of his present.

"We'll talk about it later," he said, bringing his mind to bear on the present. He glanced at Miss Fish, who was pointedly staring at her junior. "Your matron is getting a bit testy."

"Yes, I'm sure she is. She's quite strict."

"I'll leave before I get you into trouble." He started to go and then turned back, his face solemn and stern. "Don't visit the jail unless I'm with you. There are some extremely unpleasant criminals incarcerated near your friend. It wouldn't be proper for you to go there alone."

She lifted her chin and wanted to argue, but it would have been difficult at the moment. "We can talk about that later, too," she said sweetly.

He sighed with resignation, tipped his hat, and went back toward the front entrance.

Miss Fish came striding up to join her young nurse. "While you aren't rushed, Meredith, I'd like you to make up some extra iodoform gauze."

"Yes, Miss Fish," she replied, forcing herself not to groan aloud. The gauze was tricky to prepare because one had to mix iodoform with glycerin, alcohol, and ether. The sterile gauze in precut lengths was then dropped into the mixture and pressed uniformly to preserve the evenness of color. The preparer had to work quite rapidly with her surroundings as sterile as an operating room. The gauze was then rolled into strips and placed in sterile glass jars. The nurse who had to prepare it always groaned. It was one of the most difficult of the routine tasks.

"Meredith, have you ever considered taking formal training?" her superior asked suddenly. "As you know, we have several graduates of the Illinois Training School for Nurses here at the hospital, and they draw a larger salary than you do. You certainly have the qualifications to earn your diploma, and your prior experience working for your father would be taken into account, I'm sure."

"I hadn't thought about it," Tess confided, "but it is something I think I might like to pursue. I love nursing. I cannot conceive of any other career."

"Yes, I discerned that. Most attractive young women of your age are married. You have no wedding plans, no beau?"

Tess's eyes grew sad. "No, Miss Fish," she said dully. "No plans at all." And that was true—because Matt didn't want to marry her, and she couldn't conceive of marrying anyone else.

Miss Fish seemed to soften a little. "If you do decide to take the step, I know the administrator of the school. Come and see me, and I'll give you an excellent letter of reference."

Tess smiled. "That's very kind. Thank you."

"You are intelligent and skilled, despite your lack of formal training; you work harder than most of my juniors do; and you never shirk tasks," the older woman said. "Such dedication does not go unnoticed here." She nodded dismissively. "Tend to your duties, nurse. When you finish the gauze strips, you might prepare a mustard plaster for the Watkins child."

Everyone in the hospital was fond of the ten-year-old boy in the children's ward. He had a stubborn pneumonia that nothing seemed to help. Tess had been afraid at first that he had tuberculosis, but the doctors had found nothing to indicate it.

Billy was a frail and sickly child whose parents never came to visit him. They had five other children, of which he was the youngest, and both parents worked in a cloth mill. Tess had met them only once, and found them cold and unemotional. A bright and funny child, Billy was so unlike his family that he seemed not even to belong in it. The nurses petted him, to the doctors' disapproval. Even the dour and strict Miss Fish had once been seen sneaking him a peppermint stick.

"Is his chest no better?" Tess asked.

"It's no worse, at least," Miss Fish said noncommittally. "Go back on duty now."

"Yes, Miss Fish."

The next day, Saturday, was Tess's day off. It was early and she waited in the parlor for Matt to come down. She wanted to be sure she intercepted him in case he was planning to skip breakfast so he could rush straight to his office.

Sure enough, she'd been sitting on the rosewood sofa only a few minutes when she heard his footsteps on the staircase.

He was checking his pocket watch when she came to the doorway of the parlor to meet him.

He gave her a quick, wary glance.

"Are you going out?" he asked, taking in the fact that she was obviously dressed for a day out in a black suit with a white blouse and a wide-brimmed hat with jet-beaded trim.

She nodded.

"Where?"

She looked up at him and smiled. "I thought I might talk you into taking me to jail to see Nan. You said you didn't want me to go there alone. But if you won't go with me, that's exactly what I'll do."

He glared at her. "You've become something of a thorn in my side just lately."

"When haven't I been?" she retorted. She clutched her small bag tightly in her hands. "Do you have anything pressing on your schedule?"

"Not that pressing, I suppose. Jail is no place for a lady."

"That's why I want to see Nan."

"Very well," he said in a resigned tone. "Let's go. But not without breakfast."

Nan was in a small cell all by herself, but near enough to some of the male prisoners to make her uncomfortable. Tess saw at once why Matt had insisted that she not go to the jail alone. She was grateful for his company, especially in the face of the cold-eyed jailer who looked at her in a way that chilled her blood.

When he opened the cell door to admit Tess and Matt, Nan was sitting on her narrow bunk with her hair disheveled and wearing the same skirt and blouse she'd had on two nights before.

"Good heavens!" Tess exclaimed, rushing over to Nan and kneeling in front of her. "You poor dear. Hasn't anyone thought to bring you a change of clothing?"

"My sister did, but I daren't..." She leaned forward, flushing. "They watch me all the time," she whispered.

Matt's dark eyes narrowed. "I'll speak to your brother-in-law. He should be able to do something about that!"

"That's very kind of you, Mr. Davis. I'm in his bad books, even though he knows I didn't kill Dennis." She lowered her eyes. "He knows I'm going to have a baby—that it's not my husband's. I am a terrible woman!"

"Stop that," Tess chided gently. "You're not terrible."

"Certainly not," Matt agreed. "We'll do all we can for you. Have you any idea who the murderer could be, Mrs. Collier? Was there someone who hated your husband enough to kill him?"

"I did," she said miserably, folding her hands in her lap. She shook her head wearily. "I do realize that I'm the best suspect they're likely to find. I had reason to hate Dennis." She picked at a fingernail. "He didn't know about the baby. If he had, I fear what he might have done. I believe he would have killed me. He had criminal friends... or at least I think they were criminals. They probably taught him a lot of ways to do dreadful things... like kill me."

Matt leaned back against the bars, frowning. "I thought your husband was a telegrapher?"

"That's what he did to pretend that he was a decent citizen," Nan said coldly. "But he was caught up in something dishonest, with a group of men who all dressed nice and had plenty of money to flash around. I don't know exactly what they did to get the money."

"Did you hear them say anything that might give a clue about it?"

Nan pushed back her hair. "They didn't talk much around me," she said. "I heard bits and pieces now and again. Little of it made any sense to me."

"What about recent days, Mrs. Collier?" Matt asked. "Can you remember the last of these conversations you overheard?"

Nan looked agitated. "Well, just last week there were a number of men sitting in our parlor... I was working in the kitchen." She looked forlornly up at Tess, then back at Matt. "Dennis told me to make sandwiches and... and salads for them to eat with their beer... He bought beer by the keg, you know, as if he were a barkeep..." She looked around distractedly, running her fingers through her hair.

"It must have been hard on you, Nan," Tess said sympathetically. She had risen some time before and was standing next to Matt, at whom she shot a glance. Upon his nod, she prompted gently, "You were working around the kitchen, and you heard something."

"Yes, yes. Dennis said a man named Marley... that he knew how to get around locks. He said 'I'll get him to help.' "

"Marley?" Matt echoed.

"Yes, but I don't know if it was his first name or his last name. I don't even know if he was here in Chicago." She put her face in her hands. "I'm so sick. My sister fainted when they came to arrest me. She doesn't think I did it, but she's scared, too." She lifted her red-rimmed eyes. "Mr. Davis, they'll hang me if I can't prove I didn't do it, won't they?"

"No court is going to hang a woman who's in the family way," he said tersely.

"But they might not care." She moaned. "They'll make me out to be as bad as those girls who work in bordellos. The jury will all be men, and they'll convict me as sure as there's a sun."

"Now, now," Tess said gently, crossing to Nan and holding her hands tightly. "You mustn't think that way. Remember the baby and try to stay optimistic. Matt's doing all he can to save you, and so am I." She brightened. "Nan, I'll get the girls together and that will give us strength. You're well liked, and none of them will believe you capable of murder. But you'll be tried by an all-male court, and that won't sit well with our group at all." She was thinking out loud. "We might be able to help in some way."

"They won't want to help me when they hear about the baby," Nan said miserably.

"Nan, some of our members advocate having all children out of wedlock and out from under the control of men."

"Oh, of a certainty, keep men for breeding stock and then kill them..." Matt muttered.

"Matt!" Tess cried, scandalized.

Nan brightened a little. "Well, Tess, I did hear one girl say something along those lines. I'm sure she was joking," she added hastily, with an apologetic glance at Matt.

"Don't worry about offending me," he said. "I've had years of listening to Tess's thoughts on women's emancipation."

"Some of our fellow marchers have rather radical ideas," Tess had to admit. "There was a group once that advocated living like Amazons." Her face colored. "Of course, they thought men should be kept on leashes and in cages."

He chuckled. "No doubt. And I suppose you find that concept rational."

She glanced at him. "They'd have to make a very large cage to hold you."

Nan looked around her. "This one seems to hold me very well." She twisted her skirt in her hands. "What shall I do?"

"Try not to worry," Matt said solemnly. "Remember, you have us on your side. Meanwhile, there's no real alternative to leaving you here. I'm sure if there had been a way to accomplish it, your sister and her husband would have found it already."

Nan nodded. "They did appeal to the judge, but it's a capital crime, and they won't discuss bail." She turned her gaze to Tess. "Do you think you might find a book or two for me to read? It's frightening in here, and I have too much free time. Or could you bring me some wool and some knitting needles?"

"I'll do what I can," Tess said.

"Mr. Davis, please ask my brother-in-law to stop by and see me," she added. "I'm a bit scared being here alone, and that jailer... well, he's rather offensive and getting bolder with his remarks by the hour."

Matt's eyes darkened. "Don't worry about it. That can be handled. Tess, we should go."

Tess patted her friend's thin shoulder. "If you think of anything else that can help, please send word to Matt or to me."

"To me," Matt corrected. "I won't permit Tess to come here alone." He held up a big hand when Tess started to speak. "I won't argue the point."

She sighed angrily. "Brute."

"No, he isn't a brute," Nan said. "Thank you both for helping me. It's more than I deserve, especially after what happened to you, Tess. I wouldn't have had you hurt on my behalf for all the world; please believe that."

"I do believe it. You're my friend," Tess responded. "I'll do everything I can to help save you."

"There is just one more thing," Nan said suddenly, standing. "I haven't wanted to involve him... but the baby's father may be able to help you find out who killed Dennis. He got me out of the apartment after Dennis hit me. I know he didn't kill him, but he might be able to help find who did."

Matt, noting her unease, looked around to make sure they weren't being watched. "Who is he?" he asked.

She grimaced. "You've probably heard of him. Most people in Chicago have." She moved closer to him so that her voice wouldn't carry. "His name is Jim Kilgallen, but he's called Diamond Jim."

Matt's eyes widened. "Good God!"

"Do you know of him?" Tess asked.

"Who doesn't?" he muttered. "He's the kingpin of most illegal operations in Chicago, although he usually stops short of white slavery. He owns several saloons around town, two distilleries, and the biggest slaughterhouse in the city." He stared at Nan, who flushed. "Did your husband have any dealings with him?"

She hesitated, and then nodded. "That's how we met. He came to the apartment several times. Once while he was there, Dennis hit me." She sat back down. "He told Dennis that if he ever raised his hand to me again, he'd be found floating in the river. But Dennis was so strange the night he was killed that no threat would have held him back. He was out of his mind."

Matt's face went taut. Nan saw it and shook her head. "No, Jim Kilgallen wouldn't have soiled his hands with Dennis. If he'd really wanted him out of the way, he'd have given him money and sent him to New York or Miami and had him divorce me. He doesn't kill people."

"You're sure of that? Sure enough to risk your life on it?" Matt persisted.

She sighed. "Yes, I am. And he doesn't know about the baby either. Not yet." She shuddered. "I hadn't thought very far ahead. First I was going to get away from Dennis. Then I was going to get a divorce. After that I was going to tell Jim about the baby and let him decide if he wanted to marry me. He hasn't ever been married, but he's had lots of girls, prettier ones than me. Oh, it's all so sordid! My mother didn't raise me to be a bad girl! I don't know how I went so far off the beaten path as this!"

Matt, who'd seen plenty of decent girls die in brothels, didn't reply.

Tess was on the verge of tears. "You keep your chin up. We'll do something."

"I wish I was strong like you, Tess," Nan mumbled through her tears. "I was never really smart. I married Dennis because he seemed so sweet. We hadn't been married two weeks when he slugged me for burning the breakfast bread!"

"You should have laid his head open with an iron skillet right then," Tess said.

"I was just seventeen. My father often beat me for not minding him. I guess I got used to being hit by men." She looked at Tess curiously. "Don't all girls get hit that way?"

"I never was," Tess replied. "My father was a kind and gentle man. Like Matt," she added without looking at him.

"Oh, I wouldn't think of Mr. Davis as particularly gentle," Nan murmured, wiping her eyes. "Else why would he carry that great knife on his belt?"

"I only use it on scoundrels," Matt assured her. "And now we really must go. I have work waiting."

"Thank you both for coming," Nan said again. Fear was in her eyes, along with resignation. Her expression said what her voice didn't, that she never expected to be out of jail unless it was up on a scaffold waiting for the hangman.

Matt sent Tess outside the jail while he had a word with the jailer. He came out looking stern, with traces of lingering violence in his eyes.

"They should have put her in a more secure place, and with a woman matron," he said curtly. "I'll speak to Greene later and see what he can do. That damned jailer is scum."

"What did he say to you?" she asked.

"Never mind." He looked down at her as they walked. "Don't go in there alone."

Her heart skipped. "Nan isn't safe there, is she?"

"She is now," he said curtly. His black eyes met hers. "The jailer won't risk getting fresh with her again. The police commissioner is a friend of mine. I can have him behind bars if he persists, and Greene is going to let him know that in no uncertain terms."

"Good for you," she said fervently.

"But she is in a great deal of trouble," he continued. "And it's going to take some quick work to keep her from hanging. She's got a good motive for murder, nobody can give her an alibi for late on the evening her husband was killed, and she's a woman. All that is enough to convict her in the eyes of a male jury."

"It's not fair!"

"Is anything?"

She paused with him at the corner as they were about to cross the street. "What about Diamond Jim Kilgallen?"

"He may kill people, but he wouldn't do it with a pair of scissors," he replied, his dark eyes meeting her soft green ones. "The very manner of the thing points to a woman. That's another strike against her."

"Perhaps her husband had a girlfriend."

"Possibly."

"Or someone wanted to make it look as if Nan did it."

"Unlikely."

"Why?"

He took her arm, making her tingle to her toes, and drew her across the wide avenue with him. "Because in order to frame someone, you have to hate them. Nan doesn't strike me as the sort of person who generates hatred in anyone, man or woman." He gave her a wry glance and saw her puzzled expression. "You don't understand? Think. You don't like most women yourself, but you like Nan."

She smiled ruefully. "I see what you mean." They moved down the sidewalk, both lost in their own thoughts.

"Couldn't Diamond Jim have ordered someone to kill him?" she persisted.

"Certainly, but he would have sent a man, and it would have been done with a revolver or a knife or even fists and cudgels—not with a pair of scissors. Kilgallen would be the last person who'd want to implicate Nan in the murder by using a murder weapon that pointed toward a female assailant."

She couldn't disagree with that. "If Collier had a girlfriend and he'd broken off with her, that could be a motive."

"We have no evidence yet to make conclusions. Circumstantial evidence won't hold up in court. We have to have a clear motive and a suspect, and be able to prove it."

She grimaced. "This isn't as easy as it looks. Detective work, I mean." She swung her purse absently in her hands. "Are you ever going to take me to see your office?"

"Do you really want to see it?"

"Yes. If you don't mind."

"I don't. There won't be many agents in today. Most of them are working on cases around the city."

"Do you have a secretary?"

"Yes. His name is Garner. He came with me from the Pinkerton Agency. He's very efficient, and his handwriting is perfect. Anyone can read it."

"If that's a slur against my own handwriting, I'll have you remember that I never had time to do perfect script. I was too busy writing down my father's instructions, and he dictated very rapidly."

He smiled, remembering her father's idiosyncrasies. "He was a good man. I miss him."

"Oh, so do I," she said fervently. "It was so lonely in Montana that sometimes I thought I couldn't bear it without him." She paused and lifted her eyes to his. "But I should have asked you before I pushed my way into your life. I know you'd love to send me back to Montana on a rail. I'm sorry that I've upset things."

He looked astounded. "What have you upset?"

"Your life, Matt," she said heavily. "I've made you uncomfortable with my behavior, embarrassed you...."

"Nothing embarrasses me," he pointed out. "As for being uncomfortable, I'm not. You were never the sort of woman to sit at home of an evening and knit. It would have been out of character for you not to get involved in some cause."

"Your landlady doesn't like me."

"She doesn't like me either," he said, "but as long as I pay the rent, she can please herself. If I lose my rooms there, I'll find others. Chicago is a big city."

"So I've noticed. What are we going to do about Nan?"

"We're going to find the killer."

She smiled. "Both of us?"

He cocked his head and stared down at her. "Will you leave it alone if I ask you to?"

"Certainly not."

"Then, if you're inviting yourself into my case, you'll follow orders, just as my operatives do."

Her face became radiant. Her sense of adventure was kindled, and she felt more alive and happy than she had in weeks. "Okay, boss," she drawled. "Just tell me what to do!"

Chapter Nine

Matt's office was impressive. There was a huge desk and behind it a large chair, upholstered in the same burgundy leather that graced all the chairs and the divan in the large room. There was a grandfather clock on the wall and shades at the curtained windows that could be pulled against the sunlight. The floor sported an exquisite Persian rug in muted reds, and the walls were covered with framed photos of Matt with some of the most influential people in Chicago, not to mention political figures from the rest of the country. There was even one of Matt with Theodore Roosevelt!

"You know the president!" she exclaimed, staring at the photograph.

"He isn't a personal friend, but, yes, I have met him."

She picked up the gilt frame and stared at the smiling man in the picture. The autograph read "To Matt from Teddy." She placed it back into position with a reverence that wasn't lost on her host.

"I never thought much about the sort of people you meet," she said, glancing around at the other photographs. "'I suppose over the years you've gotten to know a lot of famous men."

"Any number," he agreed, one hand in his pocket as he stood looking out of the curtained window at the busy street below. "They all wear shoes and comb their hair of a morning," he added dryly.

She blushed. "I sound like a bumpkin, don't I? But then, I am. I lived in plains country with my father, very simply, most of my life. I never stayed in such a big city until I came here."

He turned, his black eyes narrowed. "You've adapted well enough."

She grimaced. "I'm not quite so sure."

He didn't move, but his eyes did. They were bold and very disturbing as they ranged over her. "It's hard to reconcile you with the memories of the young girl who helped nurse me."

Her hands were folded at her waist, her string purse dangling. "And I'm no longer young, as the matron likes to remind me," she said with faint bitterness.

"That isn't what I meant." He frowned and moved forward, stopping just in front of her. "You're more mature. Some of that flash-fire temper is missing."

"It does little good to lose control of oneself. You taught me that."

The frown deepened. "And too much self-control can be equally damaging," he said curtly. "You keep secrets from me, Tess. There was a time when you were open and truthful."

She averted her gaze to the Persian rug at her feet. "You wouldn't like my secrets." Tess sounded docile, but she was outraged. How dare Matt say such a thing! *He* was the one who was reserved... evasive... secretive.

His hand clenched in his pocket. "You and I were, and still are, friends. But you're a grown woman now, and you need more than that from a man."

She looked up at him with green eyes that flashed angrily. "I need nothing," she said through her teeth, "except your assistance in freeing my friend from jail so she avoids the hangman's noose. You don't have to keep pushing me away. I've learned my lesson quite well." She turned and went to the door, leaving him speechless—and perplexed. She checked the small watch pinned to her bodice. "I must go back on duty soon. Thank you for the tour of your office. It was quite interesting."

She gave him a polite nod and left, closing his door firmly behind her. She gave his secretary an equally brief nod and exited the building.

In fact, she wasn't on duty soon; she just wanted to get away from Matt. She went to a small park and sat down on a bench to watch the pigeons strut around the statues. She wished she had some bread to feed them, as a man and woman on a nearby bench were doing. She felt tired and drained of emotion. She'd worn her heart out on Matt, and there was nothing left inside. He was as immovable as one of those stone statues nearby, completely remote from any feeling or hunger.

He was a man without a real place in the world. Perhaps her father had done him no favor by getting him away from his own people and into a world where he didn't really belong. He lived as a white man, and it would be almost impossible for him to go back to the life he'd known when he was younger. She wondered if he ever thought about the old days with regret and loss. If he did, it was something he kept strictly to himself. He shared his fears and dreams with no one.

After a few minutes of painful reflection on the uselessness of hoping for the unreachable, she got up and went back to the boardinghouse. She was going to do something to help her friend Nan, with or without Matt's help. And she had a few ideas of her own about how to proceed.

The first thing she did the next morning was to go by Nan's apartment house on the pretext of handing out leaflets about the women's emancipation meeting. This also gave her a reason for invading the privacy of Nan's neighbors.

Women were at home at the first two apartments she visited on Nan's floor. The third was occupied by a rather irritable man, who stopped her at the doorway. But his wife, a homely yet welcoming soul with a nice smile, invited her in.

"Don't mind Humphrey, dear," she said, waving her husband away. "He's resting after an infarction of the heart, and just mad to get back to work at his job. He's a harness maker, you see. It isn't arduous work, but his doctor won't hear of his returning to it so soon. Poor Humphrey hates sitting around."

"I think most men do," Tess replied with a smile. She handed the woman a leaflet, explained what the goals of the group were, and then casually, oh so casually, mentioned that a member of the group lived in the building.

"You mean Mrs. Collier, just down the hall, don't you, dear?" the woman said, shaking her gray head sadly. "Such a nice child, and her husband such a scoundrel! We could hear him raging at her in their little apartment about her 'women's group.' Once I had my Humphrey go and bang on the door to make him stop. Her body was cut and bruised so often that I wondered how she could bear to live with him. The scoundrel seemed to try to avoid hitting her on the face, where people would see the evidence of his cruelty—though on one or two occasions he did bruise her face. And then that last night—!" She shivered. "When I think that I heard him cry out and didn't even ask Humphrey to go and see why. They didn't find him until morning. If he had been found sooner, perhaps he should still be alive." She wrapped her arms around herself. "The policeman said I heard his death cry. I shall never forget it. He called out her name. Just her name, and then, barely two minutes later, that terrible cry!"

"What name?" she asked gently.

"Why, his wife's! He said, 'Nan!' and the next thing I knew—" She leaned forward. "They said she did it with a pair of scissors!"

"Did you see her?" Tess asked urgently.

"No. I heard footsteps on the stairs and then, seconds later, the outside door open. She didn't even stop to close it, you know. No, I didn't get so much as a glimpse of her, but someone else did, and they're sure it was a woman who did it. Poor Mr. Collier. He wasn't a good man, but it's a wicked thing to kill another human being. A wicked thing!"

Demoralized, Tess got to her feet. "Thank you very much."

"Why, for what?" the woman asked with a puzzled air.

Simultaneously there was a hard knock at the door, and Humphrey went to answer it. He was belligerent only for an instant, and then his whole demeanor changed. Tess turned just in time to see a taciturn, intimidating Matt enter the apartment.

"Let's go, Tess," he said shortly.

"It's my cousin," Tess said at once to the woman. "I must go. Thank you for talking to me."

"Nice to have met you, dear." The woman nodded, smiling at Matt.

He tipped his hat at her, glanced briefly at Humphrey, took Tess's arm in a firm grasp, and drew her out the door.

He didn't speak until they were down the stairs and out on the sidewalk. "Just what the hell did you think you were doing, going to strange apartments on your own?" His tone of voice was cold, cutting.

She drew her cloak closer around her. His voice chilled even more than the sharp wind. "Stop cursing. I was interrogating witnesses," she said defensively. Her face fell. "That woman heard Collier call out Nan's name, and a little later she heard him cry out. The police said what she heard was surely his death cry." She sighed heavily. "Do you think Nan lied to us?"

He was so angry with her that he could hardly speak at all. With effort, he swallowed his rage. He stuck his hands in the pockets of his overcoat and looked down at her from under the brim of his hat. "The police established that at the time of his death Collier was sitting in a dark apartment, without even a lamp burning. He had a pistol beside him. He was obviously waiting for someone, whom he intended to harm."

He held up his hand when she started to speak. "Just a minute. Let me finish. The pistol was never fired. He'd put it on the table beside the chair, and he'd apparently just gotten to his feet when his visitor arrived. He couldn't have seen anyone well enough to recognize them in the dark. I would guess that he assumed it was his wife. He was found lying on the floor, near the door, with a pair of scissors piercing right through the artery in his neck. He bled to death in a matter of seconds."

Tess stared at him, waiting for him to say more.

He continued grimly. "It wasn't self-defense because at the time of the attack, he was unarmed. The door wasn't forced, and the assailant had to be a woman. The scissors point to it, but so does his calling out his wife's name. The shape had to have been a feminine one, which misled him, you see?"

"Yes. But it all points to Nan."

He buttoned her cloak up to her chin. "You still dress like a child, haphazardly," he remarked as he slipped the last button through its hole.

She smiled faintly. "You were forever doing this when I was young," she recalled. "I never seemed to button coats to suit you."

"Or even dresses," he mused. "The top two buttons at your neck were always fastened wrong. Didn't you ever look in a mirror?"

She shook her head. "I hated my face. It was so plain and ordinary."

He cupped her face in his warm, lean fingers and stared into her eyes. "It was never either," he said softly.

"It wasn't Sioux," she said involuntarily, and much more bitterly than she meant to.

She jerked back from him and moved away, embarrassed.

He didn't know what to say. He was too surprised to make a logical reply. Didn't she know that she was beautiful, and that it had never mattered to him that she wasn't Sioux? He had a very good reason for putting around the rumor that he didn't care for white women, and had a yen for more exotic ladies of varied extractions. But he couldn't admit any of that to Tess without explaining why. And that was a confession that she wasn't yet ready to hear.

"And you can forget that I said that," she added harshly, interrupting his thoughts. She walked on down the sidewalk without looking to see if he was behind her. "I was just a girl."

He was beside her again, more taciturn than ever. "You still don't look in mirrors."

"I only care about being clean and neat. Nothing else," she said, exasperated with herself as well as him. "Most of the patients I tend are too sick to care either."

"Obviously some of them become attached to you, as your friend Marsh Bailey did," he said after a minute. "I presume there are some single doctors as well," he added suddenly, irritated by the thought.

"Nothing of that sort goes on in our hospital," she said firmly.

"I didn't mean to imply that it did." He tilted his hat further over his forehead against the wind. "From now on, leave the questioning of potential witnesses to me."

"I had a perfectly logical reason for going from door to door. I passed out leaflets that our women's group had printed up."

He glanced at her with reluctant admiration. "Well, I'll be."

"I'm not a total idiot, Matt. I didn't just walk in and say, 'Here I am to investigate a murder; please tell me everything you know'!"

"So I see."

"Anyway, people were very nice." She clutched her leaflets and her purse. "I'm so afraid that she did it. Everyone I spoke to said that she had plenty of reason to do it. They knew that he was beating her."

"I have a quite different angle on this business," he said after a minute. "I want to talk to Diamond Jim."

She caught her breath. "He'll shoot you if you accuse him of murder!"

He cocked an impatient brow. "I don't mean to accuse him of anything. And I can't just walk into his office and start questioning him either. I thought I might accept an invitation to the party he's giving for charity. One pays so much a plate to be included on the guest list. Surprisingly enough, it's for an orphanage."

"Will you go alone?"

He searched her face. "That would make it look suspicious. I'm not known for being publicly associated with the various charities. He'd probably think I'd gone there on business, and he might think it had to do with his gambling syndicate. That could make it risky."

"Then what will you do?"

"Take a companion with me."

She averted her jealous eyes. "I see."

"No, you don't," he muttered irritably.

"For God's sake, I've told you and told you, I don't have anything to do with white women."

That last phrase was telling, but she knew better than to ask him personal questions. She might as well question a telegraph pole.

"You plan to let a man dress up and accompany you, then?" she asked with biting irony.

He smiled at her. "I thought of taking you with me."

She flushed and her heart leapt into her throat. "I don't have an evening gown."

"I'll buy you one."

Her eyes blazed at him. "No, you will not! I don't take expensive presents from men, not even from you, and certainly not an article of clothing!"

"Oh, grow up," he fumed. "Here I'm your cousin. There's nothing untoward about buying clothes for family."

Family. She lowered her eyes to the sidewalk and glowered at it. Family. What else did she expect to be to him?

"Besides," Matt said, noting her expression and forcing himself not to react to it, "this is business. The matter of Collier's murderer, remember?" He stared straight ahead. "There's a shop nearby. I did some work for the owner. You'll like her. I expect she'll have something you'll find quite nice."

She clutched her purse. She had very little money of her own, but she had plenty of pride. "I'll buy some fabric and a pattern and sew my own."

"Not to wear to this do, you won't," he replied. "In Chicago people are too aware of what one wears in general. At charity functions they go far beyond that, Tess, to sheer snobbery about apparel."

She glanced at his expensive suit and overcoat and hat. "So I see."

He met her gaze. "You wanted to fit in. This is how you do it."

"I'll try not to embarrass you."

"Thank you," he said dryly. "I'll try to return the favor."

As if he could embarrass anyone, with his innate dignity and clothes sense and elegance, she thought. But she didn't say it. He was volatile enough already.

Her thoughts returned to Nan and at last she voiced her worst fear. "What if she did it?"

"Then she'll be convicted. But we'll do what we can for her, just the same."

"Thank you, Matt," she said after a long pause.

He stopped at a streetlight and turned her toward the storefront of a very elegant women's clothier.

"You're not serious!" she exclaimed when she looked at the mannequins in the display window. "Heavens, Matt, those gowns would cost a month's salary... maybe half a year's!"

"You get what you pay for," he said without blinking an eye. "Come on."

He propelled her into the exclusive shop. An elegant woman in a becoming day dress with her hair elaborately coiffured turned from the counter to greet them.

"May I be of service, Monsieur Davis?" she asked, glancing critically at Tess's figure.

"This is my cousin," Matt told her without preamble. "She needs a ball gown."

"I am Madame Dubois," she introduced herself with a smile. "I think I have just the thing. *Un moment,*" she said, and darted to the back of the shop.

She returned, to Tess's surprise, with the most delicious white taffeta gown she'd ever seen, its sleeves and skirt tied with ribbons in softest blue and pink, edged in lace.

"It takes the breath away, *n'est-ce pas?* It was made up for a customer who gained too much weight and could not wear it when it was finished." She smiled wickedly. "But she will enjoy the *bébé* more than the gown, I daresay. Here. Please to try it on, mademoiselle. There, in the back."

She led Tess to a changing room, closed the door, and left her.

It took several minutes to remove her outer garments so that she could slip into the elegant dress. She fastened it with trembling hands, astonished at the beautiful fit.

Madame Dubois appeared just in time to fasten the last hooks in back. "You will require some assistance to close the fastenings, but surely there are other women handy, yes?"

"Yes. I live in a boardinghouse," Tess replied. "It fits so nicely! Does it look all right?" she added, tugging at the bodice. "I mean, is it not a little too low in front?"

"With a bust like yours, mademoiselle, it is perfect," she replied, smiling at the picture Tess, with her blond fairness, made in the delicious confection. She shook her head. "You will not know yourself. Come. Let us show monsieur..."

"Oh no, please." Tess put her hands over her bodice.

"Ah, I see, it embarrasses you to have your cousin see you thus. The gown will be for an admirer. I will not tell him," she whispered. "It will be our secret. I will leave you to dress, mademoiselle, but first let us remove the gown so that I may pack it for you in a box. But at once, when you arrive home, it must hang, so, for the wrinkles to fall out. You understand?"

"Yes," Tess said. She was excited not only by the feel of the gown but by its exquisite lines. She had to have it, even if it cost her a year's wages. She felt beautiful in it.

Matt was waiting patiently when she left the dressing room. Her hair was faintly disheveled, but her wide hat covered most of the damage.

"Here," he said, handing her the dress box. "Can you carry it?"

"Oh yes." Her gloved hand tightened on the handle possessively. "It's the most gorgeous thing!"

"I have also included a pair of opera gloves, my dear," Madame Dubois told her. "But you must have shoes to match..."

"I'm sure I have some at home," Tess said with her scant remaining pride.

"Very well, then. I wish you a lovely evening!"

"Thank you." Tess smiled at her and went through the door Matt was holding for her.

Once outside, he took her arm again and marched her down to a shoe store. He wasn't satisfied until she had dainty satin pumps to match the gown, and afterward they stopped at a millinery shop, where he bought her a small satin bag as well and one of the popular egret combs to complement her hairstyle.

"You've spent far too much money on me," she complained when they reached the boardinghouse in a hired carriage with her purchases.

"You could hardly go to the ball in rags, Cinderella," he told her.

She didn't look at him. "My slippers aren't made of glass, and I won't turn into a mouse at midnight."

"The carriage horses turn into mice," he pointed out.

He carried her parcels into the boardinghouse and up to her room, past a curious Mrs. Mulhaney.

"It's a ball gown," Tess told her excitedly. "My cousin Matt is taking me to a charity ball!"

"Well, it's about time you had a real social life," Mrs. Mulhaney replied curtly. "Nothing but work and that women's group!"

"I agree entirely," Matt said.

He dumped the parcels on Tess's bed, tipped his hat, and went back downstairs. He wasn't through for the day, even if Tess was.

For the next few days, she dreamed about accompanying Matt. It might be a necessary step in their plan to save Nan, but Tess couldn't help but be enthusiastic about her first ball. She hung the gown in her closet, and every so often she opened the door just to touch it and wonder at its beauty. She'd never dared hope she might get to go to a real ball—with Matt.

Back in Montana such things had seemed vaguely like fiction to her. Indeed, she'd read the fairy tale "Cinderella" and often had wondered what it would be like to have a ball gown and a handsome escort for the evening, and to go to a really fancy ball. There were barn dances in Montana, but that was a far cry from a real ball.

She counted the days until the event, working hard at the hospital and trying not to remember that it was only part of a job for Matt to escort her.

Inevitably the Saturday of the great event arrived. Tess had Mrs. Mulhaney help with fastening the gown. The older woman was fascinated by its beauty and shocked by its low-cut bodice.

"You must have a wrap, my dear," she said. "I have one that I insist you borrow. It's mink. It will be just the thing to complement that gown!"

"Mink! But I couldn't!" Tess protested.

Mrs. Mulhaney patted her arm gently. "Men never think of these things. It's quite cold, and the gown has only a hint of sleeves. I'll fetch it for you."

She went out, closing the door behind her. Tess patted her hair into place and pushed the egret comb that Matt had bought her into a particularly deep wave. She hardly recognized the pretty and very exclusive-looking woman in her mirror. Her fairness would enhance Matt's dark skin. She hoped he wouldn't find fault with her.

Mrs. Mulhaney placed the wrap around her shoulders and looked at her critically. "You look lovely. The pearls are perfect," she added, noting their faint pink hue as they lay above her collarbone.

"They were my grandmother's," Tess said, touching them with her white-gloved hand. "I'm very proud of them."

"I don't doubt it. You have fun."

"I hope to," she said. "Thank you very much for loaning me the wrap. I'll take great care of it."

"I know you will."

Mrs. Mulhaney waved Tess down the staircase, where Matt was pacing impatiently.

"I'm not late," she told him in a faintly haughty tone.

He turned and looked up at her on the staircase. Every comment he'd thought to make stuck in the back of his throat. He stared at her with black, turbulent eyes and said nothing while she slowly came down the rest of the way. Matt thought that he'd never seen anything quite so beautiful in all his life. He wanted to pick her up and carry her away, far away, so that no other man would see her. He took a deep breath, amazed to discover that he was capable of feeling such devastating jealousy.

Chapter Ten

The look in Matt's eyes made Tess so nervous that she almost tripped on the last step. She caught herself on the banister and eased her foot down onto the level floor.

"I don't have a proper wrap," she said, pulling the fur even tighter over the low bodice that she was reluctant to let him see. "So Mrs. Mulhaney loaned me this."

"You look beautiful," he said in a husky, deep tone. His face was unusually hard, and his eyes held an odd glitter.

Tess stared back at him hungrily. It was the first time he'd looked at her in exactly that way, and her toes seemed to curl inside her shoes. He made her feel like the Cinderella of her dreams.

But seconds later, the spell was broken when he abruptly and curtly said, "Shall we go?"

He took her arm and escorted her out. He was wearing evening clothes, a beautifully tailored black coat with tails and black pants, crisp white shirt, and bow tie. In his left hand he held a silk top hat and silver-headed cane. He looked impossibly handsome and elegant.

When they were in the hired carriage riding toward the hotel where the ball was to be held, he stared at her in the dim, flickering light of streetlamps.

His steady gaze made her nervous and she shifted.

"I didn't know that you were lacking a dressy coat. I assumed that you had one, God knows why."

"There's been no reason to..." She cleared her throat. "I shouldn't have occasion to wear one after tonight. I don't go out to such formal affairs... as you very well know."

He glanced out the window at the passing buildings. He didn't dare look at her too much, he told himself, or he was going to lose his precarious control. The sight of her in evening clothes, with her hair elegantly done, was almost his undoing. She'd always been pretty, even in a faded dress, but tonight she was so elegant that she made him violently possessive. It was as if she belonged in cultured society even more than he did. Combined with his own inner turmoil about his ancestry, her elegance only punctuated the differences between them and set her at a greater distance. He felt more guilty than ever about his long-held secret. He had the right to be possessive of her, but she didn't know and he couldn't tell her.

Tess was determined to have a wonderful time, despite Matt's cool indifference. Surely at least one man present would ask her to dance. Then Matt could do what he pleased—or ignore her, which he certainly seemed inclined to do. Her heart felt as if it were broken. She couldn't possibly let him see how his aloof manner was hurting her.

The hotel was emblazoned in lights, and couples in elegant clothing wandered into it in pairs. They came in sleek carriages with uniformed drivers, drawn by beautifully liveried horses, and at least two arrived by motorcar. Tess had never seen so many wealthy people in one place in all her life—in fact, she had no idea there were so many wealthy people in the world. She was awestruck by the experience.

Matt, holding her arm as they advanced into the hotel, whispered harshly, "Don't gape. They're just people."

"I've never seen any people like this," she said, with fascination plain in her eyes as she looked around her.

"Of course not," he said caustically. "One doesn't expect high fashion on an Indian reservation."

She stepped on his foot quite deliberately and smiled coolly when he winced.

"Suppose you just leave me here, cousin dear, and I'll find someone to stand with?" she asked with venomous sweetness. "I'm sure you'll be relieved not to have to keep me company!"

A maid took her wrap, leaving her uncomfortably revealed. Matt's eyes focused on the low-cut gown, the creamy tops of her breasts revealed in the most provocative way. He caught his breath audibly. He couldn't believe the gown was that modern. He'd never have let her buy it if he'd had any idea how she'd look in it. She was like a princess, and he was suddenly so violently aroused that his whole body throbbed.

He started to speak just as a handsome

young man swept between them and bent over Tess's hand, which he lifted to his lips. He'd been a recent patient at the hospital, where he'd flirted outrageously with her. They'd become friends, of a surface sort. His name was Michael Boson, and he was a wealthy young man.

"I've been waiting all my life for you," he said with breathless abandon. "Dance with me until the wee hours, and then we'll sail away to the moon on a carpet of stardust!"

Tess, relieved to have been saved from the sudden fury in Matt's black eyes, chuckled and tapped him with her lacy fan. "What a glib tongue," she teased. "I don't believe a word you say."

"Heartless girl, and you nursed me through pneumonia, too." He turned when he saw Matt. "Is this he?" Michael asked with a lifted brow, his gaze roaming over Matt's tall physique. "I might have known. He even looks like an assassin. I daresay he's armed."

"Michael, will you stop?" she pleaded.

"Michael Boson, at your service," the young man said with a wicked grin. "You're Cousin Matt, the detective. I recognize you from Tess's description. Your cousin nursed me at the hospital and then cruelly turned her back on me because I'm four years younger than she. I hardly think age is an impediment to a great love affair, myself, but she has reservations. Don't you, chick?" he added with a grin in her direction.

"Yes, this is my cousin, Matt Davis," she introduced them, and then laid her hand on

Michael's sleeve, grateful beyond measure for his unexpected rescue. She couldn't quite meet Matt's eyes. "Dance me away, Michael. Matt didn't mind bringing me, but I'd hate for him to have to spend the evening being bored stiff with me."

"It will be a great pleasure for me to spare him the inconvenience. Don't you worry, Cousin Matt; I'll take wonderful care of her, and you're invited to the wedding!"

He carried her off before Matt could reply. Tess laughed as she went into his arms on the dance floor. She hesitated, though, when he launched into a dance that she couldn't do.

"I don't know this dance. Or any dance that's at all complicated. I'm sorry," she said. "Could you teach me a step or two?"

"Heavens, girl, where have you been all your life?" he asked, dumbfounded.

"Living out west with my father, who was a doctor," she said. "We had barn dances, but nothing so elegant as this."

He grinned. "This is a waltz. It's not difficult. Here. I'll show you the basics. It goes like this..."

Matt, watching them with cold eyes, wanted to go right over there and tear Tess out of the younger man's arms. That low-cut gown was already giving him fits.

He became aware of someone nearby and turned his head. Diamond Jim Kilgallen, with a lighted cigar in his hand, gave him a steady appraisal from deep-set gray eyes. The man had jet-black hair, like Matt's own, but his was wavy. His skin was olive tan, although not as dark as Matt's. He had a broad, leonine face and he wore a thin mustache. His tuxedo was expensive, like his shoes. Matt had never seen him at such a distance before, and he knew at once that he wouldn't deceive this man with any pretext of contributing to charity.

"I know of you," Diamond Jim said after a minute, moving a little closer. "You're Davis."

Matt nodded.

"Know who I am?"

Matt nodded again.

Diamond Jim chuckled. "And I thought I was a man of few words," he said ruefully. "Do you talk?"

"On occasion."

"Hmmm. No accent. They say you're everything from a Russian duke to a gypsy." His eyes narrowed. "But you're not. You remind me of my grandfather. He was Cree."

Matt lifted an eyebrow. "I'm not Cree."

"No, but you're Indian," Diamond Jim said with quiet confidence. "A man with courage and keen intelligence, if what I hear about you is true."

"You'll hear other things, perhaps quite different things, if you listen long enough," Matt said casually.

Diamond Jim nodded slowly. "About the bowie knife, I imagine."

Matt chuckled. "I don't carry it much these days. My reputation opens enough doors without visible threats."

"It does," he agreed. His gray eyes narrowed to slits. "Your cousin over there is good friends with Nan Collier. I hear you both went to see her in jail and that you're trying to help get her out."

"Yes," Matt said. "She's in a lot of trouble. Not only because her marriage was rocky but because the murderer was so obviously female."

"The scissors."

"That's right."

Diamond Jim lifted his cigar to his lips and thought for a minute. "Damn."

"There's something more."

"Something bad, from the way you sound."

Matt didn't know how far to trust this man. Nan Collier was obviously in love with him, but how this gambler felt about her was dubious. He didn't seem a man who had a high opinion of women, and Matt knew from the talk that Diamond Jim liked women. He had plenty of them, almost every one more elegant and educated and pretty than poor little Nan.

"Go ahead," Diamond Jim said when Matt hesitated. "Spill it."

"She's pregnant."

Jim looked away, but not before his rage was visible. He took another puff on the cigar. "That son of a bitch," he said under his breath.

"Excuse me?"

"Collier," he bit off. "Somebody should have killed him years ago! If she's pregnant, it's because he forced her! She hated his touch!"

Aware of curious glances, Matt moved between the man and nearby onlookers.

The evidence was pointing more and more to some strong feeling for Nan on Jim's part.

Matt took a chance. "It isn't her husband's baby."

The expression that statement provoked was a revelation. The gray eyes that had been glittering like a knife blade grew suddenly soft. The hard face relaxed. A faint, reluctant smile drew up the hard lips. "She said that?" Jim asked, his voice quiet, awed. "She told you it wasn't her husband's?"

"She told Tess," Matt corrected. "Tess told me."

Jim stuck a beautifully manicured hand in his pocket and stared into space with that secretive smile still on his lips.

"She feels that it will make things harder," Matt said.

Diamond Jim's head turned back. "Not if they think it was her husband's," he said immediately. "No jury could convict a pregnant woman. My God, a lynch mob would form at the courthouse door, and not a single juror would go home alive!"

"You're probably right. But she shouldn't have to be in jail for a crime she didn't commit."

Diamond Jim's piercing eyes held Matt's. "I know she didn't do it. But how do you know?"

"Years of practice with guilty criminals," Matt said simply. "You get an instinct about people."

"In my business, too," the other man said. He grinned. "Of course, from your point of view, I'm the criminal."

"Criminal, hell, you're a local landmark. Visitors point you out along with the lake."

"Well, I stop short at killing innocent people. Speaking of which," he added, flinging cigar ash into a cuspidor, "how are we going to prove that Nan's innocent?"

Matt stuck both hands in his pockets. "I don't know yet. I'm working on it. I have operatives asking probing questions around her neighborhood."

"Nice of you."

"No, it wasn't," Matt said honestly, glancing toward Tess, who seemed to be having too good a time with her youthful dance partner. "I was forced into it. She"—he indicated a laughing Tess with utter disgust— "was going door to door in the apartment house. I was afraid she'd run into some man who wouldn't take no for an answer."

This produced a curious glance. "Pretty girl. Too bad you're related."

"We aren't," Matt said curtly. "It saved explanations when she came up here. Her father died. She had no one else. I'm a long-standing friend of the family."

"I'll bet that's a story worth hearing."

"I'm Sioux," he said. "I don't think another person in Chicago except Tess knows it."

A look passed between them. Diamond Jim turned his attention to his cigar. "I'm a clam,"he said after a minute. "I keep what I know to myself."

Matt didn't speak. His eyes narrowed more as he watched Tess on the dance floor.

Diamond Jim offered a cigar case.

Matt stared at it.

"No insult intended."

It took Matt a few seconds to realize what he meant. Cigar stores habitually boasted a wooden Indian at the door. When it hit him, Matt burst out laughing.

Diamond Jim chuckled. "Good to know your face isn't painted on. Have a cigar."

"Thanks. I'm partial to a good one."

"These are from Havana. Only the best." He offered a light, and Matt bent his head to fire up the stogie.

"Thanks," he said.

"Oh, I don't want any fistfights in here," Diamond Jim replied with a grin. "If your hands are kept busy, it's less likely that you'll lay out that gentleman who's dancing with your... cousin."

Matt scowled. "What do you mean?"

"You should have seen your face when you were watching her," came the dry reply. "I gather that you think any familiarity with her is a bad idea."

He averted his gaze. "She's white."

"So are you," Jim said quietly, meeting the other man's eyes. "It isn't always a matter of blood. You've lived white for a long time. Tell me that you could go back to living the old life..."

Matt puffed on the cigar. "If I'd stayed where I was, I'd probably have been killed." He stared across the room at Tess. "It might have been the best thing, too."

"Bull."

Matt sighed. "Hell."

Diamond Jim nodded to a passing woman, elegant and sophisticated with eyes far too wise. She gave him a long look, but he didn't return it.

He noticed Matt's curious glance and shrugged. "You know who fathered Nan's child, don't you?"

Matt inclined his head.

Jim smiled, his eyes warm and quiet. "I never thought about having a child until a few months ago. She likes to cook and clean house. She hums when she washes dishes, and her eyes light up when she smiles." He glanced at Matt sheepishly. "I've had more women than I can count, but they were all passing fancies. Nan didn't pass. I wanted her the first time I saw her. The longer I watched Collier mistreat her, the more I wanted to kill him and give her a good life." His eyes blazed for a minute. "I didn't kill him, but I was tempted," he said bluntly. "He hit her. I knocked him down a staircase for that. Your operatives will tell you that, because some of the neighbors saw him go down. They didn't know why, but they're not stupid. I escorted Nan out to the street and to a hotel. I had a message sent to her sister to meet her at the women's assembly. Then I put her in a carriage. We agreed that it would be safer if she met her sister and brother-in-law in public. We agreed that she wouldn't tell her sister anything about what happened, just that Dennis had hit her."

"Do you realize where that puts you?"

"Of course. It puts me at the top of the suspect list. Except that if I meant to kill a man, I'd do it staring him in the eyes—and I'd have killed Dennis with my fists, not a pair of scissors."

"Thanks for telling me the truth. I'll try to keep your name out of it. I have friends at the precinct."

"I don't have any friends," Jim said casually, "but I own a few people at city hall. Between us, maybe we can get Nan off the hook and find the culprit."

"You're a damned scoundrel."

"Oh, and I work at it, too. Except with Nan." He drew in a slow breath. "She's the only person in all my life who wanted me. Not the money, not the notoriety, just me. It's a unique experience for me, being loved."

It must be unique—and a lot more, Matt was thinking, to bring down a man like this one. He'd heard stories about Diamond Jim ever since his arrival in Chicago, none of which indicated a man with a soft heart or a weak spot.

"Shocked you, have I?" Jim asked, smiling rakishly. "Well, we all fall sooner or later, I suppose. When she's free, I'm going to marry her, in case you wondered. I'll buy her a house and pretty clothes, and spoil the kid rotten." He grimaced. "Maybe I'll go legit," he added, sounding totally disgusted. "I don't want my kid kicked around because of his father."

Matt laughed.

"You tell that to anyone and they'll find you in a dark alley one night," Jim said.

Matt only grinned.

Diamond Jim shifted his weight. "I'd rather visit Nan, but I don't want things made worse for her. If they see me in there, it'll ruin what's left of her reputation," he said curtly. "But it rankles to be here in the middle of a party while she's stuck in jail."

"It's a benefit."

Diamond Jim's big shoulders rippled. "Yeah. For the orphanage where I grew up. They needed a new roof, and the stoves were about shot."

Matt searched the other man's face and saw the years he carried.

"You got family?" he asked Matt.

Matt shook his head. "My father died at Little Bighorn, my mother and sisters at Wounded Knee." His eyes were dark with pain and anger. "Tess is all I have now." He glanced at her.

Diamond Jim gestured with his cigar. "You won't have her long if you don't do something about that," he remarked. Tess was standing beside the wall while the man partnering her was leaning on his arm just in front of her, bending over her in a proprietary manner and talking a mile a minute.

"She likes him," Matt said through his teeth.

"Maybe," Jim said. "But she's watched you all the time we've been talking, whenever you weren't looking."

"Has she?"

Diamond Jim shook his head ruefully. "If a woman like that looked at me with her heart in her eyes, I wouldn't give a hoot in hell about the differences between us. You're a damned idiot."

"I beg your pardon."

"Careful, your war paint's showing." Diamond Jim chuckled. He watched Matt control himself with a visible effort. "You give to charities, but you don't go to balls. Why are you here?"

"For a number of reasons. Mainly, for what you've already told me. I can scratch you off the list of suspects and find the real killer."

"Thanks."

Matt smiled at Jim's irritated expression. "I didn't know you from a hatbox. A man with your reputation could have done it. I wanted to know."

"You also said you were here for other reasons."

"Yes." He glanced around and moved closer. "I've been trying to get something done about the jailer who watches Nan. You aren't going to like this."

"Tell me!"

"He's making advances to her," Matt said. "Her brother-in-law's tried, and I've tried, to have her moved. No dice, despite the fact that they have women matrons for the female prisoners. And the jailer's son went to school with our mayor. Do you see the problem?"

"That's not a problem," Diamond Jim said, and for a few seconds, Matt was ready to believe everything he'd ever heard about the man. His expression was utterly ferocious. "I'll see to it."

"Thanks. I have influence, but nobody owes me political favors." Matt shrugged.

"You're a decent guy," Diamond Jim said. "I won't forget what you're doing for Nan."

"For Tess," Matt said after a minute. "She's fiercely loyal to her friends. She's fond of Nan. It's hard to turn her down when she asks a favor. She doesn't, as a rule."

"Are you going to let him walk off with her?" Diamond Jim asked, nodding toward Tess and her dancing partner.

"It looks as if she wants him to." Matt laughed humorlessly. "I taught her the bow," he mused. "And how to speak Sioux. She was more tomboy than young lady in those days. Then I went away and everything changed." He stared at her on the dance floor with an ache that wouldn't go away. "She has no idea what her life would be like if she got involved with me and the truth about me made the rounds of local society."

"Think she'd mind?"

Matt stared at him. "I'd mind."

"How old is she? She looks older than Nan."

"She's twenty-six."

"Never married?"

"Never wanted to be, she says," Matt replied. "She's a suffragist, bloomers and placards and all." He shook his head. "She says that's all she wants now, to devote her life to the cause."

"Maybe she doesn't think she has a choice."

Matt glared at him. "Sure she does. It's standing beside her, trying to hold her hand."

He indicated the man with Tess. "There could be a dozen others standing in line behind him, you know."

"Well, it's your business, of course." Diamond Jim puffed on his cigar. "But if she were mine, I'd pick her up and carry her out the door. Nothing like the element of surprise with a feisty little woman like that."

"How do you know she's feisty?"

He grinned. "Nan admires her spirit. Tess is the reason Nan decided she'd had enough of Collier. She said Tess told her that no woman had to put up with being mistreated by a man, regardless of what society said. In a way," he added thoughtfully, "it pushed her right into my arms. One minute she was telling me about the way Collier treated her, and the next she launched herself into my lap and started crying." His eyes began to glow with the memory. "It was a new thing for me, being needed like that. It began then." He sighed. "Somehow, the fact that she was married never stood in my way. I didn't give it a thought. A man who could treat her as badly as Collier had wasn't worth consideration in my book. We love each other." He stared at his feet. "I can't lose her."

"You won't," Matt said solemnly. "She's innocent. All we have to do is prove it—and find out who *is* guilty."

"It had to be a woman."

"I think so, too. That means tracking down any old flames or current flames of the elusive Mr. Collier."

"He used drugs. You know that?"

"Yes."

"It might be one direction to try."

"I'll remember. Thanks for your help."

Diamond Jim shrugged. "I'm helping myself. Nan is the only good thing that ever happened to me."

Matt searched the gambler's face and smiled. "I'll let you know what we find out. Meanwhile, it would help her most if you'd do what you can about the jailer."

"He retired tomorrow morning. Wait and see."

Matt couldn't repress a grin. The man had a way about him, all right.

His dark eyes searched the room for Tess, and he suddenly realized that she was missing. He moved forward a step, still searching.

"They went outside," Diamond Jim said helpfully.

Matt tossed his cigar into the cuspidor and started for the door. He had no idea what he was going to say or do when he joined Tess, but he didn't like the idea of her being alone with that dandy—and he wasn't going to tolerate it.

Chapter Eleven

Matt was almost to the door when a lovely young woman with dark hair, wearing a jet-studded taffeta gown, stopped in front of him. He recognized her as one of the girls who'd been giving the eye to Kilgallen.

"I know you," she said in a voice like velvet. "You're the detective. Don't you remember me?"

Matt stared at her, trying to make his mind work, not an easy thing to do with Tess outside and in the company of an amorous suitor. "No," he said more abruptly than he might have.

She moved closer and laid a gloved hand on his sleeve. "I'm Daphne Mallory," she said. "You handled a case of embezzling for my father, Hart Mallory."

"Ah, yes," Matt said.

She smiled. "I invited you to supper, but you wouldn't come." She peered at him through impossibly long lashes over the bluest eyes he'd ever seen. "Do you think if I invited you a second time, you might show up?"

He was going to brush her off. But at the same moment, Tess came back in the door just ahead of her escort, looking breathless and faintly unkempt. She fanned herself and glanced back over her shoulder as if waiting impatiently for her companion. It set Matt off.

He turned and stared into Daphne Mallory's eyes, knowing that Tess was watching. "Do you dance, Miss Mallory?"

"Indeed I do, Mr. Davis!"

He led her onto the ballroom floor, slid an arm around her, and moved her into the most beautiful dance Tess had ever watched. She'd never danced with Matt. She'd never seen him dance. She was surprised to find him so accomplished. He moved with such grace that he might have been born dancing the waltz. Her heart ached at the sight of him with that beautiful, sophisticated woman. She'd just had to fight her way out of Michael's embrace. Having led him on quite innocently, she'd found herself maneuvered out the door and almost kissed.

Part of her had hoped that Matt had seen them leave, that he might be jealous enough to come after her. But he was dancing with that beautiful woman, and it couldn't be more evident that he found her fascinating.

"I'm sorry," Michael said belatedly, hesitating beside her with a worried look. "I know that I was anything but a gentleman. I won't do it again."

Tess's eyes flashed. "You won't get the chance," she said coldly. "Why don't you go out there and find a woman with a private income and loose morals?"

He caught his breath.

"I'm sorry if I gave you the wrong idea," she said belatedly, averting her gaze. "I thought we were enjoying a harmless flirtation, not the prelude to a five-minute affair in the dark!"

He started to speak, but just as he opened his mouth, Diamond Jim came sauntering up beside Tess. He had a smoking cigar in his hand, and he gave the young man a look that clearly was intended to make the fellow feel as if he were wearing short pants.

"Scoot along, boy," he told Michael with a mocking smile. "You're out of your league here."

"Yes, sir," Michael said at once. He gave Tess a wistful, apologetic glance and walked off.

She looked up at the man local citizens

called a criminal. "You don't look like a killer," she said pleasantly.

His eyebrows shot up and he chuckled. "Thanks!"

She clutched her small bag and smiled sheepishly. "Sorry, it just slipped out."

"He saw you go out the door," Diamond Jim said, his head jerking toward Matt, who was apparently oblivious to everything except his dancing partner. "He was heading after you when you came back in."

"He was?" Her soft eyes brightened. They were so full of longing and hope that the man stared without meaning to.

"She captured him in midstride," he told her. "Although I think the way you looked when you came in had something to do with his capitulation."

"It wasn't like that."

"I know Boson," he said unexpectedly. "He's a rich layabout with a yen for virgins."

She gasped and her face went flaming red.

He smiled wickedly. "They told you I was a bad man," he reminded her. "You should have run while you had the chance."

"You... are bad!"

While he was grinning at her shocked expression, Matt caught sight of them. Very quickly he extricated himself from his dancing partner, excused himself, and made a beeline for Diamond Jim and Tess.

"Here comes trouble," Diamond Jim remarked, his eyes sparkling with mischief.

"You did that deliberately!" she burst out.

"Shhh! Don't tell him! Wait and see what he does."

Matt stopped in front of Tess, any amiability that had once touched his hard face all but a memory now.

"Leave him alone," he told her in guttural Sioux. "He's too wise for you."

She glared at him. "I choose my own companions," she replied in that same tongue. "Go back to your fancy woman!"

Diamond Jim was enjoying himself. He pursed his lips and gave them a cursory appraisal. "It isn't Russian," he murmured.

They both looked at him. Tess flushed more and Matt's jaw went rigid.

"What did you say to her?" he asked Diamond Jim in English.

"Oh, I was just warning her that Boson over there is a lazy scoundrel with a taste for virgins. You might expound on that theme. She's young for a woman her age. Very young." He excused himself and went off in the general direction of the buffet table.

"He's quite blunt," Tess said, ruffled. "Even more blunt than you!"

"He's a criminal, for all his charm. But he was right about Boson." His eyes narrowed on her bodice. He saw a faint red mark on one half-exposed white breast, and the eyes he lifted to hers were furious.

"He..." She looked around, muttered to herself at the people close enough to hear every word she said, and switched back to Sioux. "The button on his jacket did that," she said curtly. "And I hit him! You should have looked at his left cheek."

The fury went out of him. He seemed to relax, although she noticed that he had to drag his eyes away from her bodice.

"I've found out what I wanted to know," he said mysteriously, taking her arm. "We'd better go. It's getting late."

She got her wrap from the maid, and he held it for her. They said a quick good night to their host, and Miss Mallory, who was standing beside a newly acquired partner, sent a last regretful glance toward Matt and waved at him.

Once outside, Tess glared up at his profile. "Don't you want to stay?" she asked curtly. "She'll miss you."

He didn't reply. He took her arm and led her to a hired carriage. But to her surprise, he didn't give the driver the address of their boardinghouse. She heard him give other, quite surprising directions—to Lake Michigan.

He climbed in beside her, leaned back, and crossed his legs. He looked formidable and completely unapproachable to Tess. She didn't speak again. She was ashamed of her outburst. Her hands clutched her little evening bag tightly as the carriage jostled along behind the horses. The night was very cool, and she was sorry she hadn't a proper coat. The fur wrap was proving to be far more ornamental than utilitarian. Why did Matt want to go to the shore of the lake at this hour? Did he want to walk on the strip of sandy beach there?

Matt didn't enlighten her, even when they

reached their destination. He left his top hat and cane on the seat and helped her down from the carriage. He instructed the driver to wait, and taking her arm, he escorted her along the sidewalk and down onto the sand.

"It's too chilly to go strolling out here," she said through her teeth.

"Are you cold?" He stopped and turned to her. There was a full moon, and it lit his face enough for her to see its grave expression. She noted, too, that they were well out of view of the road and the carriage.

"My arms... are bare," she said.

"Your arms and your breasts," he said curtly. "I saw the way that leering jackass gaped at you. You said that a button left that mark on your breasts, but I don't believe it. You let him touch you, didn't you?"

She gasped, outraged. "As if I would let any man—!"

"You let me," he reminded her with raging anger. "Or have you already forgotten?"

In one smooth motion, he slid the mink stole away from her shoulders. She barely caught it before it hit the ground.

The next movement he made was shocking. While she was catching her breath, he bent his head and his hard mouth found her breast where the red mark lingered.

She gasped, gripped his arms, stiffened. But his lips were narcotic in the pleasure they gave. His mouth opened, and his tongue teased the flesh he had just kissed.

Quite suddenly he pulled back. His beautiful, strong hands played along the décolletage of her gown until, abruptly, he jerked the fabric, baring her breasts.

In the chill night air, he looked at the hard red nipples for a long moment before his head bent again. He took one nipple delicately between his strong white teeth and nibbled it.

She was frightened not only by his anger and the feel of his teeth but by the sensations they caused deep inside her body. She shivered.

His big, lean hand cupped her gently, and he lifted his head so that he could see her eyes. "Did I hurt you?" he asked huskily.

She wanted to say yes, she wanted to pull away and run. She wanted to lie down and draw his mouth over...

"You... bit me," she accused, shaking.

His hand softened on her body and lingered to caress her gently while he watched her shocked face. His fingers teased around the hard nipple, and he watched her shiver, knowing that it wasn't from the cold.

"Kilgallen was right," he said quietly. "You're grass green."

"Greener, even..." she whispered, realizing all of a sudden that he was as hungry as she was. Her body arched up to him. She looked at him with breathless anticipation. She never had the will to resist him. Not that she wanted to. All evening she'd thought of nothing except the hope of having him kiss her...

Her green eyes glittered with the same riotous desire he was feeling. "Please...!"

she whispered, lifting her arms around his neck. "Matt... please... do it... again!"

His heart jumped. His hand cupped her warmly, moving under her firm breast as he touched his hard lips gently to her own. He was incapable of listening to his own small voice of reason. He was touching Tess and she was letting him, wanting him. It was just as it had been on the front porch so many long days ago, when they'd enjoyed each other in the darkness. Except that he could see her body in the faint moonlight. She was exquisite. She was everything he'd dreamed of...

He nibbled at her mouth and then let his lips slide down past her collarbone. His mouth slid over the hard nipple, worrying it with his tongue until he heard her faint gasp. Then his mouth opened and moved completely over her, taking her almost completely inside the warm darkness while his tongue caressed the nipple until she arched up to him and shivered.

His tongue rolled hungrily against the underside of the nipple in a caress that made her cry out.

The sound excited him even more. His free hand slid down her back to her hips and gathered them completely against him, slowly rubbing her body into his until she could feel the hardness of him in a shocking contact.

Flustered, she pushed at his chest.

His head lifted. He saw the faint panic on her face. His hand still rested against her bare skin, and as he looked into her eyes, his hand contracted. He leaned against the seawall, his legs splayed, and he drew her between them, both hands at the top of her thighs, pushing her against the hardness of him.

She tried to protest, but he was relentless.

She shivered. Her eyes were wide, shocked, fascinated, embarrassed, and through it all, hungry. She couldn't stop looking at him as he moved her slowly against his hips.

"You're innocent," he said quietly. "But you're not ignorant about aroused men. When I was wounded, early one morning when you thought I was asleep, you lifted the sheet and looked at me."

Her face went scarlet.

"You didn't think I knew, did you?" he asked softly. "It was too poignant a thing to have openly between us. You were so young, Tess. But I enjoyed your eyes. Too much," he added with a conspiratorial smile. "And you saw how much. I heard you gasp. After a minute, you dropped the sheet and ran."

"I never thought you'd know," she said, embarrassed.

"I knew," he said solemnly. "That was when I started listening to your father about coming back east. You were only fourteen, but you had the body of a woman even then, and I wanted it."

Her lips parted. "You never gave the least indication..."

"I didn't dare," he said harshly. "You were so young, and it shamed me to feel that way about you. I gave you the only protection I could, and then I got on a train to Chicago."

It sounded odd, that phrasing about protection. She tried to focus on what he'd said, but his hands became more insistent, and he lifted her even closer to his aroused body.

"Feel that," he whispered through his teeth, watching her flush. "It's the most painful arousal I've ever had in my life, and you're a virgin!"

"Only because... you won't risk making love to me completely," she said unsteadily. "But you knew that already, didn't you?"

"Of course I knew," he said huskily. "I've always known. But you know, too, that there's no future in it."

"Why?" she moaned.

"Because there are too many differences between us in a white world. I have nothing to offer you," he said grimly. His eyes fell to her bare breasts. He touched them, hotly aware of her pleasure in his touch, her abandon. "Nothing," he whispered, moving so that she was against the hard, cold wall. "Except this..."

His lean hand moved down. He found the hem of her silky gown, and his fingers smoothed up the stocking to the fastening of her garter belt, to the soft muslin of her drawers.

She made a tiny sound of shock and caught involuntarily at his wrist, but even as she made the token gesture, he groaned deep in his throat and bent to take her hard nipple into his mouth again.

While he caressed it, her gloved hands clenched beside her head against the seawall, shivering as she felt his bare fingers slide into the hem of the muslin undergarment.

She was aware of the moistness of her own body, and faintly embarrassed that he should feel it. His hand shifted just a fraction, and she felt a spasm of pleasure so intense that she cried out.

His mouth lifted and he looked into her eyes as he touched her, watching her fight for breath, feeling her tremble.

"You didn't know at all, did you?" he whispered, his eyes narrow and adult and very intent. "And even this is hardly a drop in the ocean of what I can give you."

She couldn't answer him. She was being drawn and quartered, stretched into a sweet, painful tension that made her body move in ways to encourage and incite his touch into even more pleasurable motions. Mouth open, she gasped rhythmically as he touched her. She saw his face go hard as she suddenly went rigid all over and sobbed, arching toward him, crying as she felt a pleasure so intense that it throbbed like a hot open wound.

She shuddered and then leaned against him. Her heart was racing like a mad thing; her hands were clutching at his arms for support.

She heard his own breathing, ragged and unsteady, as his mouth pressed hotly into her throat and he drew her hand down to his flat belly, and lower, over the fabric. She felt him as she'd never felt a man in her life.

She jerked at the intimacy, but his hand moved again, and she gasped as she felt her own pleasure return as forcibly as before.

"Help me," he whispered urgently, positioning her fingers and moving them slowly against him. "No, don't try to pull back!" he groaned. "I must, Tess, I can't bear the pain!"

He pushed her hand against the heat and swollen rigidity of him. His cheek slid against hers. He trembled as he whispered to her, shocking, exciting things. And while she let him guide her, he was touching her with the same lazy rhythm, until he groaned harshly into her mouth and his own body went into the same rigor of ecstasy that he'd given her. Even as he shuddered with the pleasure, he groaned and his hand intruded again, deeper this time.

She cried out because it began to hurt.

He lifted his head and looked into her eyes. His own were glazed with pleasure, with desire. "Don't look away," he said in a stranger's harsh tone, and he nudged her legs farther apart with his knee. His hand moved again, and she felt a sharp pain, a burning.

"Matt... what are you doing?" she whispered.

"Don't you know?" He pressed against her and, holding her shocked gaze, he pushed, hard.

Her mouth opened. It was like being burned there. She stiffened and tears stung her eyes.

Then, slowly, the pain began to ease. He held her there, searching her eyes.

All at once she realized what he'd done, what she'd let him do. Her face went scarlet. She couldn't speak, couldn't breathe, couldn't even think.

"It wasn't so very bad, was it?" he whispered. His voice was tender, strained. He searched her eyes. "Do you understand what I've done?"

She couldn't manage words. She nodded.

His eyes fell to her swollen mouth and farther down, to her hard-tipped breasts. His hand moved gently and she flinched. He withdrew it slowly from under her gown, and she felt a new moisture there.

He reached for his handkerchief and curled it around his fingers before he eased the skirt up once more, still watching her face, and she felt the soft fabric against her skin. She flinched again.

"I'm sorry," he whispered at her lips. "I know it must be painful."

She swallowed. "I'm not a virgin anymore, am I?"

"Yes, you are, in the sense that I didn't penetrate you," he said quietly. "All the same, I had your virginity."

She felt him move again, and her skirt fell around her ankles once more.

"There," he said, his voice vaguely tender. "You may be uncomfortable, but you won't stain that lovely gown."

He held her afterward, without a word, until the trembling stopped. His hand smoothed over her bare back, and he murmured words she couldn't quite understand into her ear.

She stared across his chest at the dark lake, shocked and dismayed at what they'd just done. She'd never experienced anything so outrageous, even if she'd heard women talk of these experiences. Having no way to prevent children, many women indulged in such love play with men to whom they were pledged. But Tess had never dreamed of doing such a thing, until tonight, with the one man she loved most in all the world. She moved a little closer to him, shivering with pleasure.

Matt lifted his head and looked down at her. Gently he pulled her gown back up, covering her cold breasts. He found her wrap, shook the sand from it, and draped it gently around her shoulders.

"We... should go," she said in a strained tone.

"Do you want me to apologize?" he asked quietly.

She made a gesture with her head and turned back toward the carriage, so shattered that she couldn't even pretend to be calm and collected.

On the way back down the beach she paused and turned to look at him. He was as immaculate as ever, and just as remote. Nothing showed in those black eyes.

"What are you looking for in my face?" he asked.

"Regret. Guilt. Shame."

He smiled faintly. "You won't find them. I regret nothing."

"Did it mean... anything," she asked, "or was it an inconvenient itch that you used me to scratch?"

"Why, Tess, you shock me."

"I couldn't possibly shock you. Don't tease me now, Matt." Her eyes searched his. "Tell me."

"All right. Yes, it meant something," he

replied. "I've wanted you for as long as you've wanted me. But I haven't changed the way I feel about half-breed children."

She couldn't hide her dismay. She began to walk again, holding Mrs. Mulhaney's wrap closer around her cold body. "Then you want a Sioux wife, I gather?" she asked impatiently.

"I can't marry," he said, unsettled as he remembered a secret that he couldn't share with her.

"Will you be happy, living alone forever?"

"As happy as you will be," he replied. "You've never wanted to marry, have you?"

"What good would it do to wish for the moon?" she asked sadly.

"You're exquisite, Tess," he said abruptly. "All that fire and passion—waiting..."

She lifted her eyes to his stony face. "You wanted to share it tonight, didn't you?"

"Yes," he replied honestly. "I'll always want it. But what we did tonight is all we could ever do."

Her heart leapt into her throat. She stopped and faced him. "That might be enough, for both of us."

His breath caught. He stared at her, the whip of temptation on his back, until he wanted to scream.

"Yes," she whispered, reading his face in that instant, "you want it, too."

"Desire is a powerful force," he began.

She moved a step closer. "I want to lie naked in your arms, in my bed," she whispered. "I want to see you again, as you were that morning just after you were wounded. When I look at you now, I know you want me. I can see it."

His face tautened. "Tess..."

"We could lie in the light. We could... love, as we just did, with no risk of a child."

"If I had you naked in my arms, do you think I could be satisfied with what we did back there?" he asked incredulously. "God in heaven, I'd be inside you before I had your clothes off!"

Her lips parted. "Inside... me." The imagery made her shiver.

"Deep and hard and hot inside you," he ground out. "I'd lay you out on my bed and drive into you until—" He stopped, his head spinning. He could almost feel the heat of that soft, moist sheath around him, enveloping him, welcoming him. He closed his eyes and shuddered. "We have to go. Right now!"

He took her arm in a grip that hurt and half dragged her back toward the carriage.

She wondered if her feet were even touching the ground. She was on fire for him. Why oh why wouldn't he admit that they had so much more together than simple desire? They were already part of each other, but he was willing to throw it all away because she wasn't Sioux and he wasn't white.

CHAPTER TWELVE

She didn't try to talk to him. He'd become completely unapproachable. There was bridled fury even in the way he walked in the cold, rising mist back to the carriage. By the time they reached it, a light rain was falling.

The driver jumped down to open the carriage door for them. "Too much wind and cold to walk far, sir." He chuckled. "But it's fair warm in the carriage."

Matt gave him directions to the boardinghouse.

"Tuck yourselves in cozy-like," the driver said, "and I'll take you on to where you want to go."

"I think we're both more than ready to go home," Matt said as he climbed in beside Tess and the driver closed the door.

Tess drew inside herself, too sick with shame to look at Matt. She huddled by the window, staring out, Mrs. Mulhaney's wrap pulled tight over her bodice. There were very red marks there now, she knew, and not from buttons but from Matt's hungry mouth.

Matt fingered the cane he'd left in the carriage along with his top hat. He didn't know how to excuse what he'd done. He hadn't meant it to go so far. He'd simply lost his head. Having her so close, and so hungry for his caresses, had pushed him right over the edge.

The problem was, now that he'd had such an intimate taste of her, he wanted more. Much more. Which was out of the question. Playing at lovemaking was one thing. Raw physicality and the risk of a half-breed child was quite another. He didn't dare make love to her completely.

"Yes, I do," she said when they were almost home.

He scowled and glanced at her drawn face. "You do what?" he asked.

Her head turned. Her eyes glared into his. "Want you to apologize."

His head inclined. "Very well. I'm sorry."

"So am I." She looked out the window again.

"You realize, I think, that it was the only way we could indulge in any sort of intimacy at all."

She closed her eyes. "I never dreamed that people did things like that together."

"It becomes a necessity in our restrictive society, if pregnancy is to be avoided," he said shortly.

She turned and looked at him squarely, her eyes wide and curious. "Have you never taken the risk with a woman?"

"The women of my acquaintance have been sophisticated and wise in the ways of intimacy," he said, avoiding a direct answer. "Such women know how to avoid the risk of a child."

She hated hearing that, having him admit that he'd known other women. It shouldn't have come as a surprise, considering his expertise with her. But jealousy made her furious. "What a pity that such knowledge is denied to women who have more than twelve children at home and husbands too inconsiderate to leave them in peace!"

His dark eyes narrowed. "Perhaps their

need of each other is such that abstinence is not possible."

She averted her gaze, flushing. She fiddled with her small evening bag, flooded with memories of how urgent and mad it had been between them just moments ago. Her eyes closed. She could easily imagine being in Matt's arms, naked in bed, having him touch her entire body with his fingers... with his mouth...

She swallowed, then took a deep breath. "Are we ever going to get home?" she asked impatiently when she saw how distant their street still was.

He crossed one long leg over the other and studied her rigid posture. He, too, was remembering how it had been. "It is ungentlemanly to mention it," he said brusquely, "but I would have stopped, had you asked me to."

She looked down into her lap, heated embarrassment in her face. "I didn't want you to stop," she admitted curtly. "I was curious."

"So was I," he confessed. "All these long weeks, with little tastes of you that haunt me in the small hours of the night. I lost my head."

"As I lost mine." She lifted her face to his, fighting for a sophistication she wished she had. "Is it like that, Matt?" she asked, her voice lowered. "In bed, I mean? Does it feel like that?"

"Yes," he replied. His eyes searched hers in the semidarkness. At least, he thought privately, I think it does.

"Would it hurt now, after what you did?"

His dark eyes searched hers. "I don't imagine so," he said gently.

"I would like to know how it feels to make love completely with you," she said without shame. She met his shocked eyes. "I have heard of ways to prevent babies," she confessed. "Some are outlandish, but they seem effective."

He watched her without speaking.

"But I suppose nothing is without some risk, even so." She sighed and searched his face with growing hunger. "I must be a bad woman," she said in a choked tone, "because I long to lie naked with you."

His jaw tautened. "Tess!"

"Are you shocked? So am I," she said wearily. "It makes me ache to remember the heat and pleasure of touching you and being touched so intimately."

His dark eyes slid over her body. "It should never have happened."

"Why not?" she asked with genuine curiosity. "I have no betrothed, nor do you. We are adults, and we did nothing that was truly immoral."

One dark eyebrow rose. "Would you care to describe what we did for Mrs. Mulhaney and have her opinion of its morality?"

She shifted on the seat and clutched her small bag tightly. "It didn't feel immoral," she clarified.

He leaned back against the seat. "No," he agreed finally. "It didn't. It was almost reverent."

She glanced at him hungrily. "We were... like lovers."

"We *are* lovers," he corrected.

Her eyes were sad and far away. "And nothing more."

His hand slid across the seat to claim her gloved one. "Tess, you can't imagine how it would change your life if there were a child."

She looked down at his hand. "And if there were some way to prevent a child? If I could find some solution?"

"That is a pipe dream," he said shortly. "Unrealistic and dangerous."

"There is a group of women, a secretive group for the most part, which advocates birth control," she whispered. "Perhaps they have answers."

His face hardened. "Any madam in a whorehouse has such answers," he told her flatly.

She jerked her hand back and looked at him in utter shock.

He turned away. "For God's sake, let it lie. I told you that I will not take the risk. And to indulge in any more such experiments as we shared tonight is playing with dynamite. I won't indulge this obsession a second time."

She could have hit him. A child between them would have been wonderful. Marriage would have been wonderful. But while he might enjoy her body, he wanted no more from her. Least of all did he want her love or a shared future. She'd hoped against hope that things would change when she came to Chicago and they met on a more equal basis. What a fool she'd been even to have such a dream.

She stared out the window. "If that's the way you want it to be, Matt," she said.

"Yes," he said shortly. "That's how it has to be."

Nothing more was said. They went to their respective rooms, and Tess bathed her rawness away with a sense of desolation. She'd learned the lesson of love all too vividly tonight, and she had only a broken heart to show for it.

Tess went downstairs after a restless night, having relived over and over again the ball and what had happened afterward. Her body still throbbed with its first experience of passion and ecstasy. And even through the slight discomfort, it was hungrier than ever for Matt.

But if she were starving for him, there was not the slightest indication that he felt anything similar. At the breakfast table, they pretended successfully to be nothing more than cousins while Mrs. Mulhaney prattled on about how wonderful the ball must have been and how lovely Tess had looked.

It was a little surprising that as she left the boardinghouse on her way to the hospital, Matt fell into step beside her and suggested they walk. She agreed. They dismissed Mick, who smiled and winked before driving off at a clip.

"Aren't you going out of your way?" she asked.

"Not at all. I have business at a spot near the hospital." He glanced down at her with curiosity. "Are you all right?"

She lifted her head proudly. "Of course."

"I didn't... damage you too much?"

She stopped in the middle of the sidewalk and looked up at him belligerently. "You tore me," she said bluntly. "It is a natural part of becoming a woman and hardly merits such concern, especially from a man who only wanted it in such a way!"

"Tess!"

"I feel cheap, if you must know," she told him gruffly. "You feel nothing for me except lust. Had I understood that from the beginning, I should never have come to Chicago in the first place!"

He leaned heavily on his cane, aware of a man coming down the sidewalk toward them. "You don't understand why I feel the way I do."

"I know only that your stubborn refusal to lay aside your ghosts is destroying my life along with your own!"

"Ghosts, indeed!" he shot back.

"Yes, ghosts! You have no—" She paused when the man coming down the sidewalk suddenly stopped, frowned, and leaned forward to peer at Matt's rigid features.

The man was wearing a very smart suit and carrying a silver-topped cane similar to Matt's. After a moment he began to chuckle.

"Well, I'm damned! An Injun, right here in town! No wonder us poor soldiers couldn't find any to shoot out there on the plains! You all came running to the cities, like those big chiefs that travel around with Buffalo Bill Cody's Wild West Show! You in show business, boy?" He leaned on the cane, apparently discounting the stiffening of Matt's spine and the sudden glitter of his eyes. "What tribe you from?"

Matt's black eyes narrowed and glittered. His hand fell away from Tess's. "My private life is none of your concern," Matt said with exquisite diction.

The man's eyebrows went up. "Sassy, ain't you, for a redskin?"

"Let us pass," Matt returned.

The man gave Tess a thorough going-over. "Ain't you got no pride, keeping company with an Injun?" he demanded, almost spitting out the words. "No decent woman consorts with Injuns. What you planning to be, girlie, his squaw?" He laughed out loud at his own sick joke.

Tess didn't even think. She drew back and slugged him, right in the belly, right there on the sidewalk. It was a toss-up as to who was more shocked, the man or Matt.

It hurt her knuckles and she favored them, glaring at the man, who was holding his stomach and gaping at her.

"You just let that be a lesson to you!" she told him angrily. "No man talks to me in such a manner and gets away with it. What a pity you weren't in my general vicinity twelve years ago. I would have put an arrow right into your arrogant stomach instead of soiling my hands with you!"

The man was so flustered that he seemed to be beggared for a single word. He simply looked at her, babbling.

She told him then, in stoic Sioux, that he was a lowly snake with a little soul.

"What?" The man gasped to hear that language coming from her lips. "You speak... Sioux?"

"Sioux and English," she informed him, eyes blazing. "And a low dog of a murderous bluecoat soldier has less humanity than the lowliest dog in a Sioux camp!"

She turned, grasping Matt's sleeve, her face livid with fury. "Shall we go, Matt?" she asked in a choked tone. She gave the little man one last look. "Pig!" she spat.

Matt was torn between howling amusement and outraged pride. He glanced back at the man, who was gaping after them. "Well, you've ruined his morning."

"I wish I had a knife; I'd skin him like a buck deer, the vicious loudmouthed little cretin!" she said, her voice carrying down the sidewalk. The man seemed to jerk erect. He turned and all but ran from them.

"Calm down," Matt murmured. "You're shouting."

"I can't abide a stupid man," she bit off. She glared up at Matt. "There are so many of them loose in this city, too!"

Still amused and vaguely angry, he stopped in the middle of the sidewalk and looked down into her flushed face. Her aggressive behavior on his behalf would have been funny indeed, except that he disliked the feeling of impotence that came from having her defend him. "The insult was mine," he said. "The reply to it should have been mine as well."

She made a gesture with her hand. "Very

well. I'll let you hit the next man who insults you. Never let it be said that I stood in the way of men's rights."

He couldn't fight down the amusement a minute longer. He threw back his head and burst out laughing. "Good God Almighty! What am I going to do with you?"

She put her hands on her hips and smiled faintly. "Why don't you marry me?"

He looked odd. Guilty. Uncomfortable. The expression crossed his face too quickly for her to identify it. He looked away abruptly without speaking.

"Yes, I know, you'd never marry a white woman," she said in a world-weary tone. "Well, I've always known that I'd be a spinster. I suppose I'll devote the rest of my life to the women's movement and live on last night."

He shifted restlessly. "It was a moment's madness."

"It was delicious," she said in a husky, throaty tone. "I dreamed about it all night."

He wasn't going to admit that he had, too. He lifted his chin and kept walking. He didn't say another word about that, or about their encounter with a man who was obviously an ex-soldier. The experience had him churning violently inside, all his doubts congealed into a mass of apprehension and anguish.

"I don't imagine that was the first time you've had a cashiered soldier show up in town and notice your ancestry," she commented abruptly as they neared the hospital.

"No," he said flatly. "It happens from time to time."

"What do you usually do about it?"

"I ignore it," he said matter-of-factly.

"And, of course, they get the look."

He scowled. "I beg your pardon?"

"The look," she repeated. "That even, black scowl that makes people feel like insects on the sticking edge of a hat pin. I've seen you back men down with it before."

He didn't reply. He kept walking. "Even so," she continued, "most people aren't ignorant enough or uncivilized enough to be so blatantly insulting to a total stranger. Don't let it get under your skin like this."

"Why not?" he asked solemnly, stopping to face her. "Because I'm a black sheep from the czar's court or a Spanish nobleman in disguise?" He looked around them with eyes that didn't really see. "I'm a full-blooded Sioux Indian," he said, and his voice was full of harsh fury. "Nothing will change that. Nothing!"

"Why should you want to change it?" she asked.

He glared at her. "Suppose I tell you what would happen if I announced my background to all and sundry? Do you want to know? I should be an outcast even among my own men! I could conceivably lose everything I have because I'm not entitled to own property or even vote, since I don't have the rights of citizenship, which can be extended even to immigrants who don't speak proper English! Anyone who was ever in the army and fought on the plains is still my deadly enemy. There's no refuge for a 'redskin' anywhere in the United States!"

"Your skin isn't red," she reminded him. "It's a very nice bronzed color."

"Tess!"

"Sorry." She put her hands behind her and looked up at him with soft, loving eyes. "If you married me, we could put everything in my name. Your pride wouldn't like that, but it would put you outside any potential legal conflicts."

He didn't smile. He looked at that moment as if he never had smiled in his entire life.

"You're taking this too hard," she said. "The problem is that you haven't ever learned to live with your past as well as your present. You've spent twelve years denying it. But the time has come when you can't do it anymore."

His eyes narrowed on a wave of pain as he looked down at her blond fairness. "We belong to separate races. I'm Mongoloid. You're Caucasian."

"I know that. So?"

"Are you going to try to tell me that it doesn't bother you?"

She looked into his eyes with her heart in her own. "I've known you half my life," she said simply. "It never occurred to me that we were different. Well," she said with a grin, "except in the obvious ways."

Once he would have smiled at the insinuation. Now, thanks to that boor of an ex-soldier, he was overly sensitive.

"Don't," she said then, moving closer to him. "Don't let him do this to you. Matt, if you'd just stop fighting what you feel for me!"

He held up an imperious hand as he looked into her eyes. His face didn't soften one bit. "And if we had a child together? Where would he belong?"

"With us, of course," she said angrily.

He sighed roughly and ran a hand around the back of his neck. His fingers came into contact with the long pigtail and froze there, as he remembered all too well what his real background was. The pigtail was a constant reminder. He'd never thought of cutting his hair. That inconsistency bothered him sometimes. He didn't want to be Sioux. Did he?

He looked at Tess with painful longing. He'd pushed his feelings for her to the back of his mind until her attractions had pulled him right over the edge of the world.

Even if he couldn't admit it aloud, he belonged to Tess. He always had. He always would. He'd never wanted to think about belonging in any way to anyone else.

But deeper than his desire for her was his desire for her ultimate happiness. And being married to an Indian wasn't going to be to her benefit.

It didn't occur to him that he was blowing everything out of proportion, or that this wasn't the first time an ex-army soldier had recognized him as a native American. But it was the first time that it had mattered. The insults might not affect him, but inevitably they were going to affect Tess and any children they might have together.

He'd just solved a case for a client who was the product of a Negro father and a white mother. The man had fought valiantly for an inheritance that had ended in the death of a parent and the risk of prison for the son. Matt had proven him innocent of any wrongdoing, but he hadn't been able to help him secure any of the inheritance to which he was entitled.

The man had been bitter, and vocal about it. His bitterness had contributed to Matt's own doubts about any future with Tess. A half-breed child belonged nowhere in this world. The mulatto had cursed his mother *and* his father for making him an outcast, a man with no race, no roots, no future. It was a bitter memory that he'd shared with Matt, and day by day it tortured Matt more.

Tess could see the thoughts plaguing him. She knew that they were just phantoms, but he'd been running from his past for years. He was going to have to stop and turn around and look into his darkness. And she couldn't do it for him. The only thing she could do was to support him and encourage him and not push him too hard. Because as she looked at him, it occurred to her that his feelings for her were very strong indeed. If she was patient and didn't pester him about them...

"What about Nan?" she asked suddenly.

He looked at her with a scowl, as if the question had knocked him sideways. It had. He hadn't been thinking about the present or the murder case he was supposed to be working on.

"Remember Nan?" she persisted. "My friend? The one who's in jail awaiting trial for a murder she didn't commit?"

He put his hands in his slacks pockets and began to force himself to breath normally. "Yes," he said after a minute. "I'm sorry, but I had forgotten."

"We have to find the murderer," she said.

"I have to..."

She held up a hand. "Excuse me, but this is my case, too," she pointed out. "I promised to help, and I'm going to."

He wanted to argue. But it was useless. Her face told him that.

"I'm glad you're willing to see reason," she replied with a grin. "I have to go to work, but when I'm off duty, I want to see a few people—"

"You go near that apartment house by yourself, and I'll have Greene pull you in for unlawful trespass!"

She gaped at him. "You wouldn't dare!"

"Think not? Try me."

She made an angry gesture, but he didn't even seem to notice. She folded her arms across her chest. "I can talk to Nan's sister. Even Greene wouldn't deny me that!"

"All right," he said. "But only to her." He frowned again. "Why her?"

"Why not? She may know something that we don't about Nan's husband. It's certainly worth asking about."

"I suppose so."

They started walking again. A few snowflakes feathered down on them. Tess caught one on her glove and smiled. "I never really get tired of snow. But I remember one or two winters when I was hoping to see the last of it forever."

"So do I." He didn't smile. He was remembering the dead bodies lying frozen on the ground at Wounded Knee. He remembered the soldiers flinging them into a common grave with their arms and legs in grotesque positions, like the works of a sculptor gone mad.

Tess saw those memories in his face. She didn't say anything. In his present frame of mind, the less said, the better. He had to resolve his inward turmoil by himself. As much as she wanted to, she couldn't do it for him.

They stopped just outside the hospital. She turned to him, her eyes soft and green under the brim of her hat. "I suppose you have a lot of work to do today, so I won't expect to see you again."

His eyes narrowed. "Why?"

She shrugged. "I don't want to presume on your time."

That seemingly innocent statement made him wary, and curious. He peered at her face under the wide brim of her hat.

"What are you up to?"

"I'm going to a meeting tonight," she said. "I won't be at home. And since it will be bedtime before I get back, and you're usually working late these days, I won't see you again today. That's all I meant."

He looked worried. "You think I'm overreacting about what happened back there," he said, jerking his head in the direction from which they'd come. "You don't understand how it is. You don't come from the same background, even if you do know more about it than most whites."

The way he said that made her uncomfortable, as if he were trying to separate them even further.

"Is that what I've become to you now?" she asked softly. "Just another white woman?"

His jaw tautened. "I didn't say that."

Her eyes ranged over his face and met his gaze. "I'm not going to push my way into your life anymore," she told him. "If you want me to move to another boardinghouse, just say so. Chicago is a very big city. We need never see each other if that's what you really want."

He was shocked. His intake of breath was audible. "I said no such thing."

"Your eyes are saying it," she said. "You're standing there so calm and unperturbed, and inside you're seething with desire to get me into your bed, even if you won't admit it."

He actually flushed. He looked around them stealthily. "Don't talk that way in public!"

"Why? Does it embarrass you to be human?" She put a hand on her hip. "I know you don't want to remember what we did, but I'm not ashamed that we made love. If you are, that's your own problem."

"I didn't say I was ashamed!" The flush grew deeper. Now it was joined by bad temper glittering in his black eyes. "You damned nuisance!"

Her eyebrows flew up. "Look who's angry! It's a man's world, isn't it? Women don't walk away; they just lie down and get walked on!"

"I didn't walk on you!"

"You did so. You walked all over me. You said that you don't want a white wife or a half-white child, or me in your life. Wonderful. Go your own way, then, Mr. Big Shot Detective." She waved a hand expressively. "I'll go to work and nurse someone who appreciates my skills."

"Someone like that dandy at the ball who couldn't keep his hands off you?" he demanded furiously.

"Why not?" she shot back. "He doesn't care about the color of my skin!"

He started to speak, but she turned on her heel and marched into the hospital. She didn't even look back.

He turned in the direction of his office, so infuriated that he stepped out in front of a carriage and almost became part of the road.

He cursed himself—not for being dazed... and daft but for all he had said to Tess. He never should have spoken a word. He should have knocked the ex-soldier to the ground himself and beaten the hell out of him. It wouldn't have changed the way things were, but it would have made him feel better.

Then he remembered what Tess had done, and he couldn't repress a chuckle. She was a nuisance, that was true, but she had the savage heart of a warrior, despite her sex, and nobody would ever walk on her regardless of what she said.

He scowled at the sky, wondering if a blizzard was on the way. The sky was overcast, the clouds were thick and low, and the snow was increasing rapidly. He wasn't enthusiastic about being snowed in with Tess at the boardinghouse. Not that he wanted her to move.

He went on to his office and assigned his agents to the various cases that needed attention. Then he went to Nan's apartment house and set about talking to the neighbors whom Tess hadn't approached.

By the end of the day, Matt knew only a little more than Tess had learned. But it was worthwhile information. The only visitors Dennis Collier ever had were apparently well-to-do men. One in particular stuck in a neighbor's mind because he wore a huge diamond ring on his little finger. He was a good-looking man, the woman also recalled, with dark hair and a mustache, and he had a polite manner.

Matt didn't have to be told that the man was Diamond Jim Kilgallen.

When he finished talking to the neighbors, he stopped by the jail and had a word with Greene. The jailer had been replaced by a younger man. He allowed Greene and Matt into the cell with a minimum of fuss, and he was very polite to Nan Collier.

Nan was pleased to see them, but still a little downcast and very worried.

"The other jailer was gone this morning," she said, shaking her head. "I don't know why. Neither does anyone else, from what I hear." She smiled nervously. "I'm glad. He wasn't nice to be around, and he made some very unpleasant advances."

Matt didn't let on that he knew about the change or who had managed it.

"You look worn, lass," Greene said. "Can I have them bring you anything?"

"I just want to go home," Nan said with a plaintive expression. "I'm so sick. How can they believe I would kill a man, even one who beat me?"

"Plenty of women do," Matt replied. "I don't think you killed your husband, but I'm not the judge or the jury. And despite all the looking around, I can't find anyone else with a good enough motive. I can't even find a girlfriend."

"Davis!" Greene exclaimed, outraged.

"Well, I couldn't," Matt said, unperturbed. "That's a shame, because another woman would have been an obvious suspect."

"No, he didn't like women much, even me," Nan said flatly. "He was too busy pushing laudanum and alcohol into his mouth."

"Where did he get all of his narcotics?" Matt asked.

She sighed. "I don't know. He always seemed to have plenty of money, and plenty of 'medicine.' He never said where it came from."

"You might ask that moneyed criminal he ran with," Greene said angrily. "That Diamond Jim fella."

"Kilgallen doesn't use stimulants of the sort Collier did," Matt said, just in time to keep a harsh retort off Nan's lips. "He has no part of them."

"You know that for a fact, do you?" Greene asked sarcastically.

"In fact, I do," Matt replied. "I have contacts of my own in the underworld, and I don't mind using them."

Green shrugged. "Well, it was a long shot, I guess, that Kilgallen might have had him put down. I'm just worried about my wife, you know, as much as for Nan here. She's taken this whole thing hard. I haven't had two words out of her since Nan was arrested. She doesn't talk. She just sits and stares and cries."

"She thinks they'll hang me, doesn't she?" Nan asked worriedly. She wrung her hands. "Maybe they will, too. Maybe I'll die!"

"You won't die," Matt said firmly. "Not if Greene and I have to break you out of here ourselves. We know you're innocent."

That brought the first smile to Nan's face in days. "You're a kind man, Mr. Davis."

"My cousin is fond of you," he said noncommittally.

"She's such a wonderful friend," Nan said gently. "Anyone else would have turned away from me, knowing what she does. But she's loyal to a fault. It's a wonder to me she's not married. I suppose men are blind."

Matt looked away. "Perhaps they are. Blind as bats."

Chapter Thirteen

Nan's sister was white-faced and nervous as she admitted Tess to her small home. She'd been baking, Tess surmised, since she had traces of flour on her hands and apron.

"I had to do something to keep from going

crazy, so I've been making a cake," she told Tess. "Please sit down. I know what you and Mr. Davis have tried to do for Nan. I'm very grateful to you."

Tess took the small wing chair indicated and looked at the older woman with open curiosity. "You're older than Nan."

"Fifteen years," came the reply. "There were six of us, but four died in childhood. Nan and I are the only ones of our family left alive." Her eyes were sad as she added, "I lost one of my own children to a chest cold that went into pneumonia. Now I go to extremes to protect the two I have left." She sighed. "At least, I did..."

The way her voice trailed away was faintly disturbing.

She looked up again, shifting in the chair. "What can I do for you, Miss Davis?"

"Meredith," Tess corrected. "Matt and I are related through our mothers," she lied.

"Oh, I see. Well, Miss Meredith, then. Is there something you need from me?"

"Yes," Tess replied. "I need a motive for someone to have killed Dennis Collier."

The other woman's face hardened. "He was a wife beater," she said. "A bully who had no feeling for any needs other than his own. He hit my sister, again and again and again." Her eyes closed and she shivered. "She was a kind, sweet girl who never hurt a fly. And he could treat her... like that!"

"Yes, I know," Tess replied gently. "Nan isn't the sort to hurt people."

Blue eyes met her own green ones. "I'm glad

he died," Mrs. Greene said fervently. "I hope he suffered before he died! Maybe one of his fancy women killed him, and good luck to her!"

Tess jumped on that. "He did have other women, then?"

Mrs. Greene lifted her face. She seemed to be struggling for composure. She glanced at Tess and averted her eyes. "Certainly he did. Nan didn't know, but I knew. I have a friend who lived near Nan's apartment house. She told me that women came and went all the time when Nan was away at church and visiting me."

"Do you know the names of any of the women?" Tess pressed, her eyes glittering with excitement that she might have found a suspect after all. "Did your friend know who they were?"

Mrs. Greene shrugged. "No, she didn't know them. They were common women." She leaned forward. "Women from brothels!" she whispered.

Tess knew about that sort of woman because many of them ended up dying in the hospital from a host of social diseases. Her mind whirled with tragic stories. Strange, though, that a woman from a brothel would visit a man in his apartment during his wife's absence. That wasn't the usual thing at all. Most of the men who frequented brothels were respectable family men who would have done anything to keep knowledge of their indiscretions from their families. It was part of the hated double standard that the women in her group so detested.

"Why didn't he go to the brothel?" Tess

asked, speaking her thoughts aloud.

"Well, uh..." Mrs. Greene collected herself and seemed to be thinking very hard. "I suppose he wanted to shame Nan even more than he already had, what with his criminal friends being there all the time."

It didn't make sense. She almost said so. But there was something in Mrs. Greene's face that made her hold her tongue. She hesitated and then forced a smile.

"I don't suppose we'll ever know the whole truth of it," she agreed. "But the thing is, unless we can find the real killer, they may hang Nan."

Mrs. Greene's face went even paler. "I know that." Her eyes closed and she shivered. "They say that those ropes are rough against the skin," she said in a ghostly tone, touching her lace-covered neck as if she could feel the rope there. An odd gesture, an odd comment, Tess thought.

"I imagine it's very quick," she said.

"If the hangman is compassionate," Mrs. Greene said with a long, eloquent stare. "I can't let them hang my sister."

"They won't if we can find the real culprit," Tess said firmly. "You have to help me locate those women who went to see Dennis."

Mrs. Greene grimaced. "How?"

"Ask your friend to ask everyone she knows," came the reply. "And she must hurry. We have so little time."

"Isn't there anything we can do besides that?"

Tess was thinking. "I'm going to a meeting of my women's group tonight. I believe that it would show our support for Nan if we held a torchlight parade to protest her innocence and show everyone how her husband was treating her. Perhaps it would make even the court take notice!"

"It would be dangerous. Very dangerous. The last of your marches ended in a riot, Miss Meredith, and my husband told me that you were seriously injured."

"I'll be much more careful this time," Tess said, without revealing the fact that Dennis Collier himself had injured her. "Besides, it's Nan I'm concerned about, not myself."

Mrs. Greene bit her lower lip and clasped her hands together in her aproned lap. "That is a generous way to be. I wish I had your courage."

"Don't worry," Tess said gently. "It will be all right. I'm sure we can save Nan."

"I hope so. Oh, I hope so!"

After dealing with a mountain of neglected paperwork, Matt made his way back to the boardinghouse. He arrived just in time to meet a messenger at the door.

"And what's this?" he asked when the messenger, after ascertaining his identity, handed him a sealed envelope.

"A lady at the jail asked me to bring it. Gave me a quarter!"

"Here's another," he said, tossing a coin to the young man, who grinned, tipped his hat, and went away.

Matt went into the hallway, where the light was better, to read the note. He supposed it was from Nan Collier, perhaps a new lead to follow.

His surprise was visible and verbal when he read the hastily scribbled note. It read, "Have been arrested. Please come. Tess."

Mrs. Mulhaney had been walking into the hall, drying her hands on a tea towel, when she saw Matt.

"Why, Mr. Davis!" she exclaimed, as she heard him mutter a curse. "Whatever is wrong?"

"My cousin has been arrested," he said without thinking.

Mrs. Mulhaney had to sit down. By the time she got over the shock of having one of her tenants in jail, sullying the good name and reputation of her establishment, Matt was out of the house.

He waved the note under Tess's nose where she stood behind bars with a dozen other women, looking downcast and guilty.

"What the hell are you doing here?" he raged.

"Sir!" one of the matrons exclaimed angrily.

He tipped his hat. "I beg your pardon," he said politely, as his furious gaze held Tess's, "but my cousin's arrest has come as a shock."

"I don't know why," Tess said innocently. "Surely you must expect a woman of my character to end badly."

The insinuation turned his cheekbones ruddy, and he crushed the note in his big, lean hand. "Mrs. Mulhaney was almost in a faint when I left. She will surely throw us both out the door for this. She has an overworked sense of social responsibility."

"I don't care if she throws me out; I was already planning to leave. Daisy," she indicated a slightly older woman with no looks whatsoever, "has invited me to share her small house. She is a student at present. Her studies sound so interesting that I may very well enroll myself."

"Nothing of that sort matters at the moment," Matt said angrily. Too many shocks in one day were rendering his mind numb. "I'll bail you out, and then we'll go somewhere and talk."

"At this hour of the night?" Daisy asked haughtily. "Really, sir, you'll ruin your cousin's reputation."

Matt glared at her. "My cousin's reputation is none of your business, madam."

"Matt!" Tess cried.

He turned and marched out of the jail.

"Your cousin is quite dangerous-looking," Daisy said sternly. "I think the less you have to do with him, the better."

Tess stared at her. "Matt is my business." She was already regretting her impulsive agreement to share Daisy's house. It wouldn't work in a million years. Daisy obviously hated men. "And I think I won't take you up on your offer of lodgings, Daisy," she added, "although I thank you for the offer. Perhaps Matt misjudged my landlady's mood."

"I hardly think so," Ellen O'Hara said with a twinkle in her eyes. "You can stay with my sisters and me, though, Tess," she offered. "And Mr. Davis will be welcome to visit," she added with a glance at the cold-faced Daisy.

"You're very kind," Tess said.

Ellen chuckled. "Oh, you've added such excitement to my dreary life that I think I'd enjoy having you around. I know my sisters would. They're younger than me, but they're hard workers. We all work as maids for a fine family down on the lake."

"Servants," Daisy scoffed, because she was a woman of property.

"Honest work is honorable, whatever it entails," Tess told her matter-of-factly. "And I hardly think that the heart and soul of the women's movement should be the denigration of any of us by others of us. It smacks of disloyalty."

Most of the other women nearby assented loudly, and Daisy withdrew into her own thoughts.

Matt was back in minutes with the jailer.

"You have to bail Ellen out, too," she told him, indicating the plump blond girl beside her. "She and her sisters are giving me a home after Mrs. Mulhaney throws me out."

He gaped at her. "What?"

"Ellen. You have to make her bail, too."

Matt didn't say a word. He and the jailer left, and when he returned, both women were released.

"Can we see Nan before we leave?" she asked, after the other woman had thanked Matt profusely for his help.

"We might as well," Matt said angrily.

"The evening's almost over anyway."

Tess made a face at him, and she and Ellen preceded him into the area where prisoners awaiting trial were kept.

Nan was tearful and tried to hug her through the bars. "Oh, I'm so glad to see you!" she told Tess. "I'm getting more scared by the day. Have you found out anything at all? And why are you back again, Mr. Davis?"

"I've been bailing Tess out of jail," he said tersely.

"What for?" Nan asked.

"Inciting a riot," Matt said for her.

"Thank you very much!" Tess snapped at him over her shoulder.

He made her a mock bow. "You're welcome."

Nan gasped. "Inciting a riot?"

"I led a torchlight parade in support of you and gave the audience a lecture on the evils of brutality in men."

Nan laughed and then cried. "Oh, Tess, you are my friend!"

"Yes, I am, and I'm going to get you out of this somehow!" she promised. "Keep your chin up, dear. You mustn't give in to despair."

Nan touched her stomach and sighed. "I don't know if I have a prayer any more," she said. "My brother-in-law said there were no other suspects. They can't find another person in Chicago who wanted my husband dead more than I did."

"But you didn't kill him," Tess said firmly. "And we're going to prove it."

Nan managed a smile, but it wasn't a confident one. It was sad and lonely and lost.

They dropped Ellen off at the rambling Victorian house she shared with her three sisters near the railroad depot, finally accepting her invitation to have a cup of tea before venturing back to their boardinghouse.

Ellen's home was ramshackle and needed painting, and it was cold because the only heat came from open fireplaces. But it was homey, and there were no really close neighbors. The sisters made much of Ellen, Tess, and Matt, and insisted on details of the arrest and jailing. In the end they invited Tess and Matt to come again and visit. Ellen repeated her offer of lodgings. Tess thanked her and added that she might be over in the morning to take her up on it. She felt at home here already. Ellen was a kind soul, and her sisters were jolly.

"Mrs. Mulhaney won't throw you out," Matt said curtly as they rode home in yet another hired carriage.

"Yes, she will," she said. "I don't care. It might be a blessing in disguise."

He glanced at her. She made him feel even more guilty than he already did.

His face seemed to close up. He averted his eyes to the darkness outside the carriage window, broken intermittently by streetlights.

She crossed her legs under her long skirts and sighed. They were farther apart than they'd ever been.

"How do you feel about me, Matt?"

He wouldn't look at her. "As I've always felt," he said.

"And how is that?"

The carriage slowed. "This isn't the time to discuss personal matters," he said as the driver pulled up in front of Mrs. Mulhaney's boardinghouse. "We have a much worse problem waiting inside the house."

"Mrs. Mulhaney," she ventured.

"In a word," he concurred.

The elderly lady was, in fact, pacing the hall, red-faced and muttering. She stopped dead when the two of them walked in.

Tess went forward at once, without the slightest hesitation. "My friend has been falsely accused of a murder which God knows she did not commit," she said firmly. "A group of us who love Nan marched on the city jail to show our support for her, and we were arrested, by men." She lifted her chin pugnaciously. "You are well within your rights to toss me out the front door, Mrs. Mulhaney, and I will say not one word if that is your reaction. It wants courage to stand up for what is right in the eyes of God, especially if it is not right in the eyes of all men."

She stood still, waiting.

Mrs. Mulhaney went white and then scarlet. She hesitated, wiped her hands on her apron, muttered some more, and then winced. "Miss Meredith, you have placed me in an unenviable position," she said.

"How?" Tess wanted to know. "Have I done anything immoral?"

"Of course not," the older woman said at once. "It is simply the notoriety..."

"My cousin is notorious," Tess pointed out. "He often places himself in danger."

"He is a man," the landlady rejoined.

"Is a man more noble than a woman, more courageous, more valuable?"

The older woman was almost stammering by now. She grimaced. "But it is the reputation of my establishment—"

Tess held up a hand. "Say no more. I have friends with whom I can live. I will only ask that you give me until the morning to pack my things and move out."

Mrs. Mulhaney winced. "Please, Miss Mere-dith, you must understand my position!"

"Certainly I do," Tess replied. "And you may explain it to God when we both pass on to our eternal reward. I'm sure that He will understand your lack of compassion for a sister falsely accused of a crime—just as He understood the crowd for demanding the release of Barabbas and condemning Christ for crimes of which He was innocent!"

On that note, leaving Mrs. Mulhaney open-mouthed and Matt envious of her oratory, she stomped off up the staircase to her room and slammed the door behind her. There was hardly any reason for conformity now that she had burned her boats.

She took off her hat and cloak and sat down heavily in an armchair. She felt suddenly deflated—about to lose her home and the man she loved. All that had happened in one night—along with becoming a jailbird. A lesser woman would have bawled. Tess had no such intention. She could bear anything life threw at her.

Mrs. Mulhaney, confronting Matt, her face paper-pale and drawn, said, "I feel quite small."

"So do I. Eloquent, isn't she?"

"And I am wrong to make her leave? For she is doing what she thinks is right, and I am punishing her for it." She shook her head. "Oh, Mr. Davis, this modern world is not fit for women of my generation. I fear that I shall never cope with it. So many changes." She shook her head again and lifted her worried eyes to Matt's. "No one else here knows of her arrest, after all, and she is a good and kind young lady. Will you speak to her for me, and say that I ask her pardon humbly and hope that she will remain a tenant?"

Matt didn't want to say that. The tension between Tess and himself was reaching the breaking point. If he didn't move her out of his orbit quite soon, he was going to lose his head again. He couldn't reconcile his emotions with his reason, but, still, he wanted only what was best for Tess, regardless of whether it was best for him.

"Sir?" Mrs. Mulhaney persisted.

"I think that it might be a good idea for Tess to leave here," he said, surprisingly solemn.

"She plans to stay with a family of sisters who seem to have good character and at least some influence over her. She might fare better in the company of young women."

The elderly woman hesitated, but only for a minute. "I would hate to have hard feelings with her."

"I'll make sure that there are none," he promised. "Everything will be well."

She smiled wistfully. "Do you think so? I confess that I have never felt quite so bad over a decision. Thank you for your help, Mr. Davis." She hesitated. "You will stay?"

"Of course," he replied.

She smiled again, excused herself, and went up to bed. So did Matt, but not to sleep. He sat in a chair by his bed and let his mind go back to the ex-soldier's cutting remarks.

Since he'd come east, he'd been spared most of the racial prejudice that his relatives suffered on reservations all over the Dakotas and Montana. He lived as a white man, was treated as a white man. By denying what he really was, he'd escaped all the hardships of trying to live as an Indian in a white world. He'd been hiding here in Chicago since 1891. After his schooling he'd begun to play a game of make-believe, pretending to be something he wasn't. And for what? For wealth and prestige and influence, the things that Tess had once said would make it possible for him to stay here even as an Indian. Certainly the Indians who traveled with Buffalo Bill's Wild West Show had managed to live among whites. But, he wondered, did any of them aspire to white society, or were they content to be curiosities?

Tess had such faith in human nature, he thought cynically, and he had so little. He'd seen the worst of people, since his young manhood. Except for Tess and her father, he'd known little kindness from whites while he wore a breechclout and carried a bow and a quiver of arrows. Tess knew him as he really was, as he had been. She'd never seemed to mind. In fact, she'd been proud of him. She still was, despite his own misgivings.

He felt uncomfortable, remembering how she liked to revere the past and the life they'd lived. She had no shame that her father worked among Indians. She had no shame that she adored Matt. She spoke Sioux without inhibition, and she had a temper and a wild, independent spirit that he admired.

She made him feel ashamed of the way he'd acted. He was afraid of the truth, but Tess wasn't. She had the courage of her convictions. She was utterly fearless, as she'd been tonight, leading a procession to the jail to protest the arrest of an innocent woman. She walked the last mile for people she cared about... which encompassed most of the human race. It didn't really surprise him to realize that she'd have done the same thing for him, even if she hadn't loved him.

He got up finally and stripped to his drawers, loosing his black hair from its braid so that it fell down to his waist. He looked in the mirror above the dresser and glared at his reflection. With his hair down and stripped like this,

his Indian heritage was so obvious as to be blatant. No one who saw him so could ever mistake him for anything except what he was.

He groaned, hating himself. What had Tess said about mirrors? That she hated her face because it wasn't Sioux. He cursed his own doubts. It wasn't that he'd be unwilling to have the truth generally known. But eventually it would kill him to watch Tess react to the insults and the degradation of living with him if people knew what he was. She was strong now and she fought. How long, though, could a woman fight before she fell into despair? She was so bright and beautiful, so courageous. He hated to think of her spirit being crushed by one too many a cruel insult about her Indian husband. And for him to live on the reservation now, after he'd lived so long in Chicago, was unthinkable. He knew in his heart that regardless of the way things worked out, he could never again live as a Sioux.

He turned away from the mirror, thinking about tomorrow when Tess would leave and he wouldn't see her every day. Dear God, how it would hurt to lose her. And, he admitted, he was going to worry about her, across town with her friends.

What if she made another enemy like Dennis Collier? She wouldn't be totally defenseless because he'd taught her to take care of herself. But he felt more protective of her than ever.

The soft knock on the door surprised him. He went to open it just a crack.

"Matt?"

Tess was standing there, her hair down, her robe pulled and held together at the neck of her silky gown.

He opened the door and glanced both ways, pulling her quickly inside. He shut the door and looked down at her narrowly.

"What do you want?" he asked shortly.

Her eyes caressed him, fascinated with his lean, hard body, with the way he looked with his hair loose and so long.

"You looked like that twelve years ago," she recalled wistfully. "My eyes fed on you."

His chin lifted. "What do you want?" he repeated tersely. Her rapt appraisal was making his body react, and he didn't want her to see it.

"I forgot to tell you about what I found out from Nan's sister," she said.

He glared at her. "It couldn't have waited until tomorrow?"

"I won't be here tomorrow. Not long enough to talk, at least, and you mentioned an early meeting, didn't you?"

He nodded.

"I won't stay long."

He hoped not. His body was aching. He motioned her into an armchair.

"Aren't you going to sit down?" she asked.

"Is it going to take that long?" he asked mockingly.

She sighed. "All right, I'll be brief." She related the things Mrs. Greene had said about the prostitutes and her promise to try and find out the identity of those who went to Dennis's apartment.

Matt scowled. "No, that can't be so," he said after a minute. "I've done some delving into Collier's noctural wanderings on my own. They were to opium dens, not brothels. And a man doesn't bring a prostitute to his own home, Tess."

"Why not?" she demanded. "If he wanted to shame Nan, why not?"

"Because the apartment manager would have known, and he'd have been thrown out into the streets," he replied. "Besides, a man with senses as dulled by opium as Collier's isn't capable with a woman."

"What do you mean?"

"I mean that he can't be aroused in that state."

"Oh."

"You should know," he persisted. "Your friend Bailey was under the influence of laudanum, wasn't he?"

"Yes, but I had no occasion to see the effects on him in the sense you mean," she said simply. "The only nude man I've ever seen is you."

His black eyes slid over her face, her softly waving blond hair, her body in the clinging fabric. "Was there anything else you wanted to tell me?" he asked, his voice beginning to sound strained.

"Only that Edith Greene is very upset about her sister. It's heartwarming to see how much she cares for Nan. I never had siblings."

"I remember."

Her pale eyes went over him like hands. The aching hunger in them was as visible as her heartbeat. She got to her feet, trying not to give away her feelings. "I'll go back to my room now," she said huskily. "I didn't mean to disturb you when you were ready for bed."

"I'm not," he said curtly. "I don't wear anything to bed."

"Oh."

The silence in the room was thick with tension. She looked at him and couldn't look away.

"Do you have any idea how dangerous this is?" he asked roughly.

She couldn't get words out. She nodded.

"I want your eyes on me. God help me, I want nothing in the world more!" he said tersely.

As he spoke, his hands went to the fastening of his drawers. He slipped it and let them fall to the floor. He was aroused and exquisitely made, so beautiful a physical specimen. Tess audibly caught her breath as she looked at him openly.

He let out the breath he had been holding. He went to the bed and stretched out on the cover, his hair splayed out around him, his body rigid, trembling faintly with desire.

She moved to the side of the bed, her eyes like saucers, hesitant and hungry all at once. "What do you want me to do?" she asked.

His head turned, and his black eyes glittered up into hers. "Anything you want to do."

Her hands shook. She let her robe fall to the floor, and her hands were on the straps of her gown.

"Anything except that."

She swallowed, shivering. "Don't you want to see me?"

His jaw tautened. "With all my heart. But it's too dangerous."

"Please." She slid the straps down, holding his eyes. "Please. Let me. I want to, so badly!"

He grimaced, but he didn't speak as she let the fabric slither down her slender body, revealing every secret of its contours to him.

He closed his eyes for an instant and shuddered.

"I'll die if this is all I can have," she managed to say in a tortured voice.

He sighed in sheer, sweet defeat. "So will I." He held out his arms.

She went to him, trembling as he drew her down with him and turned, pulling her nude body completely against him with her legs tangling in his, the evidence of his desire pressing hot and swollen against her belly.

"Oh, Lord." She groaned as he rolled over with her and over again, their bodies touching intimately, sliding together and apart, the glory of skin against skin holding them spellbound. All the lights were on, and she wasn't embarrassed. He was gloriously formed, and she loved the sight of him.

He lifted himself a little away from her and looked for a long time before he bent to her breasts. Even then he was slow and tender, every movement a whisper of pleasure.

Her body moved against him, blindly searching for what he'd given her before, there on the beach. He obliged her in tender, breathlessly invasive ways, his lips traveling from her breasts over her soft belly to sensitive spots inside her thighs. And all the while she whimpered, a fist against her lips to keep from crying out her pleasure in the stillness of the night.

His long hair fell around her like a black cloud as his mouth worked its way back up to her swollen mouth and possessed it. One long, muscular leg slid between both of hers. While he kissed her, he pleasured her with his expert fingers, teasing and probing and exploring until she arched up against them and let him fulfill her in a firestorm of ecstasy.

And even that wasn't enough. Her tormented eyes looked into his as he brought her hand to his body and guided its slow, trembling strokes.

"There must... be a way," she whimpered. "Oh, God, I want you. I want all of you, inside my body!"

"Tess!"

She was under him, against him. He had no willpower, no strength to resist her. She moved between his legs while he looked at her in anguish, too enthralled to stop her.

Her body lifted. She tugged at his hard thighs, guiding him, softly pleading with her eyes and her lips.

She was... against him. His eyes closed as he felt her softness, felt her warm and moist femininity pleading to be filled.

He looked into her eyes, searching them while his body poised on the knife-edge of disaster.

One of her long, white legs curled around his, and she lifted, shivering, feeling the hardness softly beginning to bury itself inside her. She swallowed. Her lips parted. She could barely breathe. He wasn't fighting her. He was... watching her.

She was too weak. She tried to lift further against him, but her body shivered with the effort. She bit her lip and sobbed as he hovered there, neither advancing nor withdrawing.

It was too late, he thought with resignation. She could be pregnant from the touch of him like this, when he was excited. There would be no more risk regardless of what he let her do.

With a faint smile, holding her gaze, he let his body relax, and as it relaxed, he penetrated her so deeply that she gasped in shock. Even with his initiation of two nights ago, there was still a flash of pain, and muscles unused to invasion were stretched in new and awesome ways.

He moved experimentally from side to side, feeling her response to him as she stiffened and her hands dug into his back.

"It was painful," he whispered, moving seductively against her. "It won't be again. Lift your legs around my hips."

She obeyed him, fascinated by the hot glitter of his eyes, by the sudden sensuality of his body as he enforced his possession of her with sharp, faintly violent little motions that sent her mad with pleasure.

"Don't cry out," he whispered above her. "The sound of passion is unmistakable."

Under them, the springs were audible. She looked at him with mingled pleasure and apprehension.

"Yes," he whispered. "We're going to make too much noise, especially when you start writhing under me. And you will writhe, Tess."

He drew away from her, causing her to cry out softly in pure fear of the loss of him.

He got up from the bed and lifted her, his face taut, his eyes blazing.

"You'd let me have you in the living room with the doors open," he observed, his eyes narow and appreciative as they gazed at her trembling body. "And I'd take you there, without a qualm. You see how violent this is, how uncontrollable? I tried to warn you, and you wouldn't listen. Now we both have to take the consequences."

"I want you," she whimpered.

"You're going to have me," he said huskily. "As much of me as you can take, for as long as I can hold out."

He laid her down on the soft rug and stood over her, his body taut and vibrant with unsatisfied passion. With a rough sigh, he went to the door and turned the key and latched the bolt.

He moved over her with mindless intent, seeing the way her legs opened for him, the way her breasts went taut. She was completely without reserve, shuddering already with the promise of ecstasy. Her eyes were blind with it, her hands seeking, shaking.

When he went into her, she shivered and sobbed.

His lean fingers went to her soft hips and dug in, jerking her to him in quick, rough movements that only intensified the hot throb of her body. Her arms fell back beside her head, and she arched, crooning in a husky, pleading cry as she met his eyes and watched him take her.

He'd never dreamed that Tess was capable of such sensual abandon, such blatant passion. She matched his sharp movements, bit her lip bloody keeping the cries from escaping her tight throat. He was above her, inside her, rising and falling with beautiful rippling muscles, sensual rhythm, his eyes hot on her as he taunted her body with his.

She sobbed with frustration, grasping at the elusive sweetness and groaning when she couldn't quite reach it. He pushed and pulled away, twisted and rolled, laughing deep in his throat as she went impossibly high, only to fall back and wait for the next wave to carry her up again.

"Stop it..." she choked out, lifting in a shivering arch. "Make it stop... make it stop... please! Please!"

"Don't scream," he whispered roughly.

And then it was fierce and violent and demanding. He drove into her with such ardor that she climaxed almost at once, but before she could recover, he took her up again on a tidal wave of fulfillment that grew and grew and grew until she bit into his shoulder to keep from screaming and her body went into helpless convulsions that shook them both from head to toe.

Only when she was near unconsciousness

did he give in to his own need and fulfill it. He thought that he would never survive what he felt then. He closed his eyes and shuddered and shuddered until his body felt bruised from the force of the pleasure he felt.

They lay together, bathed in sweat despite the chill of the room. Her hair was as damp as his. She couldn't breathe properly. Her body felt as if it had broken in several places during that maelstrom. She clung to him with real fear that he might want to lift away.

"What is it?" he whispered at her ear.

She clung tighter. "I don't want you to move away."

"I'm not going to."

She relaxed and felt him move against her with sensual pleasure. She shivered involuntarily at the sensations he provoked.

"Can you feel me, deep in your body?" he whispered.

"Yes!"

"I can feel you, like a soft, wet cocoon." He brushed her ear with his lips. "When I can think again, I'll never forgive you for making me do this."

"I don't care. Maybe I'll die right now, and we'll never have to separate again. We can be one person forever."

The words disturbed him. His hand smoothed over her soft hair, and he lifted his head to look down into her eyes. Sated. She was sated.

He felt an earthquake of possession. Then he lifted his torso so that he could see how intimately they were joined together below the belly.

She followed his eyes and caught her breath.

He saw her curious expression and lifted just enough so she might see.

"Man and woman," he whispered. "Male and female. See how we join, how we couple, how we mate."

Her eyes, fascinated, looked up into his. "Yes. How we mate."

His jaw tightened. He looked down again and moved, deliberately, watching the quicksilver ripple of her body as he rekindled the ecstasy they'd shared. He moved again and his teeth clenched.

He didn't want to. He was going to stop. He was... He pushed down hard and then again and again, watching her face as he took her with desperate passion.

"Yes," she whispered jerkily, lifting to meet him. "Yes, yes, yes!"

She went over the edge almost at once, and he watched her.

"Don't close... your... eyes!" he bit off.

Shocked, she opened them just as the pleasure arched her in helpless, uncontrollable spasms of fulfillment. He watched her feel it, and seconds later he gave in to it and let her watch him.

The intimacy of it was unbelievable. When he collapsed against her, shaking, she stroked his long hair with a feeling of utter wonder.

"We looked at each other," she rasped. "We looked... right at each other!"

"I never thought that I might want to watch a woman," he whispered roughly. "I saw your eyes the instant you gave yourself. It was beautiful to see."

"So were you," she murmured. She clung to him. "Dear God, what are we going to do?"

"I wish I knew," he said heavily. He rolled over onto his back, drawing her so that she lay half over and against him. His body still throbbed from the ecstasy she'd given him. He could barely breathe at all.

"I'm not sorry," she whispered. "I'll never be sorry!"

"Neither will I. It was exquisite, reverent," he said quietly. "The most beautiful and wondrous experience of my life."

She smiled against his broad, damp chest. "Thank you for saying that, even if you don't mean it."

He rolled her onto her back and looked down at her solemnly. "Oh, I mean it. I couldn't lie about such extraordinary loving."

She searched his eyes, aware of the way he was looking at her now, with possession and pride and the lingering traces of desire. There was something else, too; something dark and warm and constant that he'd never let her see before. She couldn't quite decide what it was.

His hand swept down her body, gently, exploringly. "You belong to me completely now," he said. "In every way there is."

"And you belong to me, Matt."

"You don't understand. There's more to it than this feverish passion we've just shared. Much more."

She searched his eyes. "Yes?"

He drew in a long breath, and his eyes closed briefly. "I'm going to have to tell you," he said after a minute. "I've put it off for years, but after what we've just done, it really can't wait any longer."

He lifted away from her and got to his feet, moving to the water pitcher and bowl on the nightstand. He poured water into the bowl and took two flannel cloths and wet them, pausing just long enough to wring them out before he sat down on the rug and handed one to Tess.

He bathed the sweat from his body while she did the same to her own.

"Did you bleed?" he asked.

She flushed. "No. The other time I did."

He smiled gently. "It made this time much better than it would have been."

"I realize that." She laid the cloth aside and looked at him with eyes that worshiped him. Nude, he was as beautiful as any statue in a museum.

"I like the way you look without your clothes, too," he murmured with a smile.

She sighed. "What is it that you have to tell me? Something unpleasant?"

"Not really." He leaned back against the bed and pulled her across him, so that her breasts pressed softly into his chest. "Do you remember the day we went up on the butte, and Old Man Deer came to see us there?"

"Yes," she murmured, closing her eyes. She felt loved and safe and secure. She wanted this closeness never to end. "I remember."

"He didn't happen upon us," he said. "I asked him to come."

"Yes?"

"He was a shaman, and a relative of mine.

That meeting was soon after you'd looked at me under the sheet."

She felt a little embarrassed. "I remember that, too."

He smiled. His hand smoothed over her damp hair. "I was afraid that something might happen, even though I did everything in my power to keep a safe distance between us." He sighed. "Perhaps I foresaw what happened tonight. Either way, I wanted to protect you. There was only one way to do that. And Old Man Deer did it."

"Did what?"

"Do you remember the ceremony he performed with us, Tess? It was before you were fluent in Sioux."

"Yes."

"I never explained it to you."

"I know. I wondered why."

"Because there was no need for you to know. What he did wasn't binding in your world. It was only binding in mine. In the world I knew then," he corrected. "But if anything had happened, it would have protected you."

"How?"

He hesitated. His hand stilled in her hair. "He married us, Tess."

Chapter Fourteen

Tess wondered if she'd gone mad. For a minute she didn't say anything. Then she began to realize what Matt had just said.

She looked up at him, stunned. "He married us?" she parroted.

He nodded. "By Sioux custom," he said. "Even though I didn't give your father any horses to pay for you," he added, tongue in cheek, "or go through the usual courting rituals. Old Man Deer knew how I felt about you. Some Sioux girls marry at the age you were then, or even a bit younger. For all your youth, you were every inch a woman." His eyes went over her hungrily. "No less a woman than you are now."

"You never touched me."

"I watched you bathe one night. A shameful memory. You never knew I was there. I thought your body was the most beautiful I'd ever seen. It still is."

"And you made me feel guilty for looking at you!"

He smiled. "We wanted each other even that long ago. It was inevitable that the bonds holding us away from each other would snap if we spent too much time together. After the other night, when we touched so intimately, well... I knew, I believe."

"Are you sorry?"

He shook his head. "Nor should you be. Whites might condemn us for being this familiar with each other outside a legal marriage, but by Sioux law, you and I have been married for twelve years."

She drew in a sharp breath. She glared at him. "And you've been an adulterer."

He cocked an eyebrow. His eyes danced with amusement, but he didn't answer the charge.

"You knew nothing of our marriage. Besides," he murmured dryly, "perhaps the experience I gained insured the pleasure I just gave you."

She colored prettily and curled closer to him. "It was a little frightening, that pleasure."

"Yes." He drew her closer. "I've never experienced anything like it."

She nuzzled closer. "Can't I sleep in your arms?"

His heart jumped. "I want that. More than you know. But what we've done is hardly permissible in this society."

"And you wouldn't like telling people how we married, and under what circumstances."

He didn't reply. Pleasure had numbed his doubts for a time, but as he looked at her, the apprehension came back full force. He frowned and suddenly his big, lean hand spread out against her soft, flat belly.

She uncurled and let him touch her there, her eyes meeting his. She knew exactly what he was thinking. "Would it be so terrible if it had happened, Matt?"

His eyes were troubled. His hand moved gently. He didn't speak.

She looked at him, filled with hunger for his child. What would he do if she were pregnant? Would he send her to one of those sophisticated women of his acquaintance who would know how to get rid of it? Her face contorted.

He glanced at her eyes and saw that expression and scowled. "What is it?"

"Those women," she said hesitantly. "You

said they knew how to stop a baby…" She bit her lip until it was bloodless.

"Oh… no," he whispered quickly. His hand pressed hard against her. "No. I would never, never ask such a thing of you!" he said, and sounded properly horrified that she'd even mentioned it to him.

She felt a little less panicky, but she was still worried. He'd said too often that he didn't want a child with her. She'd tormented him into doing what she wanted, without any consideration whatsoever for his fears. Only now did she feel guilt.

"If it happens," he said curtly, "it happens. I won't say that I regret how we came together tonight. I wanted you to the point of madness. I couldn't have drawn back."

"Neither could I. But I'm sorry if I made you do something you regret."

"How could I regret going to paradise in your arms?" he asked softly. "Because I did. And so did you."

She closed her eyes and laid her cheek on his chest. "What do we do now?"

He didn't answer her. He couldn't think of any way to answer her. They'd taken the ultimate risk together, against his better judgment, against his wishes. But he couldn't blame her for what had happened. He'd wanted her as passionately as she'd wanted him. And he could hardly regret such an earthshaking climax. It had been as he'd always dreamed it would be. Now he had to live with whatever consequences came of it. He could only pray that none would.

They dressed again, reluctantly, and she went to the door, looking back at him with haunted eyes.

"Don't worry," he said quietly. "We'll take one step at a time."

"Mrs. Mulhaney wants me to leave."

He nodded. "Not really, but it will be for the best if you go." He looked at the rug where they'd been together. "It will happen over and over again until we're eventually discovered together and disgraced," he said softly. "That's as inevitable as sunrise now."

She drew in a slow breath. "I suppose it is." Her eyes roamed his face and body with quiet delight. "You won't cut me out of your life entirely when I leave?"

"Don't be absurd," he replied. He smiled, trying to lighten the somber mood. "After all, we have a case to solve."

"Nan!" She caught her breath. "Oh dear, I forgot all about her!"

His lips tugged up. "I should hope so, under the circumstances!"

She smiled roguishly. "Well, it was rather hard to concentrate. Under the circumstances."

"Go back to your room before someone catches us together in this state of undress. Shameless hussy," he teased, making his words sound like an endearment.

"Look who's talking."

He grinned. "Good night."

She said it in Sioux, her eyes adoring him

one last time before she slipped the locks and, peering down the hall, eased out of his room and quickly back to her own. She locked her door and leaned back against it with trembling legs and a shaking heart. Matt had made love to her, on the floor, with all the lights blazing. She was still breathless with excitement. She wanted to do it again and again. But she was going to have to move out. And how was Matt going to feel now that his passion for her was spent?

How would he feel tomorrow, in the cold light of day? Would he be angry at her tempting presence in his room so late at night? Would he be worried about the risk of pregnancy? Would he ease her out of his life and push her away if there was no child? How did he feel about her and what they'd done?"

She lay down, but she didn't sleep at all. Her mind, numbed by passion earlier, was starkly alive now.

Tess didn't know what to expect when she went downstairs the next morning, dressed in her nicest suit, with a suitcase in her hand. It took all her courage to put on a brave face and not let anyone see her apprehension as she walked as far as the dining room doorway.

Mrs. Mulhaney looked up very guiltily from her plate.

"I used the telephone to call for a hired carriage, Mrs. Mulhaney," Tess said, noting with disappointment that Matt wasn't among the diners. "I've included the amount of the charge in my bill for this week." She proffered an envelope.

Mrs. Mulhaney got up and came out into the hall, her hands buried in her apron, as they always were when she was nervous.

"I would have said nothing if you had remained," she told Tess softly. "None of the others know anything of what happened. But Mr. Davis seemed to think it best that you go to your friends. I do hope that there are no hard feelings..."

"Don't be silly," Tess said, regretting the harsh things she'd said to the poor woman the night before. "I could never have hard feelings for someone who's been so kind to me. Forgive me for the awful things I said to you," she added. "I didn't mean to sound so self-righteous."

"I didn't take offense. Your friend is in a great deal of trouble, and you want to help her. Anyone could understand that. You will be all right, my dear?"

"I shall be fine. Ellen and her sisters are good girls. We'll do well together. Good-bye, Mrs. Mulhaney."

"Good-bye, Miss Meredith."

The carriage was waiting outside. Mick Kennedy ferried her luggage out to it and put her inside.

"Where to, miss?" he asked kindly.

She gave him Ellen's address.

"Aye, that'll be Miss O'Hara," he said with a grin. "I know all the O'Hara girls, and that's a fact. There's not a finer bunch of lasses in Chicago, and no hint of scandal about them."

"I hope not to cause any," she said demurely.

"You? And that's a fine joke, it is." He chuckled as he closed the door and hopped up into the driver's seat.

Tess sat back with a sigh, shaking her head. Mr. Kennedy had no idea how much scandal Tess had caused in her young life, and how much more she was likely to cause. Her hand went to her stomach, and she closed her eyes and dreamed. She'd never been so certain that she and Matt had a future, despite their differences.

Ellen was happy to see Tess. She was given her own room, although there was little time to acclimate herself because, like Ellen and the others, Tess had a job to go to.

"Sure, our work isn't as noble as yours," Ellen teased, "but then, you're more educated than we are."

"Bosh," Tess said. "I've had more advantages. That's all."

"I'm glad you're to stay with us," Ellen added gently. "I had a feeling your Mrs. Mulhaney might kick up a fuss when she heard what you'd been about. A proper lady, she is, and runs that boardinghouse like a convent."

"She's very nice," Tess said. "She even loaned me a mink stole when Matt took me to a charity ball."

"She never did!" Ellen exclaimed. "Who'd have believed it?"

Remembering what had happened while she was wearing the stole made Tess color just a little, but she controlled it quickly, bade Ellen a cheerful good-bye, and took herself off to the hospital.

She hoped that Matt's absence that morning at breakfast wasn't an omen of things to come. Then she remembered him telling her that he had business to attend to and had to get a very early start. It was like having the sun come out after a bad rain. She smiled and then began to hum. Now if only she could find a way to get Nan out of jail and make Matt face his past and, of course, obtain the vote for her sex, life would be wonderful indeed. Two out of three, however, wouldn't be at all bad.

Matt had gone to work to fetch Stanley. He had a job for the young man that was going to require extensive stealth and courage. Stanley had been overjoyed that his boss had finally trusted him with something more dangerous than filling fountain pens with India ink.

But when he learned the specifics of this new assignment, his heart fell.

"You want me to go into a bordello?" Stanley asked plaintively. "But, Mr. Davis, I promised my mother—!"

"I don't want you to *do* anything in there," Matt said irritably. "I want you to ask questions. I've uncovered some new evidence in the Collier murder. I want you to check out his associations with any of the women in there." He nodded toward the notorious house of ill repute.

"By posing as a"—Stanley swallowed—"client?"

Matt felt his patience wearing thin. "By posing as a detective, Stanley," he said shortly. "You look trustworthy and, forgive me, non-threatening."

Stanley eyed his boss warily. "Why don't you go?"

"Because I had to identify the madam in an assault case when a man who was shot in that house. She'd recognize me immediately and tell her girls not to give me a scrap of information."

"You said it was going to be a dangerous assignment," Stanley muttered, feeling betrayed.

Matt clapped him on the shoulder. "By God, it is, son," he said solemnly. "Just think, you could be raped."

Stanley gave him a glare that was impressively dark.

"You could be shot," Matt added. "The bouncer carries a gun. So don't make any threatening moves."

The younger man brightened. That was more like it. "I'll do my best, sir. What do you want to know?"

"If Dennis Collier was a frequent customer, if he had a regular girl there, and most importantly, if he ever invited her to his home."

Stanley let out a breath. "That's a tall order. But I'll try." He straightened his tie and his bowler hat, and with a jaunty smile, he walked down the street to the bawdy house.

Matt waited for him outside, his eyes wary. It was a dangerous neighborhood, that was no lie, and the bouncer inside didn't like detectives very much because of Matt. He couldn't let the boy be hurt, but he needed the information badly.

Ten minutes passed. Matt glanced at his watch. So far, so good. He was mentally congratulating Stanley on his success when he heard a commotion down the street and a series of thuds on the back stairs of the house of ill repute.

Fearing the worst, Matt dashed through an alley and almost through an occupied clothesline as he made his way to the back of the house.

Stanley had gone crashing down the steps. He was groggy and bruised, and a huge man with a pistol was coming right down after him. The boy wouldn't stand a chance. The women were leaning out windows, and Matt knew that they'd swear to whatever the madam told them to.

His heart raced as he reached under his jacket for the bowie knife he'd worn just in case of trouble. He was glad he had it. He slid it quickly out of its sheath, waited to make sure the gunman meant business, and took it by the tip.

"You little worm, nobody talks to these girls without paying. This is what you'll get for your trouble, nosey parker!"

"Leave him alone," Matt called, his voice even and threatening.

"And who's going to make me?" the bouncer drawled, turning the pistol toward Matt.

He cocked the pistol just as Matt drew back and threw the knife. It sailed through the air with such force behind it that it went straight into the bouncer's shoulder through his suit jacket. He gasped. The gun discharged harmlessly in the air and then fell to the ground as he grabbed his shoulder with a harsh groan.

Stanley gaped as he watched Matt stride forward without the least hesitation. He kicked the gun out of the man's reach, threw the bouncer to the ground, placed a booted foot against his chest, and withdrew the big knife with a single jerk.

He held it steady with the tip pointed toward the downed man, and for an instant it looked as though he might use it again.

"God Almighty, don't!" the bouncer wailed. "I'm just doing my job!"

Stanley was holding his breath. He stared at the older man over that blade, and it was like seeing him for the first time. The irritable, stoic man for whom he'd worked these past years was a stranger. The shape of his face and eyes, the steely glint, the ease with which he handled that knife all added up to a totally unknown quantity. And he knew at once that Matt wasn't an exiled Russian or a gypsy or an Arab prince. Having seen similar skills in Buffalo Bill's Wild West Show, which he'd attended several times, he no longer had any doubt about his boss's mysterious ancestry.

"Stanley, are you all right?" Matt asked curtly, but his eyes never left the bouncer.

"Y-yes, sir," the younger man stammered. He clambered to his feet, shaky and nervous as he grabbed up his hat.

Matt leaned down and wiped the blade of the knife on the jacket of the wounded man. His eyes met the other man's coldly. "You're a lucky fellow," he said softly. "There was a time when I'd have killed you without a second thought for pointing a pistol at me."

He stood erect then and slid the blade back into its sheath. His eyes didn't leave the downed man, even when he motioned for Stanley to join him as he started back down the alley.

Stanley followed him at a respectful distance, ruffled and bruised and a little nervous of the man he worked for.

Matt stopped as they reached the busy sidewalk and looked at the younger man with piercing eyes. "Are you sure you're all right?"

Stanley had to nerve himself to speak. "Yes, sir, Mr. Davis."

"What happened?"

"I'd found a girl who knew Mr. Collier," he choked. "I was talking to her, just talking to her, when that man burst into the room and said I was getting something without paying for it. He told me to give him twenty dollars or get out. I was trying to do just that when he started tossing me around."

"He won't toss anyone around for a while."

"No, sir, he won't." Stanley looked at the sheathed blade with faint fear. "I never saw anybody in Chicago throw a knife like that, except in Bill Cody's traveling show."

"No?"

Stanley didn't dare ask the question that was sitting on his lips. He imparted what he'd learned instead. "Mr. Collier knew this girl, Lily. He liked her to hold his hand and listen to him talk about how bad his wife treated him. He never wanted to touch her or do anything with her. Only listen. But she never went to his house, and none of the other girls had anything to do with him, just Lily." His face was solemn. "She says she's seventeen years old, Mr. Davis. She isn't pretty, but she has a sort of dignity about her, and she's a sad girl. She said that she always liked Mr. Collier because she didn't have to grit her teeth and do the things most men wanted her to." He flushed. "I felt sorry for her."

"I feel sorry for all of them," Matt said flatly. "They're little more than slaves, and the madam who runs that particular establishment could chew through ten-penny nails. She cares nothing for the girls, only for her profit. And when they become diseased, as they inevitably do, she kicks them out without a penny."

"Can't the police do anything?"

"They can close the house down," he said.

"And she'll go out of town and open another one. As long as there are men who want that sort of thing, there'll be women who'll provide it. That's a basic fact of life in the city."

"I suppose so. It's sad, all the same."

Matt was frowning thoughtfully. "This makes no sense," he said. "I was told that Collier brought prostitutes to his apartment house. What you've learned seems to put paid to that."

"Could there be another place where he had women?" Stanley asked after a minute. "Or perhaps it was a woman who wasn't working in a brothel."

"I don't know. I'll have to look into that."

"Can't I help, sir?"

Matt's lips turned up, and the frightening look of him went into eclipse. "You haven't lost your taste for detecting, Stanley?" he teased gently.

Stanley grinned and flushed together. "No, sir. I guess it gets into your blood."

"Then I'll let you pursue this. But I'll need to go back to my source for further information first."

"Thank you for trusting me to do it, sir. I'm sorry if I seemed to let you down back there. I was stunned from the fall," he added defensively.

"Stanley, I've been thrown down staircases a time or two. I remember how it felt."

The young man nodded, but his expression was eloquent when he looked at Matt.

"Is there something else?" Matt asked.

Stanley started to speak. Then he thought

of how he liked his job and the risk he'd be taking to speculate on Matt's background. He smiled instead. "Not a thing, sir. I'll go back to the office and clean up."

"Good man."

"Thank you, sir!"

Matt watched his operative walk away; clearly the young man was confused. Stanley had to have guessed how Matt had learned to use that knife, but he respected him too much to actually ask the question. It hadn't been fear, because Stanley might be cautious about making him angry, but he wasn't afraid of him in any physical sense. So why had Stanley let the matter drop without a word? It was a question that kept Matt brooding for a long time.

He remembered Tess and the night before. She wouldn't be at the boardinghouse when he got there, and he felt lonely already. He was going to have to get used to not seeing her every day, and that might be a good thing. They needed a little space while he came to grips with the sudden shift in their relationship. He didn't know how he was going to cope with it. He knew only that he was going to have to find a way. He wasn't going to lose Tess. Not now.

Matt wanted to see her in a public place. Because of their changed relationship, it would be dangerous for them to be alone. He stopped by the hospital just before her shift ended and went over to meet her coming down the steps toward Mick's carriage.

Tess stopped dead when she saw him, but under the wide brim of her hat he could see that her eyes lit up.

He smiled, too, moving forward. He didn't touch her. They simply stared at each other with barely contained longing.

"How are you?" he asked.

"I'm fine. I like it at Ellen's house, and they're good company."

He nodded. "I'm glad."

"Have you something for me to do on Nan's case?" she asked, guessing his reason for coming to her.

"In a way," he said. "We found a girl in a bordello who was keeping company with Collier. The problem is that she had no intimate relationship with him and doesn't know anyone at that particular house of ill repute who did."

"That's interesting," Tess replied. "Mrs. Greene said that he had lots of women."

"I wonder if she really knew," he replied thoughtfully. "Maybe she was guessing."

"She sounded to me as if she knew exactly what she was saying. What reason would she have had to lie about it? She hated her sister's husband, because she knew how he treated Nan."

"Perhaps we looked in the wrong place," he said. His eyes narrowed. "I might ask Kilgallen," he added. "He has contacts all over the city, some of which might be in some of the more successful prostitution rings. He might know more than Mrs. Greene did about Collier's infidelity."

"Something worries me about that," she murmured as they went along the sidewalk together. "You said that Dennis Collier wouldn't be—well, able to perform with a woman when he used opium. And yet when he wasn't using it, he seemed to be working or running errands for his shady friends."

"He was running errands for Kilgallen at first," he told her. "But he got mixed up in the opium trade. Then he started using that devil's substance, and I'd guess he had to have more than Kilgallen paid him to support his own cravings. He made extra money by passing along information that came over the telegraph about shipments of cash. You've heard of the yeggs, I'm sure."

"Who hasn't?" she asked, fascinated. "Collier seems to have been involved in a number of foul deeds." She shrugged. "But it still has to be a woman who killed him," she said miserably. "And although I don't really think Nan did it, there's something I haven't told you."

He stopped. "What?"

"There were splatters of blood on her gloves the evening Dennis was killed."

His indrawn breath was audible. "Why didn't you say so in the beginning?"

"Because you'd have thought exactly what you're thinking now, that's why!" she returned angrily. "The blood convicts her automatically, isn't that what you think? But she said that it had come from carving up a chicken. Surely you know that chickens bleed after they're killed!"

He stared at her steadily. "Why would she

have a live chicken, Tess?" he asked solemnly. "She'd have had one from the market. And those are drained of blood before they're sold."

Chapter Fifteen

"Oh, dear." Tess groaned. She felt as if a terrible weight had been placed on her shoulders. She actually slumped. "Oh, dear!"

"Are you in a rush to get home?" Matt asked suddenly.

"Heavens, no."

He took her gloved hand in his. "Come on!"

Mick drove them to the police station, where Matt asked him to wait. Matt wanted to talk with the officer who'd found Dennis Collier's body, but discovered he was out on a case, investigating a domestic disturbance. Matt persisted until he got the location. He thanked the officer at the desk and tugged Tess out the door again.

He gave Mick the address where the officer was supposed to be.

"You aren't just going to walk in there in the middle of a free-for-all?" she asked, breathless with excitement.

"Only if I have to," he promised. He glanced at her with mischief in his black eyes. "Don't you think I can handle myself in a fight?"

"It isn't that. These people seem to walk around armed half the time, judging by the number of knife and pistol victims we get at the hospital..." She drew in a sharp breath, remembering Wounded Knee. "Sorry. I didn't mean to say that."

"Don't walk on eggshells with me," he chided gently. "I've learned to live with the bad memories."

"But not with anything else about your past."

"I'm working on that." He studied her curiously. "It really doesn't bother you, does it?" he asked suddenly.

"That you're Sioux? Of course not."

Her eyes were steady, intent on his, utterly fearless. He smiled. "Why?"

"Because you come from a proud people who lived on the land and took excellent care of one another for hundreds of years before white people started trying to own the earth." She smiled sadly. "I remember that your people were appalled if they saw a white mother hit a child. Sioux children were never hit. They were taught respect for their elders, and right from wrong, but they never felt the sting of a belt or an angry hand."

"That's true."

"And I remember the sharing, how the most respected people were always the poorest because they were also the ones who gave away the most to those in need." She shook her head. "Material things don't mean very much to the People. But white folks can't live without the symbols of their wealth. They have to have the biggest houses, the most opulent furnishings, the most expensive clothing... and all around them, little children are going hungry."

"Which one of us is Sioux?" he murmured dryly.

She glared at him. "I'm Sioux inside, and you're white outside."

His eyebrows arched. She sounded absolutely outraged.

While he was trying to come up with a reply, the carriage pulled to a stop. A police wagon sat outside a tenement. Loud noises and crashing sounds came from just inside the building.

"It sounds like a full-scale riot," Tess ventured.

"It probably is." He got out of the carriage and paid Mick. Then he helped Tess out. They proceeded toward the steps.

"Lady, don't you go in there; it's dangerous!" the driver of the wagon called to her.

Tess gave him an affronted glance and kept walking.

"Sir, aren't you going to stop her?" the man called to Matt.

Matt chuckled. "If I stop her, who's going to protect me once we're inside?"

The policeman sat there with a blank expression, hardly able to believe his ears. Tess giggled. And so did Mick.

"And that's what I love most about you," she murmured as they made their way into the apartment building. "You never did treat me like a helpless child."

"I have reason to know that you're not. Who was it who shot an arrow at a Cheyenne who was firing a Winchester rifle at me?"

"Those were wild, free days," she recalled. They paused in the hall, where the noise was beginning to decrease a little. "Bill Cody offered me work in his Wild West Show. I was a novelty—a young girl who could shoot a bow and speak perfect Sioux."

"You never told me!"

"You never asked," she pointed out. "Besides, I kept hoping you might one day get tired of Chicago and come back. You didn't."

"There was too much sorrow for me there, too many bad memories. But Old Man Deer went with Cody. I saw him often when the troupe performed here," he added surprisingly. "He told me how bad things were at Pine Ridge after we left. He said the people were all ashamed of being Sioux after the massacre, as if Wakan Tanka had let everyone down by giving the whites such a victory. And of course, medicine men were banned from practicing their craft. Well, you know all the rest. One had to be white or one was worth nothing. So the Lakota Sioux felt that they were worth nothing."

"Is that how you felt, too?"

He nodded. But as he looked down at her, there was something different in his expression, in his eyes.

"But something's changed," she began.

"Yes."

"What?"

"Today, my young associate bit his tongue to keep from asking about my ancestry. Not because he was afraid of me," he added. "But because he was awed."

It was a strange choice of words. "I don't understand."

"I threw the knife at an armed bouncer who threatened to shoot me." He chuckled. "He was impressed. But he likes me too much to embarrass me. Imagine that?"

She grinned. "Of course I can. I've held you in awe since I was barely a woman."

He pursed his lips, looking oddly rakish and devil-may-care. "Maybe I should approach Cody for a job myself. Apparently he's found a way to reinstill pride in the People, by showing the world what the warriors looked like."

"It's cheap."

"It's educational," he corrected. "And it's embarrassing the government," he added with a wicked grin. "Some of the old war chiefs are becoming world famous."

"That makes it acceptable even to me," she assured him.

He started to speak just as three burly men with cut and bruised faces came storming out into the hall while a policeman they glimpsed on the floor of the apartment called for them to stop.

"Shall we?" Matt asked Tess.

"Of course we shall."

He tripped the first man and helped him headfirst into the wall. Tess walked into the second one with her knee, and when he bent double with the pain, she brought her knee up again and laid him out cold on the floor with the force of it.

The last one skidded to a stop just as the policeman came staggering out into the hall with a pistol and cocked it with a loud warning shout.

The man stuck his arms up, gaping at the two men on the floor and the people who'd put them there.

"Sir, I'm eternally grateful." The policeman panted, dabbing at a deep cut on his forehead.

"Oh, I only settled one for you. She"—he indicated Tess—"knocked the second one down."

The policeman stared at her. "She did?"

"I'm an old Indian fighter," she told him with a straight face.

"I'm not quite an old Indian," Matt murmured, smiling slowly, "but she can still throw me when she wants to."

The policeman chuckled, not quite sure what to believe. He called to the men in the wagon, who came and dragged the three men out.

"We'll need the ambulance, too," the policeman called to the driver. "They'd almost done in their poor father in there."

"We'll send it."

"I am a trained practical nurse," Tess said. "May I be of help?"

"Indeed you may!"

She was led to the man, who was cut and bruised and concussed. She did what little she could for him while Matt spoke to the policeman.

"They told us we might find you here," Matt said to the policeman after he'd introduced himself and Tess and explained why he'd come.

"What I need to know is what sort of condition the Colliers' kitchen was in when you got there," Matt asked straight out.

The man looked taken aback by the odd question, but he recovered quickly. "Well, it was a mess," he said. "She'd butchered a chicken in there and left feathers and parts of it in the sink after she'd boiled the rest. She told us that she'd gotten it from a neighbor who killed it for her but didn't dress it. She did that and cooked it for a guest they had earlier that night, and in the rush to get to her women's meeting, she'd left the cleaning up. I never thought that quite rang true."

It wasn't true, Matt thought, remembering what Kilgallen had told him. The mobster had said that he'd knocked Dennis down the stairs and taken Nan away, calling for help from her sister and brother-in-law. There hadn't been time to clean the kitchen first. And it did indeed verify what Nan had told Tess about where the blood on her gloves had come from. He could have cursed. He was still no nearer a solution to the murder, and Nan was running out of time. The trial was next week.

He pursued one more line of questioning before he gave it up. "I wondered if anyone told you about Collier having loose women in his apartment when his wife wasn't home?"

"Good Lord, no," the policeman said. Then he paused thoughtfully. "Well, not loose women," he amended. "Someone certainly saw a woman run out of the apartment just after Collier screamed on the night he was murdered.

But she was dressed in dark clothing and wearing a hat. The witness I talked to said that she was skinny and hatchet-faced." He shrugged. "That didn't sound like Mrs. Collier to me, but you know how witnesses can mix things up sometimes."

"Yes, I do." He was trying to put a face to that description. Tess beat him to it. Her eyes met his, and she was suddenly pale. She knew who fit that description to a tee. And it was the last person she'd ever have accused of murder. Until now.

She didn't say a word to Matt, though, in front of the policeman. She did what she could for the downed man until the horse-drawn ambulance came. The two attendants knew Tess from the hospital, and they smiled politely and asked after her health as they loaded the victim onto a stretcher and took him away.

"Thank you for your help," Matt told the policeman.

"Thank you for yours," he returned with a wary, still not quite believing glance at Tess. "They've got Mrs. Collier in jail for the murder, you know," he added.

"We know," Tess said. She wished him a good evening, grabbed Matt's hand, and pulled him out the door.

"You've remembered something, haven't you?" he asked her once they were clear of the building and out of earshot.

"Yes, I have! Matt, don't you remember meeting someone who meets the description the policeman just gave us?" she asked, her eyes wide and bright with excitement. "Someone who hated Dennis Collier and admitted that she was glad he was dead?"

"Of course!" He let out a breath. "My God, Nan's sister—Edith Greene!"

"Exactly!" Tess exclaimed. "Don't you see, she was sending us on wild goose chases, giving us false clues, trying to keep us from seeing that she was the one with the best motive for murder, after Nan."

"Is she that hard-hearted," he asked slowly, "that she'd let her own sister be hanged for what she did?"

"I have a feeling that she did it on the spur of the moment, that perhaps he tried to hit her or threatened to go after Nan and kill her. I don't think she went there to do it."

"Neither do I," he concurred. "Well, Miss Detective, where do we go from here?"

"Let's go and visit Mrs. Greene and see if we can flush her out!"

"Officer Greene will be at home," Matt said. He shook his head. "God, I hate it for his sake. He'll never live it down, not at his age."

"With a good attorney, she might get off. God knows, there's no law against killing treacherous poisonous snakes," she muttered coldly.

He chuckled amusedly at some secret joke.

"What are you laughing at?"

"In our own language, we are Lakota, or 'alliance of friends.' But the whites called us Sioux. Some people say that it means 'enemy,' though in what language I do not know. Others say it's a shortened version of an Ojibwa word, *nadewisou,* which means 'treacherous snake.' "

"You never told me that," she reminded him.

"I'm not a treacherous snake," he pointed out. He grinned. "But Collier was. And maybe we can offer Mrs. Greene hope. I know a damned good trial lawyer in Texas who'd come up here and defend her if I asked him to. He was with us in Cuba, in Roosevelt's volunteer regiment."

Her breath caught. "You never told me that, either—that you were in Cuba! Neither did Dad. He knew?"

"Yes. We decided to spare you. You'd have worried," he said simply.

"I suppose you were sure of that?"

He turned and looked down at her with old eyes. "I suspected you loved me with passion when you were fourteen. You grew older and never married, and your father said you still talked about me constantly, years after I came to Chicago. He, too, suspected you were in love with me. I never minded that you came to Chicago. I was only trying to cope with my doubts about our differences. I was protecting you, just as I always have. It's only today that I've suddenly realized how little you require protection. You truly have the heart of a warrior." He smiled as he saw her surprised look. "Didn't you realize that I could have refused to meet you at the station? If I hadn't wanted you around, I could have helped you get a job in another city. I could have taken you to one of the Christian homes, any one of which would gladly have given you board. But I didn't, did I?"

She shook her head. She sighed. "You wanted me here?"

"I love you. Didn't you realize?"

It was snowing a little. The chill was getting so bad that even her warm wool topcoat didn't help much. Her feet were freezing inside her cotton stockings. And still she stood there, gaping up at his beloved face.

"Why else would I have asked Old Man Deer to marry us?" he whispered, touching her cheek with a gentle hand. "And denied myself women for twelve years?"

"Denied yourself?" She did gasp out loud then. "But you said... !"

"I said that I'd had encounters with sophisticated women," he replied pleasantly. "And I have. I've held them and kissed them, and caressed them." He grinned. "But I never slept with them. I was a married man, for God's sake!"

She hit his chest and shook him and groaned furiously, and he pulled her into his arms right there in the middle of the sidewalk and kissed her breathless.

When he let her go, they were getting pointed stares from passersby, not all of whom were outraged. Some were frankly amused.

"Now, let's go and see what we can do for Mrs. Greene. We can wait. Nan can't."

He took her arm and drew her along with him. Seconds later his fingers locked firmly into her own, and she wondered if it wasn't to hold her down to the sidewalk. She surely would have floated, in her state of utter euphoria, if he'd let go of her hand.

Mrs. Greene invited them into her house with a curious expression and led them to the sitting room. She offered coffee and they accepted, passing the time of day with a courteous but very puzzled Officer Greene, who'd arrived home from work only minutes before.

When Mrs. Greene brought the coffee tray, Matt got up to take it from her. Her hands were shaking. She smiled perfunctorily and sat down next to her husband as Matt placed the tray on the side table.

"Would you pour, Miss Meredith?" Edith Greene asked in a tight voice. "My nerves are unsettled today; I can't think why!" She laughed nervously.

Tess obliged her, passing cups of coffee to everyone before she settled her cup and saucer gingerly on her lap.

"This is a strange time to come calling, if you'll forgive me saying so," Officer Greene said.

"I'm afraid it isn't a social call," Matt replied solemnly. "We've done some investigating, and we have a suspect in the Collier murder case. In fact," he added with studied carelessness, "we know who did it."

"For God's sake, girl!" Greene exclaimed as his wife spilled coffee all over herself.

Her hand was scalded, and she covered it with her napkin for just an instant before she looked at Matt with hunted eyes. "How did you find out?" she asked in a strained tone.

"A neighbor saw you run out of the apartment."

"That's a lie!" Greene exploded, but Matt silenced him with a lean hand and a quick glare. "Let me say at once that I don't believe you capable of cold-blooded murder, Mrs. Greene," he added quickly. "And I know an attorney who will represent you at trial. He'll get you off. Collier was a rat and everyone knew it, and enough people could swear that he was beating your sister frequently to convince a jury of his character."

Mrs. Greene could barely get her breath through sobs and tears. She put the napkin to her eyes and leaned forward over her lap while her husband sat and gaped at her with pure horror.

"I would have told, rather than let her go to the gallows. You must believe that." She wept harshly. "I was afraid, so afraid!"

"There's no reason to be so afraid," Tess broke in. "Please tell us what happened."

She dabbed at her eyes and fought for control, glancing nervously and apologetically at her husband before she began.

"Nan had come to that meeting looking like death warmed over and with bruises on her pretty face. She said that Dennis had sworn to come after her and kill her, and she didn't even want to go home with us because she was so afraid that he might hurt us." She smiled dully. "We persuaded her. But he"—

she nodded toward her husband—"had to go back to work. And he'd no sooner left than Nan got really scared."

She paused for breath. "I went to see him and told him I'd send Nan home if he'd promise not to hit her again. I didn't mean it, of course. I just wanted to put him off. He seemed to me to be dangerously drunk. Well, he said if she didn't show up, he'd bring his pistol over and kill her. And the way he was talking, I didn't doubt for an instant that he might actually do it.

"I was scared to death, but I thought that maybe I could talk him out of doing anything stupid. I thought I could scare him into backing off and leaving her be. You can reason with most people if you really try, can't you?" she added plaintively.

"Not with a drunk man, you can't, and you shouldn't have tried, you crazy woman!" Greene groaned, catching her hand tightly in his.

"I know that now, dear, but I was afraid to let you know because he might have killed you if you'd gone instead of me." She drew another breath, and her complexion paled. "I left. Then I decided to go back. It was dark in the front hall of the apartment. He came into the foyer. It was so dark that he didn't recognize me. He said 'Nan?' real loud, so loud that you could have heard him on the landing. I closed the door and leaned back against it. My knees were shaking, and my mouth was so dry, I couldn't do much more than say his name. And then he moved, and I saw it."

"Saw what?" Matt prompted.

"The pistol," she continued. "He had a pistol. It was lying on the table beside him. He laughed real softly and said he was going to take care of me once and for all, but first he was going to make me give him what I was giving that rich mobster I was going around with. He still thought I was Nan. He was drunk. Staggering drunk."

"Go on," Tess said.

Mrs. Greene's eyes looked haunted. "He got up and came toward me. He started cursing me, and he raised his fist. I knew he was going to hit me, and if he did, I wouldn't have a chance. Nan's sewing basket was sitting on top of her treadle machine, where she always kept it. I fumbled in the basket and felt for her scissors. He came at me and I ducked so that his fist hit the door instead. He screamed and I just..." She had to swallow down nausea. Her eyes closed as she shuddered. "I stabbed out wildly. He staggered backward, still screaming, and fell. I didn't even wait to see where I'd stabbed him; I just jerked open the door and ran." She bit her lip, sobbing. "I never meant to kill him. As God is my witness, I was just trying to keep him from killing my poor sister!"

Tess went to sit beside her on the rosewood sofa and put her arms around the older woman. She began to rock her gently.

"I should have said all this right away, the very minute they arrested Nan." She wept piteously. "But I was so afraid of the shame I'd bring on my husband and my little children! It just tormented me. I'm glad it's over," she added in a defeated tone. "I don't care if they hang me. I killed a man. I have to be punished."

"You killed a snake," Matt said. "They ought to give you a medal. Don't worry," he told Greene with a confident smile. "I'll cable Jared Dunn in Fort Worth and ask him to defend you. He'll come, even though he and his wife spend most of their time watching their baby son grow," he added amusedly.

"You think this Dunn fellow can save my wife?" Greene asked huskily.

"I know it," Matt told him. "It was a clear case of self-defense, and I can dig up twenty witnesses who'll swear to Collier's low character and your wife's sterling one." And he could, because Kilgallen would provide them—after all, Edith was soon to be his sister-in-law.

Greene was still powerfully worried, but his face cleared a little. "Well, my darlin'," he said, "I guess we'd better make a trip down to the station house."

She nodded, wiping her eyes. She gave Tess a watery smile. "I'm sorry. I've never even hurt an animal."

"Collier was worse than an animal," Matt said coldly. "He got what he deserved. I'm only sorry that you and your sister were caught in the middle."

"You're very kind, Mr. Davis," she said.

"You'll cable this Mr. Dunn, then?" Greene asked him.

"At first light," Matt promised. He got to his feet along with Tess. "We'll go with you to the station and take Mrs. Collier to a hotel…"

"You'll do no such thing," Greene said gruffly. "She'll come to us, where she belongs."

"You're a kind soul yourself, Officer Greene," Tess said gently.

He almost blushed. "Well, Nan's a good girl, even if it might seem to be a different story. What with the child and all," he said uncomfortably.

"I think you've got a few surprises coming about Nan and that baby," Matt murmured. "But I'll let you find them out yourself. One shock in a night is enough."

Nan was released, to her joy and sorrow, because her sister had to take her place in the cell. She thanked Tess and Matt profusely and then went home with her dejected brother-in-law.

She could help him with the children, she said, and smiled at the thought of her own expected child.

"What will Kilgallen do, do you think?" Tess asked when they were outside the station house in the biting cold wind.

"I think he'll marry her out of hand without waiting anywhere near a decent period of mourning," he chuckled. "That's what I'd do."

"You? The very conservative Mr. Davis?"

He looked down his long nose at her. "I don't feel as conservative as I've been in past years," he confessed, smiling. "Perhaps I'm about to break out of my own mold."

"My heart shivers at the thought," she teased.

He caught her gloved fingers in his and took them to his mouth. "I'll escort you back to Ellen's house. Then I have a few things to tend to. It may be a week or more before I see you again." He was solemn all at once. "Don't lose faith in me, Tess. I won't let you down."

"I never thought that you would," she said quizzically. She smiled. "I love you."

He sighed. "And I love you. I hope that we have a hundred years to enjoy each other."

"And a son and daughter to keep us company," she said with dogged optimism, expecting him to argue.

He didn't. He just smiled. The conversation on the way to Ellen's was pleasant but not intimate, and he left her at the door with only a soft kiss for comfort.

A week later Matt sent the society section of the *Chicago Daily Times* to her at the hospital by messenger.

She waited to read about a wild west troupe and studied first the accompanying large photograph that covered most of the top of the page. Pictured were several Oglala Sioux men who were appearing with Buffalo Bill's Wild West Show in a special Chicago performance before they traveled on to New York City. Among the Sioux dignitaries were two minor chiefs, a medicine man named Old Man Deer, and right there, in the middle of them all, Matt Davis, local detective, in full regalia right down to the warbonnet, looking every inch a credit to the tribe.

The article read "Famous Chicago detective Matt Davis poses with comrades from the Oglala tribe in South Dakota. Mr. Davis was known by the name Raven Following when he fought the white soldiers during skirmishes in the Indian Wars until the bitter defeat of the Sioux at Wounded Knee on December 30, 1890. Mr. Davis spoke with pride of his heritage and passed several hours speaking in his native tongue with the members of his tribe and with Bill Cody. The next appearance of the Wild West Show, which Mr. Cody calls an educational spectacle rather than a sideshow, will be in New York City."

It went on to detail the movements of Cody's troupe, including plans for a European tour. Tess stared at the photograph with mingled pride and delight. Underneath it, written in bold ink, was a question: "Would you marry this man?"

It was the middle of a workday. Tess didn't even take time to think that she might be fired outright for what she did next. She took time only to find her purse, then ran out of the hospital, in the cap that was never supposed to be worn more than a hundred yards from the front door, her apron flying as she hailed a passing carriage, the newspaper held tight in her fingers.

Christmas was on the way, and everything

was gaily decorated, from streetlights to front doors. She barely took note of the gay garlands adorning the streets as she stared impatiently out the window on the way to Matt's office. It was a dream come true, she thought, a miracle. Whatever had caused him to reveal his heritage so publicly? She was so proud of him that she could have burst.

The carriage finally got through the noon traffic and deposited her on the sidewalk in front of Matt's office. She handed the driver all her change and ran into the building and up the staircase.

Stanley was in the hall, looking at some papers, when she came tearing up the steps.

He grinned like the Cheshire cat when he saw the newspaper in her hand. "Isn't it swell?" he exclaimed. "I knew, or at least I suspected, but I had too much respect for Mr. Davis to pry into his private affairs. Imagine that, he led a war party! And he told me that the Oglalas have a proud heritage. Crazy Horse was Oglala, and so was Red Cloud, who fought the whites to a standstill back in the 1870s!"

"Yes, it is a very proud heritage," she agreed.

Matt had heard her voice. He came to the door of his office. He was hatless, and his glorious black hair was loosened for the first time in public—and in daylight, she thought with a scarlet blush. He looked magnificent.

"What do you think?" he asked her in Sioux.

"*Wachia ka cha i bedush kien che,*" she replied. "I am happy when I see you."

"And I am happy when I see you," he returned in English.

"My go-gosh, you speak Sioux?" Stanley stared in fascination at Tess.

"Indeed she does," Matt told him. "And she can shoot a bow and skin a deer and ride a pony bareback. I taught her those things, back in Montana."

"You're cousins, of course. Are you Sioux, then?" Stanley asked politely.

"We're not cousins," Matt returned. "That was a fiction to keep people from asking too many questions. Actually, Stanley, Tess is my wife."

"Yes, I am," she replied. She and Matt gazed at each other with such love that Stanley was faintly embarrassed.

"Only among the Sioux, though," Tess added.

"Only until I can find a minister to perform a ceremony that's legal in Chicago," Matt told her with a chuckle. "Stanley can give you away. Would you like that?"

Stanley gasped. "You would... honor me in such a way? Oh, sir!"

Matt clapped him on the shoulder affectionately. "You're a fine young man, Stanley, and I'm going to give you a lot more work in the future. You've proved yourself to me in every necessary way. You're a credit to my agency."

Stanley beamed. "Thank you, sir!"

"Thank you, Stanley."

The young man, red-faced with pleasure, beat a hasty retreat to his own office. Tess went with Matt into his. He closed the door behind them and leaned back against it to study her.

"I gather your answer is yes?" He nodded at the paper she still held in her hand.

"Yes!"

He moved toward her, glancing at the photograph. "It's rather flattering, isn't it?"

"You're very handsome," she replied softly. "And I love you with or without long hair."

He grinned. "I'm glad."

She held the paper up. "Why?"

"You taught me the futility of running from the past," he said simply. "You never run from anything, Tess, and I never used to. But I'd let myself become demoralized by what happened at Wounded Knee. When I finally turned around and looked into my darkness, all I saw there were shadows without substance." He drew her close. "Our children will be unique," he murmured, bending to her surprised mouth. "And I want a lot of them..."

She didn't say another word. Her lips parted under his hard mouth, and she clung to him with every ounce of her strength. They would be beautiful children, she thought, and she would be grateful every day of her life that she had helped Matt make his peace with the past.

Snowflakes struck the windowpanes, and the wind was howling. Tess seemed to hear sound from far away: the rhythm of drumbeats and the sizzling of campfires. A noble people were rising up from the ashes of their ancient civilization. Their voices called across the years, across the miles, and breathed beauty into the faraway future.

One day, she thought, the Oglala would once again be a proud nation, a nation of educated men and women who would challenge prejudice and demand their rightful place in the world. Women would do that as well. The outcome was as inevitable as life itself, as certain as the happiness she would share with her own Raven Following. And the two of them would be vanguards in the fight to make those dreams come true. Her heart was full... of love, of hope.

Epilogue

CHICAGO
LATE AUTUMN, 1938

Tess squeezed her husband's hand, and he shot her a grin. They were watching their daughter, their second born, being sworn in as the first woman to hold public office in the state of Illinois. Her brother, a famous trial lawyer who fought for the rights of all minorities and especially of the Sioux people, stood at her side. His dark good looks drew as many admiring glances from the women present as his sister's beauty drew from the men. The weather was blustery, promising yet another cold, snowy winter, and the windows rattled. It sounded like sweet music to Tess.

How her savage heart had gentled, Tess thought, remembering the wedding and the joining with this man at her side that had produced these wonderful and accomplished children. She and Matt had married during

Christmas week in a lovely ceremony that led to a gloriously happy marriage. Of course, Matt was obliged to bail Tess out of jail from time to time—until the early 1920s. There was a great drop in the frequency of those trips to police stations in 1920 when the amendment to the Constitution giving the vote to women passed both houses of Congress. They stopped altogether in 1924 after the passage of the Indian Citizenship Act, giving citizenship and the right to vote to all native Americans born within the territorial limits of the U.S. She glanced across the room, where the now very upright citizen Jim Kilgallen, whom no one for twenty-five years had dared call Diamond Jim, sat with his beloved wife, Nan. Nan's sister, Edith, represented by Jared Dunn, had been acquitted of murder and had received a suspended sentence for manslaughter all those long years ago, and lived far away now, in the South.

Sighing, Tess thought about how Matt had once worried so obsessively about having children who would have to bridge two worlds. Through the passing years, all those doubts of his had vanished.

"And you thought our children would end up as victims," she chided him in a near whisper as their tall, slender daughter placed her hand on the Bible in preparation for taking her oath of office.

Matt, his hair laced with silver, as was Tess's now, held her hand warmly in his and chuckled softly. "While you never had a single doubt about their potential." He pressed her fingers closer to his and looked lovingly into her age-lined green eyes. "Tell me now, before we take her and our son and his companion to dinner, do you regret any part of our lives together?"

She frowned thoughtfully, and mischief flared briefly in the pale eyes that met his dark ones. "Well, maybe just one thing."

"What?"

She leaned close and pulled his head down so that she could whisper in his ear without fear of being overheard. "I regret that we can't go back and do it all over again!"

The glorious light in his eyes was eclipsed only by the wonder in his achingly tender kiss. And if people stared at the elderly couple kissing so devotedly in the audience in front of God, a handful of reporters, and half of the Chicago political machine, they didn't mind at all. Neither did their daughter, who chuckled unashamedly as she shook hands with the governor and stepped down from the stage to join them. As for their son, he raised an amused eyebrow and shared a secret smile as he walked over to join the pretty girl in the front row.

"I thought you said both your parents were Sioux," the girl remarked.

He glanced at them, love shining in his eyes. "They are."

"But your mother's complexion is so fair and—"

"It isn't her complexion that makes her a Sioux. It's her heart."

He would have expounded on that theme, but Tess waved to him, standing in the circle of Matt's strong arm. She was laughing like a young girl in the throes of her first love. And in her heart, she was.

Matt drew her closer. For an instant he imagined that he heard the thud of the hooves of fast ponies racing free across the plains, and the throb of the drums around the campfire, and the melancholy falsetto of the singers. The old days were gone forever. Men could fly without wings, and motion pictures were rewriting the history of the struggle over possession of western lands. But when Matt closed his eyes, he could hear the wind whisper to him, of brave deeds and harmony and boundless freedom. His children would never know those things. But he and Tess had lived the old ways.

"What are you thinking?" Tess asked softly.

He opened his eyes and looked down at her. "I was remembering the sound of old voices raised in prayer songs."

She moved closer and laid her cheek against his jacket. "One day," she whispered, "the old voices will sing to us again, and we'll ride our ponies across the plains."

He kissed her forehead with tender lips and drew her even closer. "Together."

She smiled. "Of course, together. God would never divide a soul. And ours is a shared soul."

He laid his cheek against her silver hair. He couldn't find the words to tell her how strongly he shared that feeling. But he didn't have to; she already knew.

Above Tess's head, their son and daughter were grinning wickedly. Matt didn't move a muscle. He just winked.

DIANA PALMER lives in the northeast Georgia mountains with her husband, James, and their son, Blayne Edward. She spent sixteen years as a newspaper reporter and columnist. She has a bachelor's degree in history and is working on her master's. Since 1979 she has written more than eighty novels. Her numerous awards include seven Waldenbooks bestseller awards, four B. Dalton bestseller awards, two Bookrak awards and a Career Achievement Award from *Romantic Times*.

She is also known to romance fans as Susan Kyle and Diana Blayne.